P9-DCI-195

Also by Quinton Skinner
Amnesia Nights

14 DEGREES BELOW ZERO

14

DEGREES BELOW

ZERO

A NOVEL OF PSYCHOLOGICAL SUSPENSE

QUINTON SKINNER

Ⓥ VILLARD   NEW YORK

A Villard Books Trade Paperback Original

Copyright © 2005 by Quinton Skinner

Published in the United States by Villard Books, an imprint of The Random House Publishing Group, a division of Random House, Inc., New York.

VILLARD and "V" CIRCLED Design are registered trademarks of Random House, Inc.

Library of Congress Cataloging-in-Publication Data

Skinner, Quinton.
14 degrees below zero: a novel of psychological suspense / Quinton Skinner.
p. cm.
ISBN 0-345-46543-1
1. Victims of violent crimes—Fiction. 2. Parent and adult child—Fiction. 3. Fathers and daughters—Fiction. 4. Coma—Patients—Fiction. 5. College teachers—Fiction. 6. Single mothers—Fiction. 7. Minnesota—Fiction. 8. Widowers—Fiction. I. Title: Fourteen degrees below zero. II. Title.

PS3619.K565A613 2005
813'.6—dc22   2004061220

Printed in the United States of America

www.villard.com

9 8 7 6 5 4 3 2 1

I have placed my happiness on seeing you good and accomplished, and no distress which this world can now bring on me could equal that of your disappointing my hopes.

—THOMAS JEFFERSON, *in a letter to his daughter*

ACKNOWLEDGMENTS

Thanks to Alička Pistek, Mark Tavani, Brynnar Swenson.
My loving gratitude to Natasha and Gabriel for providing an
abundance of (often inadvertent) inspiration.

Thanks always to Sarah.

14 DEGREES BELOW ZERO

10 DEGREES BELOW ZERO

INTRO. PEOPLE LIKE THIS MUST HAVE THEIR SHARE OF PROBLEMS.

The ancient Chinese philosopher Chuang Tzu once enjoyed a vivid dream of being a butterfly—swooping, beating his wings, riding the currents of the most minute disturbances in the atmosphere.

When he awoke, he was forever troubled. He could never answer, to his satisfaction, whether he had been a man dreaming he was a butterfly, or whether he was now a butterfly dreaming he was a man.

When he went down the slope in the snow, his mind was in a riot. He tried to overcome gravity and deposit himself unharmed at the top of the tree-lined trail. It was no good, of course. He was unable to out-will reality, to bend time and happenstance, to reverse the sixty seconds that had seen him battered, his consciousness fractured. He knew that he might never recover from this.

His eyes sent to his brain a series of snapshots: the denuded trees, the whiteness of the snowstorm broken by black spots of rock, his own breath forming trails in the winter air as he fell.

He slid and tumbled, his rage unfolding. Big clumps of snow fell from the sky and landed in his eyes. He craved revenge for what had just happened, but his body ignored his commands, sending back spiky blasts of pain from his extremities and a blast of panic from his chest as his wind was knocked out.

Gravity continued to do its thing and he fell. He began to roll, and then remembered what was at the bottom of the slope.

The river was partially frozen and covered with floating snow. From the top of the hill it had been a thing of beauty, winding in serenity through the city. Down here it was noisy, its currents sounding like a long exhaled breath. He looked up and caught a glimpse of the bridge, with cars going past, and wondered if anyone could see him.

The thin ice snapped like a glass tabletop. The sound was muffled by the snow and cold; it was as though the elements had conspired to make his death as quiet and uneventful as possible. He tried to grab hold of something, anything, and gasped when the freezing water enveloped his shoulders and legs.

Get up. Just stand up. Don't let him get away with this.

He was in the water now. A deep part of his mind urged him to stay alive, but he couldn't get his arms and legs to work. His cold-weather gear started soaking up water, and he felt himself begin to sink.

Up above, in the snowstorm, an airplane passed. Inside they would be worried about their landing. But they would be warm.

Then the water was up around his face. It was black and too cold to be believed. His eyes and mouth remained above the surface, and he sucked in air in panicked gasps. Water filled his ears.

Get up get up get up get up get—

The air was . . . no, that wasn't air. Was he breathing water? He wasn't breathing. He was *drowning*. Pain seethed through his arms and legs, into his chest. He couldn't feel his hands and feet.

This isn't good. I don't want this.

He could hear the river singing a sleepy song. He tried to remember where he was. He had fallen. He was in the river. He could still see the sun but it was filtered through an aqueous gauze.

Someone get me out of here. Please.

He was on the bottom of the shallow water. The sun had gone out. He tried to remember the sound of his own name. He—

—remembered holding a photograph. It showed a man in his forties, with thick dark hair and upright posture. Next to him was a younger woman, obviously his daughter—the resemblance between them was striking. In between, holding both their hands, was a beautiful little girl in a flower-print dress, her bangs hanging over her forehead, caught in mid-sentence, talking to her mother and grandfather. To one side was a handsome man of about thirty, in a blazer and open-necked shirt; he stood just apart, as though not sure whether he was allowed to get too close to the family—or if he wanted to.

It was a sunny spring afternoon at the farmers' market. In a second photo, the young woman turned to the handsome man and kissed him on the lips. The older man made a point of diverting his granddaughter's attention. They were good-looking, well-dressed people. They seemed comfortable and happy together. They were worthy of envy. They showed little sign of what they had just been through.

The father and the boyfriend shared a glance. In a third photo we might try to discern what passed between them, but the image revealed little. They smiled with their mouths and not their eyes. They looked through each other, rather than allowing their gazes to meet.

People like this must have their share of problems. Everyone does. At the market they smelled the hay, the flowers, the cotton candy. Each in their various ways tried not to think about sickness, loss, resentment, and the shadowed corners of the will that had to be checked. They appeared a picture of happiness. He remembered that day. He—

—he was trying to talk, but the freezing water burned his throat and the centers of his eyes clouded over with the awful whiteness of the void.

1. ALL HER FEARS DISSOLVING FOR A SECOND OR TWO.

Even in her sleep she could taste her mother's grilled-cheese sandwiches: crackling on the outside but rescued from dryness by a fatty residue of butter coating her tongue, the cheddar inside melted perfectly and peeking innocently around the bread crust. It smelled of calmness, security, and warmth.

"Something to drink, Jay?" her mother asked.

"Milk," Jay mumbled through the first mouthful of the sandwich.

"Excuse me?" Jay's mother said; she was beautiful but looked tired, with her long hair tied back and a suggestion of shadow around her eyes.

"Milk," Jay said more clearly.

"Is that how we ask for something?"

"Can I have some milk, please?" Jay blurted out.

Her mother nodded with satisfaction and went to the kitchen.

Jay heard the sound of the refrigerator opening and the milk being poured. She had another bite of her sandwich.

The light streaming in through the dining-room windows cast pools of reflection on the wooden tabletop. Jay made sure not to leave crumbs. Her father wasn't home—he was at work—but she had trained herself to avoid the looks of irritation her carelessness provoked. He made Jay tense and worried. She loved him so much that she grabbed hold of him whenever he was near, pressing herself to his leg or arm, her thumb making for her mouth, all her fears dissolving for a second or two.

The milk was in front of her. Jay couldn't remember her mother bringing it. Somehow she knew none of this was real, but it felt so good she didn't want it to stop.

She lived in a place called Minnesota. It was a very cold place where people knew how to behave themselves. It was actually only cold for part of the year, but that cold was so profound, so shocking and even terrifying at times, that it cast a shadow over even the hottest and sunniest days of summer.

Jay's mother was gone. She had left. That's right, she had left.

The house was quiet. It was three stories including the spacious attic, full of comfortable furniture and a kitchen always stocked with food. Though she was in a little girl's body, Jay could remember growing to adulthood there. She'd snuck cigarettes by the big elm in the backyard, and lost her virginity in her room one afternoon when she was supposed to be at school. She loved the house, for all its residue of pain and disappointment.

Another bite of the sandwich. The crispy pan-fried bread gave way to the hot, liquid core. The place was entirely quiet, the way it had often been when she was a teenager, with her father off somewhere and her mother silently painting in the sunporch—no music, no talk radio, nothing but Anna's endless meditation on the back garden. It had grown increasingly quiet during dinnertime as well, the laughter and storytelling between Jay's parents having shifted to a more muted song of things unsaid that Jay could never entirely penetrate.

She got up from the table. Strange, she was so short. The top of the table was at about shoulder level. How old was she? Five? Six? She reached up and felt the soft outlines of her cheeks, the feathery wisps of her shoulder-length hair.

The living room was as she remembered (when *was* it?), with stacks of magazines and books everywhere, her own and her parents', with Anna's gardenscapes on all four walls.

Anna. Jay's mother's name was Anna. And now she was gone. She had died.

Jay sat on the worn-out sofa under the room's largest window, raising a small nimbus of dust that dispersed around her. From there she could see the open door to the sunroom, and make out the workbench where Anna kept her paints, rags, and brushes. Jay tongued out a stubborn bit of her sandwich from the back of her teeth, enjoying the flash of a flavor she hadn't tasted in . . .

She was never going to see her mother again.

With an emotion resembling panic Jay thought of the closet upstairs where Anna kept her clothes. She knew everything was just as Anna had left it; Jay's father, Lewis, was too benumbed by grief to get rid of them. Jay had an urge to go up there and lose herself in the smell of her mother's stale perfume and the feel of the dresses Jay used to press her face against.

But she couldn't. She willed herself to stand, but it was impossible. She might as well have been cemented to the couch.

The room began to break apart as though it wasn't real. Of *course* it wasn't real.

Her bedroom was suffused with the morning chill. Weak light insinuated its way through a crack in the curtains. Jay stretched her body and remembered where she was, and when it was.

Next to her slept a man. Stephen. That was Stephen. He slept with his arms folded, his chest rising and falling, his handsome face tense as though he was working out some unsolvable problem. Somehow he sensed Jay waking up and shifted toward her a couple of inches.

Jay was twenty-three. She wasn't a little girl any longer, though she could taste the grilled-cheese sandwich of her dream and, almost gasping, remembered that she had been in the presence of her mother just moments before. She had asked for the milk correctly, after some prompting. She had pleased her mother one more time.

She shook her head because it wouldn't do to start the morning crying. There was a *real* little girl down the hall, after all, and Jay had to be strong for her. She had to be strong in spite of how certain she was of her own weakness.

It wouldn't be irresponsible to doze for ten more minutes. Ten more minutes, and then Jay would launch herself out of bed and transform into a domestic whirlwind effortlessly getting Ramona ready for school and then heading to work. It would be easy. It would be simple, in a way that it never was before.

2. MAYBE HE NEEDED TO HAVE A WORD WITH STEPHEN.

N ow he had to walk the dog every morning before work—the beast had needs. Lewis had named it Carew, after the baseball player, and had regretted the decision ever since. Rod Carew, in his playing days with the Minnesota Twins, had exemplified subtlety and finicky precision. Carew the dog, in the prime of his canine days, was the polar opposite. Carew the dog was spastic, perpetually overexcited, and utterly oblivious to the finer points of his master's moods.

Lewis Ingraham held Carew's leash in the chill air, the breath of man and beast condensing in the gray morning, with the leafless trees and dim blues and whites of the autumn morning. And a thought occurred to Lewis.

He had come to realize—or at least believe, with the heartfelt conviction of a man uncovering an essential truth until then hidden beneath the mundane surface of things—that Carew had single-handedly (granting the beast, for the moment, the symbolic gift of hands) tipped Lewis's life from stoically bearable to entirely unpalatable. Oh, the fucking *dog*. The walking, the feeding, the constant emotional thirst for attention—they all entailed an added level of obligation and toil, and had transformed an otherwise flat but satisfyingly habit-ridden stage in a man's life into a hectic, fecal-tinged routine of unrewarding strife.

Not that it was all Carew's fault, to be fair.

It was acceptable to Lewis to admit that he didn't like his dog, and never really had—he was a man untroubled by some of the more unseemly aspects of his personality. The dog had been a gift from his daughter Jay, and as such was laden with so much symbolism and implicit significance that it was nearly unthinkable for Lewis to, say, simply unleash the animal and encourage it to amble from sight and disappear forever. Actually, no, he had tried that. The dog always came back.

The day they went to get the dog had been a scorcher, burning with heat and humidity. Lewis had been hungover and numb with grief. They'd gone together to Animal Control with Jay's daughter Ramona—Lewis's granddaughter, his consolation prize for continuing to exist. The thought of Ramona enlivened Lewis's step and robbed the sting from the morning air. He remembered going that day to the derelict city facility near downtown, nestled near the steel prison of the automotive impound lot, on a mission to get a dog for himself. It was understood that the dog would also be Ramona's—that Lewis would care for it, and that it would provide him with a supplemental reason for continuing to live, but that Ramona was also gaining a dog-by-proxy, saving Jay the trouble of adding more direct responsibility to her aimless and fairly feckless young womanhood.

Funny, he hadn't thought about that day in a while. The dog was also Ramona's. And Ramona *loved* Carew.

"You might not realize it," Lewis said to the dog, who looked up with perked ears. "But you just earned a reprieve. Again. You fucking mutt."

Yeah yeah yeah, Lewis, the dog said. *You're the man.*

Ramona had selected the spotty, shaggy thing—it had the wild-eyed look of the career convict who had come to enjoy prison. Jay had paid the adoption fee (still more symbolism) that sprang Carew from his death sentence—it was just a few days from euthanasia, according to the tag on its cage. Then she paid for the veterinarian visit, a one-stop extravaganza including Carew's neutering, delousing, and treatment for kennel cough. Jay had granted Lewis the gift of a living being, a companion, an entity to dilute his solitude.

How long had it been since Anna died, anyway? Soon it would be closer to seven months than six. Her clothes still hung in the walk-in closet in their bedroom—*his* bedroom, where he rarely slept now. His shirts, suits, and shoes were all in the guest room, Jay's former bedroom, to which he'd transferred many of his things after his only child left for college. He used it as a dressing room, and he liked to see himself in the full-length mirror hanging on the closet door. He liked to inspect his naked body, proud of his flat belly and strong thighs—he still ran at least three times a week around Lake of the Isles, no matter the weather. He took care of himself, and had a better physique than a lot of the soft, doughy twenty-somethings he saw padding around his neighborhood. But he didn't make a point of it. No one needed to know he was vain about his body, or his full head of hair, or the way time had carved his features into a mask of masculine solidity.

Anna had been attacked by pancreatic cancer, and it rotted her out from the inside. She was like waterlogged wood at the end, soft and porous. In the last couple of weeks she smelled terribly. Lewis had burned incense constantly. He had camped out on the sofa downstairs in a mess of pillows and blankets and books. He slept only a couple of hours at a time, vigilant for the sound of her coughing or moaning in a semiconscious stupor of pain and narcotics.

"Sit, Carew," he said to the dog, who had spotted another canine on the other side of the street. A female, Lewis thought, but his assessment was certainly clouded by the creature holding its leash—a girl of about twenty-five in those hip-hugger pants and spaghetti-strap top that was apparently handed out as a uniform these days. *She* didn't seem cold, but Lewis's hands were shaking.

Lewis, at forty-seven, prided himself on not being the sort of man who took untoward notice of girls almost half his age— girls, he reminded himself with a wince, who were essentially the same age as his daughter.

"I said *sit,*" he growled, more loudly. Carew did not comply. Carew had gotten a taste for chaos during his wild, predomestication days, and ran wild through the house and slept on the sofas. He was most definitely not getting with the program. The dog *knew* that Lewis was in no condition to train it.

In a full-fledged pique, Lewis jerked on Carew's leash—all right, granted, probably *too* hard, but how else was he to get his message across? The girl across the street looked up, and a flash of concerned consternation played across her admittedly pretty face. Lewis imagined himself through her eyes: an old guy, bundled up though it wasn't really that cold, losing his shit and committing borderline animal abuse.

Lewis smiled and gave her a *what're-you-gonna-do* shrug. She would have been in his range, back when he was young. Now it was out of the question. It was unsavory to even think about it. But he thought about it.

The girl gave Lewis a little half-smile, noncommittal, and

went on her way. Her ponytail bounced on her shoulder blades as she walked.

Now why the hell had she given him a look like that? All right, he was dressed far too warm in his hooded sweatshirt and black burglar's cap. The girl was sleeveless, her arms fetchingly lithe and tanned. It wasn't his fault he was bundled like an old man—the goddammed antidepressant his doctor had forced on him made him feel high and giddy in the morning, his face and fingers borderline numb, and random pains and chills flitted through his chest cavity. Maybe the girl wouldn't have been so standoffish if she'd known that he'd just lost his wife. The pretty ones always thought they were above you—and all because of a chance genetic fluke that inspired behavior in men that was, in the end, little more than a complicated mask over extremely simple desires.

He could have had that girl when he was younger. He was sure of it.

He'd been married to Anna for twenty-five years when she died. He couldn't say they were all good years, especially when he was younger, more angry. The last years, before she got sick, were also no picnic. But time had passed, they had stayed together. Sometimes he thought they shouldn't have. But there was no point thinking about it now.

Lewis and Carew reached the empty park. It was silent and still, too early for the children to be out.

"Here we are, boy," Lewis said, his voice morning-hoarse. "Your earthly paradise—Dogshit Park."

Lewis walked gingerly through the grass, fastidiously avoiding the plethora of turds that decorated the turf. They were like synesthetic land mines, their sight and smell permeating his oversensitized consciousness and senses in a way that had been the norm for the past year, since Anna had learned she was sick.

Taking in a measured breath, Lewis massaged his chest. He was light-headed, and everything seemed unreal. He tried to will the world back into focus, to make everything take on the somber tones of reality. He sent out internal feelers for the catastrophic explosion of pain behind his sternum that would be the last thing he ever felt.

It didn't happen. He didn't die. He came back to himself.

There was a big sign posted: CLEAN UP AFTER YOUR DOG. Someone had painted over some of the letters, and now it read: LEAN AFT YO DOG. Everyone apparently felt they had a special dispensation from the rules, anyway, because there was shit everywhere. Lewis counted a half-dozen mounds before he found a clear patch of grass and unclipped Carew's leash. He wasn't supposed to let the dog run free in the city, but fuck it. He felt a certain sympathy for Carew's plight—it couldn't be easy, living with Lewis.

Carew took off and ran a big circle in the grass. He looked back with undisguised doggy affection, his big tongue hanging out.

Yeah yeah, Lewis. OK OK yeah.

"Yeah, OK to you, too," Lewis called to him. "Now go play. We have to get home soon."

There was another sign in the neighborhood that read: BEGIN ONE WAY. Someone had obscured two letters to make it read: GIN ONE WAY. The gag rankled him every time he saw it. The better joke, obviously, was to erase the GIN and make the sign read BE ONE WAY. Wasn't that apparent to everyone?

Lewis took his cell phone out of his pocket and, with surprise, realized that he was smiling. He was too emotional these days; it was as though some defensive barrier inside him had been breached and couldn't be put in place again. For the moment it was working in his favor, though, because the sight of Carew's mottled brown pelt gave him pleasure. He thought of the animal's not-disagreeable smell, and the satisfying clack of his claws on the hardwood floors at home, and the feeling of Carew's body against his when they watched TV on the sofa together. And Lewis felt all right.

After dialing a familiar number Lewis pressed the phone against his ear and, with his free hand, fished for a cigarette in the pocket of his sweatshirt. He managed to get the thing lit before Jay picked up.

"Hello, what?" she mumbled. "Dad?"

For the moment he had no aches, no chills, no heaviness of heart and mind. The sound of his daughter's voice was a warm fire on a winter day—he could melt, he could die. He lived to hear her call him Dad. He loved her like music, like light. She and Ramona were all that he lived for, and he knew how much they needed him.

"How did you know it was me?" he asked, watching Carew digging in the grass.

"Who else would call so early?" she said.

"Early?" he repeated, an unintentional note of mockery in his voice. "It's almost seven-thirty. I'm out with Carew. Isn't Ramona out of bed yet?"

A moment of silence.

"Dad, it's more like ten after seven," Jay moaned. "Ramona's asleep. I need to rest, Dad. You're twenty-five years ahead of me in melatonin depletion. Is there something important you want to talk about?"

"What do you mean, you need to rest?" Lewis asked her. "What time did you get to bed last night?"

Another pause. Lewis had miscalculated. He shouldn't have asked her that, at least not in that *tone*. Jay and Anna had always been major sticklers in the matter of Lewis's *tone*—he was too cutting, too acerbic, too *something*. He wasn't sufficiently empathetic. He had been made to understand that sometimes he *came on too strong.* He lacked warmth. The criticisms of the mother had been passed on to the daughter. At least some part of her still lived.

"Stephen was here last night, if that's what you mean," Jay said. She was waking up, her voice turning sharp.

Lewis took a drag on his cigarette. He needed to be alert. He was entering a conversational wilderness.

"Honey, you know I didn't mean anything," he told her. "Did Ramona at least get to sleep at a decent hour?"

Jay let out a long breath. "Yeah, Dad, she *did.* She's *fine.*"

"You make it sound like I'm giving you a hard time," Lewis said. "Truce, all right? I just called to talk to you. It's a beautiful morning—cloudy, but the sun's coming out like a big bald head. You remember that song?"

"Yeah, Dad, I do." Softer now.

"You should get up," Lewis told her. "Get your day started."

Carew was fussily smelling trees, the grass, turds. His back twitched with the olfactory explosion of the park. Lewis winced as a plume of cigarette smoke found his eye.

"So you're walking the dog?" Lewis heard the sound of his daughter adjusting herself in bed.

"I already told you that," he said. "Hey, did I hear Ramona? Does she want to talk to Grandpa?"

"Ramona isn't up yet."

Lewis realized, all at once, that Stephen was in bed with Jay. He had spent the night there, in Jay's little two-bedroom apartment on the far side of Hennepin Avenue, about six blocks from Lewis's house. Lewis had suspected Stephen of sleeping over before, but it was an apprehension he'd never had confirmed.

She wasn't required to live like this. Jay had an open invitation to come home, to bring Ramona, to unite what was left of the family. Of course, should that happen, Lewis knew he wouldn't approve of allowing Stephen to spend the night.

What was this doing to Ramona's psyche? He was no kinky Freudian, but things were hard enough for the little girl—she was growing up with a single mother, and she almost never saw her father. And now the confusion of seeing a boyfriend parading in and out of her mother's room, the sleepy male face at the breakfast table, Stephen half-clothed and giving her mother confidential caresses to commemorate the erotic adventures of the night before.

It had to be harmful to Ramona. It pained Lewis to think it, but the girl wasn't being given an optimal upbringing. Of course, raising concern of any kind would only serve to cleave a yawning chasm of enmity between himself and Jay. She was stubborn, proud. She might move away. She might disappear.

Lewis took a jagged breath and caressed his breastbone. *Not yet, can't die yet.* His head swam with fear. He calculated his chances of surviving the morning at ninety-six, maybe ninety-seven percent. Very good odds, but he felt his world narrowing.

What made it all the more unbearable was Stephen himself. Stephen was a tenure-track professor at the university, in the graduate program that Jay herself might have been starting this fall—if she hadn't gotten pregnant at nineteen and dropped out after her second year of college. Now Jay was twenty-three. Stephen was nine years older. Stephen: Mister Perfect, Mister Intellectual. He hadn't fooled Lewis for an instant, not from the moment—the very *millisecond*—they first met.

"Dad?" Jay said. "You still there?"

"Yes, honey," Lewis said, trying to remember how he talked when he sounded normal. "Can I please say good morning to Ramona?"

"She isn't up, Dad," Jay said again. "And there isn't time. We're going to have to hurry to get her to day care on time."

So Lewis was to believe that Ramona wasn't awake yet, although in the same breath Jay was talking about rushing her to day care—a day care that, not insignificantly, Lewis paid for. Precisely when had his discourse with his daughter devolved into worthless half-truths and arm's-length parrying?

"When you were Ramona's age, your mother and I always got you into bed by eight o'clock," Lewis said. "That way, you were nice and rested in the morning. We didn't have to drag you out of bed."

Indistinct sounds on the phone.

"Jay, did you—"

"What did you say, Dad? Sorry."

"Is someone there?" Lewis asked, the words escaping him despite his best intentions. "Did Stephen spend the night?"

Lewis briefly considered walking home, getting into his car, and driving the short distance to Jay's apartment. Perhaps this was a conversation best conducted in person. Maybe he needed to have a word with Stephen.

"Dad, don't take this the wrong way," Jay said. "But it's just not your business."

Zing. In a heartbeat, Jay had turned cold and disapproving—an elegant diversionary strategy, something else she had learned from her mother.

"I could consider it my business, since it pertains to the general welfare of my granddaughter."

"I can't talk to you when you're like this," said Jay. "I'll call you later, Dad. I'm glad you're enjoying the morning. I really am."

"Don't get offended. Please," Lewis rushed to say. "You know I'm always thinking about Ramona. She's only four years old."

"I know how old my daughter is."

"Then you also know that at her age—"

"Good-*bye*, Dad."

"Jay?"

"*What?*"

"I love you, sweetheart."

A big sigh, the biggest of the morning, then the longest gulf of silence.

"I know, Dad."

Lewis's daughter hung up on him.

Carew squeezed out a magnificent shit just then, three logs' worth. Lewis leashed up the dog and pondered the crap as though it were an abstract sculpture at the Walker museum. He took a look around.

Fuck it. If no one else cared, why should he? Let someone else clean it up—or, better still, step in it.

3. IT WAS KIND OF AN UGLY THING.

O f *course* Jay loved her father. He was always able to overlook her transgressions, to absorb the impact of her mistakes, to point out for her where she was going wrong. He had always been unremittingly generous with her, never sparing of his time, or himself. When she was a little girl, other children had been jealous of her over her parents. The other kids in the neighborhood had shut-down materialistic disciplinarians to deal with—real white-bread Minnesota die-hard conformists, no matter what package they advertised in the form of Democratic politics and Unitarian activism. Jay's parents were always different. Anna had been an artist once, and beautiful, with a sort of innate grace that Jay could never attain. Anna never gave a damn if Jay smoked pot or went out with boys, so long as Jay maintained her integrity. And Anna would even go so far as to give Jay a pretty coherent definition of what that integrity comprised.

As for Lewis, well, half of Jay's adolescent friends had serious crushes on him. They talked about it right in front of Jay. And these were *real* crushes, the kind where they seriously thought about her dad as a sex object. It was gross, she had been obliged to act disgusted, but secretly the whole thing filled her with a transgressive pride. She knew she should probably spend some time on the couch one of these days and unravel all of that old shit. When she could afford it. When she wasn't waiting tables for a living.

It was kind of an ugly thing, come to think of it, the way she had always felt *jealous* of her parents—the way they always seemed to have their lives together, the way they always seemed to be in love despite having been married for about a hundred years. Jay had felt small in comparison to them—not in the normal sense, but smaller as in *inferior*. They were hard to live up to. And Jay's guilt had always been compounded by their unflagging support, their constant attempts to boost her up, their refusal to judge anything she did.

Today Jay woke up and ached with the absence of her mother. In his usual fashion, Lewis had somehow sensed this and tried to make it better. He liked to take charge. He always tried to make everything all right for those he loved.

God, he was always around.

"I take it Lewis deduced that I stayed over," Stephen said. "And that he wasn't particularly happy about it."

"It's none of his business," Jay said, replacing the phone in its cradle.

She could see Stephen's face in the mirror over the dresser. He slipped into his default expression, the one that guardedly revealed his general haughty disapproval for the small-mindedness that he was forced to deal with on a daily basis. Of course he never expressed outright contempt, or anger—those were implicit. That was the thing about Stephen. Jay thought she might be in love with him, but he was stronger than her, and more elusive. It was really quite hard to ever pin him down on anything.

Stephen knotted his silk tie and smoothed his wavy hair—it was a rich brown, like a nice suede coat. It curled around his ears and accentuated his long nose and high forehead. God, he was really nice to look at. Not that Jay was a frump—in fact, she had long enjoyed a reputation as a beauty, in opposition to her own opinion. She had an unpleasant sense that she wasn't as attractive as Stephen, on the abstract level at which a man's appearance contrasted with a woman's.

But why exactly did she think that? Because Stephen did? Had he expressed that to her on some subliminal level, or was she simply being paranoid?

Jay had no clothes on, and as she sat up in bed her blanket slipped down and she saw herself in the mirror: her belly was flat, and she had small breasts with nipples that stood up in the cool morning. She had fine black hair, and a face that looked young enough for her to get carded when she bought American Spirits at the SuperAmerica on the corner. *Not bad.*

There was a noise, and Jay looked to the doorway. Ramona was standing there in her Hello Kitty pajamas, rubbing one eye with a clenched fist.

"Good morning, Mama," Ramona said.

Actually, she spoke in an accent that was virtually indecipherable to anyone outside a small circle composed of her mother, grandfather, and, with sporadic success, her day care providers. Ramona's vocabulary comprised a galaxy of words and precocious expressions, but her pronunciation lagged behind other children her age. The "G" in Ramona's greeting was little more than a hopeful fiction, beyond the skill of her struggling tongue. Her "D" sound was a glottal choking off. Her "ing," on the other hand, brought joy to Jay's ear. Ramona had mastered that sound, and it was like high-pitched bird music to her mother.

Stephen finished fussing over his tie and looked at Ramona with a self-conscious smile. Ramona's speech troubles invariably made Jay feel protective. She hated it when people made Ramona repeat herself over and over—something that Stephen had only recently learned not to do.

Jay suddenly realized that her daughter was staring at her breasts. Or—it was amazing how early children developed these attitudes—she was staring because Stephen was in the room, with a sort of opprobrium over her mother's nudity.

Jesus—did Ramona feel some sense of ownership over these breasts, more than two years after they ceased to be a source of nourishment for her? Stephen was certainly obsessed enough with them, always touching her nipples, always wrapping his lips around them in bed and grazing them with his teeth as though about to bite her.

Not for the first time, Jay had a sense of her body as existing largely as a vessel for the pleasure of others. Wasn't that a hint of ownership gleaming in Ramona's eyes as she stared at her mother's nakedness?

A look of ageless wisdom passed over Ramona. She glanced at Stephen with a tired resignation. *Once mine, now his,* she seemed to be thinking, with her long legs planted in the doorway. Every now and then Jay got glimpses into Ramona's inner life, all the minor triumphs and major heartbreaks.

Jay pulled her blanket up to cover herself. "Time to get ready, pumpkin," she said. "Want me to make you some toast?"

"What are *you* doing here?" Ramona asked Stephen, her singsong delivery blunting the edge of her interrogation.

Stephen laughed. "Right now I'm getting ready for work," he said. "What are *you* doing?"

"This is my house," Ramona told him. "I don't have to say."

Stephen smiled bigger, flashing teeth. "Can you make a picture for me today at day care?" he asked her. "Something nice, like those boats on the lake we saw the other day?"

Ramona stared at Stephen, but Jay saw her daughter warm a few degrees. "Maybe," she said.

"Fair enough." Stephen bent at the waist to bring his face closer to hers. "That's good—don't make any promises. You're a terrific artist. Don't force your creativity. It'll come on its own."

"Sweetie, why don't you wait for me in the kitchen?" Jay said.

"You have to put clothes on," Ramona observed.

"That's right, I do," Jay replied.

Ramona padded off, elbows swaying, and Jay got up. She paused in front of the mirror and saw Stephen looking at her with a pleasingly intent expression. He came over and put his hands on her hips. Last night they'd had very gentle sex, careful not to wake Ramona. Jay wondered what it might do to a little girl's mind, hearing her mother fucking away in the next room. People had always fucked, after all, it wasn't as though Jay had invented it—and people might have been fucked up by fucking, and all that it entailed, but people weren't walking around in psychotic fugues because they once heard some thumps and groans through a wall. Still, she imagined all sorts of Freudian scenarios playing out, writ large in the form of Ramona's hopelessly neurotic adulthood. She didn't want to say anything to Stephen about it, because he would come up with all sorts of theories—he *taught* Freud, after all, and Lacan, and Adorno, and a whole pack of crazy Germans and Italians Jay had never gotten to because she'd dropped out of college. Never mind that she'd tested off the charts in elementary school, forget the inordinate pride Lewis had taken when the authorities informed him that his daughter was a "genius." Now she waited tables. That was reality in its most unadulterated form. She was ill equipped to talk psychoanalytic theory with Stephen—and unwilling to subject her daughter to his thinking, for the objects of his observations tended to be painted in stark and unflattering light.

"I have to stop at my place to get some notes." His hand slipped down to cup Jay's ass. He was a whole head taller than her, and possessed of a ropy musculature. Despite herself, knowing that Ramona was as likely as not spying from the hall, she pressed her bare stomach against the blue cotton of his shirt.

"You look nice," she said.

"Thank you," he said in a husky voice.

"You're teaching a class this morning?" she asked, realizing she had to defuse the sexuality that was springing up between them.

"Two, actually." He smiled. "Are you ever going to get my schedule straight?"

"Why bother? It'll just change next semester." She pulled away and slipped on panties, a pair of jeans, and a Pavement T-shirt she'd owned since she was a senior at Minneapolis South. She looked in the mirror and saw that she looked the same as she had then, with the addition of dark circles under her eyes and the removal of a few pounds of baby fat. "And what about my work schedule? Have you memorized that?"

"Well, actually, I have," Stephen said, grinning. "You're working dinner shifts Wednesdays, Fridays, and Sundays. Thursday and Saturday you work lunch—and every other Monday. Otherwise you have Mondays and Tuesdays off."

"You suck," she said.

Stephen put his arms around her and kissed her forehead. God, he could be such a prick. He was a tenure-track professor at thirty-two, a Young Gun in the Cultural Studies department and the author of an upcoming book. Jay had met him at a dinner party a year-and-a-half before, when she was still part of a circle of high-school and college friends. Then, as now, Jay was *sorting things out,* but she sensed that Stephen was only going to tolerate her stasis for so long. He treated Jay with undiluted respect, and he seemed to view Ramona as a real person rather than as a frightening hindrance, as other men did. Yet she sensed him growing impatient with her, more and more as time passed. She sniffed his hair, which smelled like her shampoo, and thought that often he regarded her more highly than she did herself.

It was impossible to imagine life without Ramona, without her incessant moods, her tornado of disorder, and the quasi-spiritual miracle of her very being. Jay was capable of contemplating in the abstract other courses her life could have taken. Each one was like a mini-life she hadn't lived, but could faintly remember, like an echo from a dream.

Finishing college wouldn't have hurt. At one time she had planned to pursue a Ph.D. and teach. Now she could get no traction on her life. She already felt too old and lived-in to sit in a classroom full of callow, self-absorbed adolescents—they'd be just a few years younger than her, yet separated by a gulf of experience.

Anna had "loved" Stephen—her words, a direct quote. She had also, in so many words, warned Jay not to surrender too much of her emotional sovereignty to him, not while she was so young.

"In ten years you'll likely be someone else," Anna had said. "He won't. He'll be the same person."

"You were just thinking about your mother," Stephen said, running a finger along her cheek.

She couldn't speak.

"Do you want me to talk to Lewis?" he asked.

"And what would you say to him?"

Ramona called out from the kitchen, her voice so squeaky that Jay wondered: what, are the girl's vocal cords a *millimeter* long? How could such a high-pitched sound come from a human? Ramona called for her again, louder now, in the tone of royalty demanding the attention of a servant.

"I'm *coming*, Ramona!" Jay yelled, and was startled to hear her mother's voice coming from her mouth.

"First I'd tell him he needs to back away and lay off you a little bit," Stephen said calmly, ignoring Jay's exasperation. "I'd tell him he should stop calling you four or five times a day and bumming you out. He's overbearing, negative, and profoundly depressed. I'm not sure if he knows all that, but I would bring it to his attention and suggest that he see a shrink or a therapist."

"Stephen—"

"His mood is like a contagion—"

"*Mama!*"

"He swoops in on you, and by the time he's finished he's sucked all the joy right out of you."

"*Mama!*"

"I'm *coming*! Stephen—"

"Let me finish. Every time he calls you, you go from well-adjusted to neurotically anxious in the span of about two minutes. God knows what Anna endured being married to him, but now that she's gone Lewis is turning all his energy on you."

"Stephen, that went too far."

"I apologize," said Stephen. "But it doesn't mean I'm wrong. And part of the reason you haven't been taking any positive action in your life lately—"

"Is because my mother *died*, Stephen. She died of cancer, and it took a while for her to die, and it was horrible, and it completely fucked me up—"

"*Mama!*"

"Ramona, *stop it*!" Jay screamed. Stephen flinched.

"I know, Jay," he said quietly.

"And also because I'm a *mother*, and because I've been alone, and because it takes all my energy just to present myself as a functioning human being in front of my daughter."

"Please, she shouldn't hear this," Stephen said, putting a hand on her shoulder.

"I *know it*!" Jay snapped. "But I can't help fucking up all the time."

"That's not true. You don't fuck up all the time. You're one of the least fucked-up people I know," Stephen said in a level voice. "That's just the way your father makes you feel. You have a great mind. You're very young. But Lewis will drag you down with him if you allow it."

"That's too much," Jay said. She found a box of tissues on the dresser and blew her nose.

Her thoughts fell into a familiar downward cascade. Ramona, Stephen, her job, her father, her *life*—all of it blurred into a single insurmountable problem that made her fingers tingle and left her wanting to levitate and never come down again. Her room looked shabby and small, with its beat-up postcollege furniture and vomitous green color scheme. She smelled stale sex rising from the sheets. All of it, *all of it*, became a spongy fear that expanded inside her, which would grow and magnify throughout the day until Ramona's bedtime, when she would be so tired from all the worry and uncertainty that her eyes and back would burn. How to argue with the dread when the dread might be right? Maybe things were going to keep slipping away from her. Maybe Stephen really just liked to fuck her, and would eventually get tired of it. Maybe she would still be wearing a Pavement T-shirt in ten years.

She was a single mother who waited tables.

"Mama?" said Ramona from the doorway, looking up sheepishly. "Can I have breakfast now?"

"Of course, sweetie," Jay said. "Mama's really sorry she yelled at you."

Ramona turned on her heels and ran down the hallway with heavy steps. She never acknowledged Jay's profuse apologies. Jay couldn't tell whether it was because the offense was already forgiven and forgotten, or whether something deeper and dark was going on.

Jay ran her hands through her hair and shrugged at Stephen. It was so early in the day.

"Look, I'll talk to him," Stephen said. "I'll be tactful. I know how to dance around with people like Lewis."

"No. No, let me do it."

"That won't work," he replied. "You go into these conversations with your father full of resolve. Then he batters you with his sarcasm, and all that loving manipulation he throws your way, and then you're right back in it. You're a little girl again."

"Maybe," Jay said, heading out into the hall.

"Maybe nothing," Stephen called out from her room, though not without kindness.

Jay made for the kitchen and put on a Lifter Puller CD. There was toast to be made and milk to be dispensed. Ramona was going to be late for day care once again. There were so many things that needed to be done.

INTERLUDE. IN THE CAR, THERE WAS NO WIND.

Ramona had a lot of secrets. Some of the secrets were good, and others were bad. There were some secrets that she wasn't sure were which, but in order to find out she'd have to reveal them to a grown-up, and then they wouldn't be secrets anymore.

You could talk about some things to grown-ups. Other things you had to keep to yourself. Ramona's mama was beautiful and smelled good and was really smart. She also got mad really fast. There were a lot of things that Ramona knew Mama wouldn't understand.

Like the car seat. Ramona kind of liked it. It allowed her to sit up high, so she could see the trees going by. She liked to count the dogs on the way to day care.

"Three," she said. It was a black dog on a leash. She held up her bear so that it could see, too.

"What, honey?" Mama asked, looking in the mirror.

"Nothing," Ramona replied.

The thing about the car seat, actually, was that Ramona hated being strapped inside it. It reminded her of the electricity chair she saw one time on TV when she was watching a movie she wasn't supposed to be watching. Someone had pushed a button, and the man inside it had died. Ramona sort of wondered whether her mama had a button like that someplace.

"Four," Ramona whispered. That one looked like a nice doggy. She made sure that Bear could see it. Grampa Lewis had a very nice doggy named Carew. Bear loved Carew as much as Ramona did.

One time one of the fish in the tank in Ramona's room died, and Ramona cried for a long time. She was still waiting for the fish to come back, but it hadn't, not yet. Ramona wondered what was taking so long, but this was one of the secrets she didn't want to talk about with Mama.

Because when you died you went away. Ramona wasn't sure what had to happen for you to come back, but she figured she'd find out soon.

Mama was cussing at the car in front of her. Mama wasn't supposed to cuss. No one was, but they did it anyway. One time Ramona said *goddammit* and Grampa Lewis got real mad and sort of yelled at Mama about it. Mama said that Ramona probably heard it from him. Ramona was supposed to never say that again.

It looked windy outside. It was getting colder. In the car, there was no wind. That made Ramona feel kind of sad, because she liked the wind even though it messed up her hair.

A lot of things made Ramona kind of sad. She didn't know why. That was another secret. She wasn't supposed to be sad, it bothered grown-ups. So she didn't tell them when she felt that way.

Like now.

She liked Stephen but didn't want him to know it. It wasn't a big deal. She had been really surprised to see him in their house this morning. Ramona wondered what Stephen and Mama did when they closed the door. She suspected it had to do with butts, or Mama's vagina. She wasn't sure.

Stephen kind of wanted to pretend he was Ramona's daddy. She didn't like that. Ramona had a daddy, though she didn't like him. She sort of didn't like men. Some of her friends' daddies were all right, in a way, but she wouldn't want any of them to be her father.

She liked Grampa Lewis. A lot. He was tall, and handsome, and he gave Ramona candy and told her not to tell her Mama about it. He was really strong, and sometimes when she was with him she wished he would kick someone's butt so she could see what it would look like. She knew he could kick pretty much anybody's butt if he wanted to.

The sky had a lot of clouds. It was going to get colder, maybe tomorrow. Ramona remembered winter. It felt like hurting inside.

Grown-ups were hurting all the time. Their bones popped when they walked. Grampa Lewis cracked and popped all the time. It was funny.

"I'm craziest about that dog," Ramona told Bear. It was a special dog, all black with white spots on its face.

"What did you say, honey?" Mama asked.

"Nothing," Ramona told her.

You couldn't tell grown-ups the whole truth. They wanted it, but you couldn't give it to them. That was how it worked. Ramona didn't make the rules. They were always asking questions, with their big faces and big eyes. You had to figure out what they wanted to hear. Otherwise they would get mad, and they might not give you treats and presents. Mama was hungry for Ramona all the time, hugging her, touching her, asking her how she felt. It was nice, but sometimes Ramona pretended not to hear Mama, and pretended not to notice her.

Because she was the Perfect Princess. Sometimes she was *both* Ramona and the Perfect Princess, but that was hard to explain and she was still working it out. The Perfect Princess talked to Mama sometimes, giving Ramona a place to hide and not deal with all the things that Mama wanted from her.

And if Ramona answered all of Mama's questions, there would be none left. And then Mama might die like Grandma.

She wanted to ask Mama when Grandma was coming back. Grandma was Mama's Mama. That was magic. The Perfect Princess thought dying was like going on a vacation. There were trees there, and water. Grandma was having a nice rest.

Sometimes Ramona wondered if Grampa was kind of a bad man. He was nice to her, but he wasn't always nice to other people. Sometimes he was, but it was also weird how he acted.

Now they were at day care. It was time to visit with her royal subjects: the younger kids. She would pretend the older kids weren't even there. Mama opened the car door and undid Ramona's car seat. Ramona slid out.

"What are you thinking about?" Mama asked. "You've been so quiet this morning."

"Nothing," Ramona said.

"Oh, come on," Mama said with a laugh. "You have to be thinking something. Everybody is thinking of something."

"I love you, Mama," said the Perfect Princess.

"Oh, honey," Mama said. Her eyes got watery and she kissed the Perfect Princess on the forehead.

Ramona liked her mama. The Perfect Princess wasn't sure. The Perfect Princess didn't really like anybody.

4. A SINGLE MOTHER COLLEGE DROPOUT WITH RAVEN BLACK HAIR.

There were a number of things on Stephen Grant's mind as he made his way to his late-model Volkswagen. There was a thin stratum of logistical fretting—the stop by his house, the things he needed to pick up there—then a layer of mental preparation for his classes that morning, which was not dissimilar in nature from the sort of all-around readiness evinced by an actor who was starring in a play later that day. Stephen liked thinking on this level, letting half-formed memories percolate in a stew of ephemera. It was probably why he had become a teacher—for, unlike many of his colleagues, he viewed himself as a teacher first, an educator even, and a theorist second.

He wished these were the only thoughts that preoccupied his consciousness as he started up the car and glanced back at the brick apartment building where Jay and Ramona lived. Stephen, it turned out—and it pained and embarrassed him on some level to admit it—was an actual *human being* who required companionship and suffered a deep primordial longing for the daily dramas his fellow *Homo sapiens sapiens* were so adept at creating. On a purely intellectual level, he wanted to be emotionally self-sufficient. He would even forgo his penis, that tyrant and benefactor, if the reward were to be total freedom from the weaknesses and caprice of *other people.*

Stephen flipped on his heater. It wasn't terribly cold yet, but he was from California and had yet to acclimate to the tundra. The U. of Minnesota was a fine enough school, and given the hiring climate in the humanities he was lucky to have landed a tenure-track job there, even given his standing as a complete badass and object of fear and envy from the silverbacks in the department. Still, the U. had the distinct misfortune of being situated at approximately the same latitude as Moscow. This meant vividly painful winters, sheets of slippery ice, Stephen's black car coated in road salt and sliding through stop signs in a miasma of slush and snow. Winter was coming in a matter of weeks—Stephen's third in Minneapolis. The dread was almost enough to distract him from his driving.

He had an ordered mind, and he doubted whether those who knew him earlier in life understood how psychically disciplined he had become since his dope-smoking, acid-dropping college days. Everyone back home remembered him as a stoner, a burnout, which kind of pissed him off. Now he went to the highest-level academic conferences, where people had heard of him and listened to his latest talk on Lacan or even Borges, for God's sake, when he wanted to mix things up. When he went home he was cast as the bad boy. Shit, so he had acted like Syd Barrett for a few years. Now he was turning into Edmund Wilson. People couldn't let go of the past—*their* problem, not his.

There was a prime parking spot right in front of his duplex. He jogged up the steps, snatching yesterday's *New York Times* in its blue plastic wrapper and tossing it on the table inside. Jay lived in postcollege splendor—she had some decent furniture her parents had given her—but there was no denying her age, which was demonstrated by the presence of milk-carton bookshelves in her living room. Stephen was a full-fledged adult with money and a good job. He had polished wood floors, an antique built-in sideboard, chandeliers, glassed-in book-shelves . . . all this shit that made him feel really good about himself. He'd grown up with money—quite a bit of it, actually, some of it filtering down to him still—but his parents had basi-cally been well-heeled hippies who preferred the reek of in-cense, dust, and cat litter. Now Stephen aspired to elegance, quiet, and dignity—three things his parents would have had trouble recognizing, much less epitomizing.

Papers, papers . . . notes. Stephen went through the things on his desk. He glanced up at the mirror and mussed his hair a little. He cultivated a slightly unkempt image. The girls he taught responded to it and, while he would most certainly never engage in any impropriety with any of them, at any time, on any occasion, he was not averse to being an object of attraction. To as many of them as possible. It was healthy in a sense; it fos-tered a patient-analyst sort of transient romantic attachment. At least, that was what *he* thought. He wasn't going to share *that* particular theory with anyone soon. He started stuffing his briefcase. It was getting late.

When he got back in his car and was driving, other matters in Stephen's life began to surface. Such as the aforementioned Jay and Ramona. And that fucking prick Lewis.

It could be said that taking up with a woman nine years younger was not the best way for Stephen to establish a conven-tionally respectable profile in his department. A woman not much older than his students, a single mother college dropout with raven black hair, toned, flawless skin, and unbelievable thighs. Well, anyone who would *say* such a thing would surely be motivated by their insane jealousy over their incapacity to duplicate Stephen's achievement. Stephen, on more levels than one, was *the man.*

His heart leapt in a giddy fashion as he hit the freeway for the short drive to campus, as he thought of last night and making love with Jay while the moonlight shone through the window, her breasts—God *damn,* those perfect breasts—pressed against his chest while she whispered to him to remember to be quiet. Jay was the most attractive woman Stephen had ever been with, bar none—and it was no small added bonus when he brought her to faculty dinners and watched his colleagues try to suck in their bellies and ingratiate themselves to her in a postmodern ironic fashion while their wives looked on in a decidedly nonironic mode of detachment and pity. Stephen had been with plenty of pretty girls. He was no slouch. But Jay's physical essence was like sweet ambrosia. He had a hard-on now from thinking about the sight of her naked or, better yet, just in panties and a sheer tank top, lounging in her room, seemingly unaware of what an utter hydrogen bombshell she was.

This was not to say that Stephen was sexist, or didn't value women for their intellect—*please.* He'd had all that nonsense drummed out of him aeons ago. He couldn't have been with Jay if her physicality hadn't been wedded to a powerful mind. She was young, a little callow yet, and educated largely in a haphazard, autodidact fashion. Still, she had a history of being regarded as intellectually extraordinary (and now Stephen's heart gave a very different kind of lurch, as he entertained his insecurity over the possibility that she was smarter than him) that dated from her childhood, and it certainly wasn't too late for her to accomplish things. That is, if she could somehow become motivated to raise herself from the semidepressive rut that currently constituted her days.

It was a rut that, he had to admit, was making her somewhat less attractive. *Somewhat.* He knew he shouldn't be so hard on her. She had lost her mother just half a year ago—and what a mother, so knowing, so magnetic, so *hot* (and Stephen winced as he took the exit ramp off the freeway, knowing what an awful thought that was, no matter how profoundly true it was).

Stephen knew it couldn't be easy being a single mother. Jay had the misfortune of getting knocked up early in her sophomore year, and had let her bad luck derail her academic career completely. The father was up in Oregon someplace, utterly useless, never visiting or sending money. *His* name was Michael, and he was working on his family's organic farm—or, to hear Jay tell it, was probably smoking pot all day and goofing off like a post-hippie, Pacific Northwest Hud, eternally juvenile, of no use to either Jay or Ramona.

The real problem, as Stephen saw it—now he was driving into the comforting fantasyland of the university (God, the *girls*)—was Lewis. Stephen exhaled sharply. Lewis, what a creep. A manipulative narcissist of the highest order, an overbearing browbeater who—and here Stephen was entering into dangerous territory, but he had earned his right as a *thinker* to do so—had in a sense possibly caused Anna's cancer. Stephen would not have been surprised to learn that her fatal illness had been some sort of mind-body self-sabotage ploy to escape her husband, the only means at her disposal since, for some reason, she seemed to be sincerely devoted to the man.

Lewis used to work at American Express, in a real high-level corporate management gig. He made piles of money, and Anna never had to work. He styled himself the benevolent upper-middle-class patriarch while scarring the women in his life with his constant needs for validation, collaboration, and approval. Lewis never left his wife and daughter alone, never gave them space to breathe. Stephen had seen it. Now Jay was alone, without the buffer of Anna to absorb Lewis's poison.

If only it had been Lewis who had died.

And then, ten minutes later, Stephen was teaching his class. His mind moved on two tracks at once. He was talking about Kafka, and Musil, stuff he could do in his sleep and often did.

But he was also thinking about Lewis, about having a talk with the old boy. Maybe Stephen could cajole a little sense into him. It wasn't impossible. Stephen could be forceful.

As forceful as Lewis? That remained to be determined.

And now Stephen opened up his book and read aloud to his class.

Someone must have been telling lies about Josef K., for without having done anything wrong he was arrested one morning.

"Someone tell me what that means," Stephen said to his class with a tight smile.

5. HIS CONTINUED WILLINGNESS TO WEAR THE MASK OF LEWIS.

L ewis took the bus downtown. He could have driven his Lexus, but it cost money to park it—he was already overextended on payments on the thing, bought a couple of years ago when he was living another life. His old job at American Express had come with a corner office and prepaid parking in a downtown ramp. His new job came with an employee discount.

It was still impossible to believe that Anna had left the world before him. He'd gone through his decades of on-and-off smoking, his mood problems, the negativity that had cast a pall over his adult life—hadn't that been enough to finish *him* off early? Wasn't that supposed to be the *design*—that he would die before her, that he would never be left alone?

He got off the bus at Seventh Ave. and winced as he was enveloped by the cloud of smoke the thing discharged pulling away from the curb. Despite himself, he still loved downtown in the morning. People were clenched up with the shock of being alive, and the low-angle sun poked from between the buildings like the eye of God. It was splendid.

He was still doing all the clichéd widower things. He woke most mornings and, just for a moment, was considerate of her side of the bed until he remembered that the bed was now all his. When he woke on the sofa downstairs, he searched his memory for whatever transgression had landed him there. He sought out her brand of cereal on the supermarket shelf. He wondered when she was coming home. Everything in his environment promulgated a sense of disbelief.

There, rising above the street, was the building where he used to work. Lewis imagined what was going on up there, on the twenty-second floor, where he once had an assistant and thirty-five people working under him. The company had offered him a leave of absence when Anna was close to death; it had been a chance to walk away and return when he was ready. But he never got ready, and after several months the offer was politely rescinded. Lewis's old peers were incapable of understanding that the man who worked in the corner office no longer existed. He couldn't understand the job anymore, the client services, the supervision, the meetings. Maybe he had never liked it. He certainly hadn't been *happy* there. But now he sure as hell could have used the money.

The sidewalk beneath his feet, as he stood there with people passing, was as solid as anything got. The thing he couldn't grasp was the dissolution of Anna's physical form—the fine lines of cartilage that had formed her nose, the skin stretched over her shoulder blades, her upper lip, her toenails. They were all gone, burned to ashes and poured into Lake of the Isles at midnight, per her typically romantic request. Now, when he ran around the lake two or three times a week, he thought of her resting there. How *useful* all of those body parts had been to her, and for so long. Some of them had had their uses for Lewis, too. Now they were all gone.

All this was hard enough to take without considering all the times when he'd wished he was free, and rid of her, both before and during her sickness. Well, he got his wish. And he had hastened it along, in his usual well-meaning way.

Stop thinking about it.

In the third-floor employee lounge at the Marshall Field's department store Lewis hung up his coat on the peg reserved for his use. He hugged his sides and tried to will away the chill that had descended upon him while walking Carew—and wasn't that a kick in the ass? Done in by the cold already when it was going to be about forty degrees more frigid in a matter of weeks. Maybe it was the antidepressant. Lewis was unconvinced that anyone knew entirely what those pills did to people. True, Lewis was no longer explicitly suicidal, as he had been a couple of weeks before. The powdery little pills had taken care of that for him.

Maybe it was just aging. There was always *that* to contend with: shortness of breath that could not go unobserved, pains in the belly that could never again be dismissed as innocent.

"Lewis. Good morning," said a voice behind him, a voice belonging to Guy Boyle.

"Guy," Lewis said, his voice coming out hoarse.

"Whoa. You coming down with a cold there?" asked Guy.

"Let's hope not," Lewis said.

"Yeah, I hear that," Guy countered. "My kids all have a case of the crud. Looks like maybe winter's coming early."

"Don't say that," Lewis replied. "We'll all be cursed to six months of snowstorms and frozen heads."

"Pardon?" said Guy.

"I meant frozen *pipes*," Lewis said.

Guy laughed. "Ah, I'm not worried," he said. "The winters here aren't as cold as they used to be. You noticed that? We haven't had a real serious cold snap in years."

"I guess a lot of things are different now," Lewis told him, feeling his grin tighten.

Guy's expression froze into affable neutrality. Guy was a career man at the store, with a hearty and seemingly organic love of men's apparel and the intricacies of selling it. He worked in the suit section, the high-end stuff. He was ostensibly Lewis's superior but, because of their similarity in age, he generally treated Lewis as a peer. Guy had three kids, and he and Lewis related to each other as family men until, naturally, something would touch upon the subject of Anna. Lewis understood that he was a bit of a tragic figure in men's wear. Word had spread quickly about his executive past, and the mysterious fall that had necessitated a career change in the early autumn of his years.

Lewis found out about the job from an ad in the Sunday paper. He had just been informed of the hiring of his replacement at AmEx, and so he had just stopped agonizing over calling the office to either resign or announce his comeback. He had gone downtown the next day, applied, met Guy. They hit it off right away. Lewis had confided in Guy about Anna, about how he needed a change. Guy thought that Lewis would fit in fine in men's wear—a tight-knit fraternity of more than a dozen men of varied age. Lewis had started work the next morning. The job paid less than a quarter of what he had been earning previously.

"How's that granddaughter?" Guy asked. "You have to bring her in again sometime. She's a peach."

A peach. So far, Lewis had been remarkably successful at not resenting Guy's bland, insipid optimism. Remarkably, commendably successful.

"She's doing just fine," Lewis told him.

Lewis had spent his boyhood in the suburbs of Chicago, moving to Minneapolis for college and meeting Anna there. She had been lithe, distant, always seeming as though she had just woken from a dream or was about to enter into one. She had been an art student, while Lewis was studying for his MBA. Her friends and rival suitors had thought him conventional, uninteresting. But he had landed her.

"Had coffee yet?" Guy asked him.

"I think I'm going to hold off," replied Lewis. "Caffeine is starting to make me anxious these days."

Guy gave Lewis a funny look which suggested that he had *heard* of this thing called anxiety—an exotic ailment that afflicted women and non-Minnesotans—but had never heard a grown man confessing to suffer from it.

Lewis's heart gave a kick. His hands were cold, almost numb. His mind felt sharp enough, though, to realize that this was going to be one of those very long mornings in which instants stretched themselves into mini-eternities.

"Well, come on out with me," Guy said, a hand on Lewis's shoulder. They left the sterile comfort of the employee lounge for the brightly lit and empty sales floor. The store would open in ten minutes. A Latino man Lewis's age was hurriedly buffing the floor with a machine that looked as though it was about to swallow its master. The sales crew was gathered around a table piled high with neatly folded and stacked neckties. Today the shift was manned by, in addition to Guy and Lewis, Leonard, Dan, Ken, and Vincent. They were all about two decades younger than Lewis, though they were no more energetic or motivated than Lewis on his better days. Lewis worked assiduously to avoid condescension in his dealings with them.

He used to buy a lot of clothes in this department. He remembered buying clothes from his new coworkers, though he couldn't be sure—he'd never paid enough attention to remember their faces or names in the past.

"Ken's going to the Vikings game Sunday," said Vincent when the old men joined them. The younger guys were all drinking coffee from paper cups bearing the name of the store.

"Lucky bastard," said Dan.

"Who'd you have to blow to get the tickets?" asked Leonard.

"Keep it clean, boys," Guy said, glancing around to see if any of his superiors had heard.

"Seriously," said Leonard. "Forty-yard-line tickets for the Packer game. Six rows back. Do you ever run out of luck?"

"Father-in-law," Vincent said sagely. He blew a cloud of steam from the surface of his coffee.

"That right?" asked Dan, eyes narrowing behind his glasses.

Ken shrugged, his shirt rustling. Only about twenty-five, and getting fat.

Dan groaned. "In-laws. It's like a fucking tax built into your life. And you never pay it off."

"*Boys,*" Guy said.

"At least yours live a half a mile away," Vincent said. "You know what my wife did? Gave her mother a key to our house. I said, 'It's your problem if she comes in while I'm giving it to you in the living room.' "

"What'd she say to that?" Leonard asked, approvingly scandalized.

Vincent sipped his coffee. He had wolfish blue eyes. "What *could* she say?"

"Your wife lets you give it to her in the living room still?" Dan asked. "Man, mine's gone all vanilla. Only at bedtime. Says it makes her sleepy."

"I can see you having that effect," Vincent told him.

"It's not my fault," said Dan. "It's marriage. Best thing I ever did, worst thing I ever did."

"We still do it in the living room," Leonard offered. "Got me a blow job on the couch last weekend."

"Bastard," Dan said.

Lewis folded his arms. This was vulgar stuff, and he'd never been at home in the locker room. Still, it was more lively than the discourse in his house these days.

"All right. Enough." Guy stiffened and held up his hands to restore order. The younger guys, one by one, tossed their coffee cups into the trash. The store would open in minutes, and this crew of sex-obsessed hoodlums would transform into helpful experts on silk, cotton weaves, and modern synthetic fabrics.

Lewis was trying hard not to think about numbers. Eight, for instance: there were eight years left on his mortgage. He and Anna had bought the house so long ago that it had nearly tripled in value, but still the payments were a considerable monthly expense. Then there were the taxes, and the utilities—God, it cost a fortune to heat the place, to say nothing of the sewer charges and electricity. The cable bill was up to a hundred bucks, but he couldn't part with *that*. Then the car insurance, the monthly bus pass, the gifts for Ramona, the hundred bucks he slipped to Jay on a regular basis.

Adding it all up, Lewis was losing money working this job. He was, admittedly, losing less money than if he wasn't working at all (already tried that), but his finances were slipping quickly into the abyss. He'd had good health insurance, but Anna's sickness led them into a labyrinth of co-pays and elective treatments that gutted their savings while helping Anna not at all. Even when Anna had argued against it, saying it was no use and she felt death coming over her, Lewis had insisted they try everything. Anna had argued he should save the money for Jay and Ramona.

Anna had turned into a drain. She got sick and drained

everything out of everyone around her, and then she was gone. Lewis recalled, for perhaps the thousandth time, the moment she died.

"What about you, Lewis?" Vincent asked amiably. "You a football fan? Never heard you talk about it."

"No, that's not for me. I'm not one of you conformist morons drooling every Sunday in front of your homoerotic corporate gladiator combat," Lewis did not say, but wished to.

For hadn't he earned—through the virtue of his years, the long slog through his days, his endurance and continued willingness to wear the mask of Lewis Ingraham—the right to resent these men younger than himself? He thought of Stephen, that interloper in his life, bedmate of his daughter, that arrogant pedant who wielded his intellectualism over Jay like a cudgel—Jay, who had showed so much promise, who had shone so brightly and so beautifully, who had been destined to provide a cosmic corrective to Lewis's corporate sell-out and Anna's spent talents. It had all gone so fucking wrong. Anna and Lewis had tried to get Jay to stay in college when she got pregnant; they had practically begged her to move back in their home, as well. Anna even offered to basically raise the baby after the father bailed out and fled to Oregon.

But would it have worked? Lewis never liked babies—too chaotic, too unrewarding. And Anna . . . she had good intentions, but she had been increasingly incapable of keeping her own boat afloat by then. She'd been putting on weight, getting scatterbrained and out of touch, letting the house go to holy hell. Lewis resented all of it, every day. He felt as though Anna had let him down. He may have even undermined the possibility of Jay coming home and staying in school, now that he thought about it.

"How can you propose to take care of a new baby," he might

have asked his wife one night, when they were alone and words had grown cheap and plentiful, "when you can't keep house, and you can barely take care of yourself? Or me."

That was how he remembered it. He might have been wrong.

Lewis looked up at Vincent, whose smile was frozen. Vincent was newly married, barely thirty, living in a new house. It was still all new for Vincent.

"Football, yeah. Well, not really," Lewis said. "It's all right, I suppose. It hasn't been the same for me since the days of Tarkenton and Chuck Foreman."

"You remember all that?" Vincent asked.

"Ahmad Rashad," Dan muttered.

"He's the guy who does those shitty shows," Vincent scoffed. "Michael Jordan's bitch, man."

"Dumb-ass!" Dan crowed, triumphant. "He used to be one of the best receivers in the league. Right, Lewis?"

"That's right."

"Gentlemen, we are now open," Guy announced. Several customers had appeared on the floor, like guerrilla insurgents previously hidden but now emboldened to come out into the open. They wandered as though dazed, stunned and disoriented by the array of goods as well as the tall mirrors strategically placed to prevent shoppers from achieving a cohesive picture of the space.

Lewis wandered over to a big wooden cabinet filled with expensive folded dress shirts—he was wearing one of them, a cotton-blend Calvin Klein with a flat back and double stitching. He'd bought it full-price about eighteen months ago, back when he was at his old job and could afford such things.

He tried to breathe regularly as he allowed himself a moment's contemplation of the depths of his financial pit. Many of his monthly bills were paid automatically on his credit cards, which kept the dogs at bay but also created a rising balance to which astronomical interest rates were regularly and sadistically applied. There were still medical bills left unpaid—thousands of dollars' worth, in fact. It was not going well.

The house was his, and it was beautiful and replete with equity. He could sell it, but what then? An apartment, neighbors upstairs and down? A life diminishing by degree, until there was nothing left of him?

Pain stabbed his chest, right behind the sternum. Lewis rubbed the bone, trying to will it away. It hurt all the time. He could die at any moment.

"Excuse me," said a woman his age. "Do you work here?"

Lewis turned and tried to stay calm. He had to be strong. He had to survive. Jay and Ramona would be bereft without him.

"Yes, of course," Lewis said, pleased by the note of incredulity in her voice (could someone like *him* really be *working* there?). "What can I help you with?"

"I'm buying shirts for my husband," the woman said. She wore sunglasses perched atop her blond head, and she had a pert, athletic figure. She was one of those well-preserved housewives who had haunted the ill-lit corners of his fantasies. "Your shirt is very nice. Did you buy it here?"

"Yes!" Lewis said, brightening and leading her to the display. "You have a good eye. This line of shirts is comfortable, elegant, and they wear well. And we have a very extensive selection of colors. Shall I select a dozen for you? Or two?"

The woman laughed. "So you work on a commission, I take it."

Lewis clasped his hands. "Customer happiness is my greatest satisfaction, far more than any financial consideration."

She laughed again, more genuinely this time. She looked Lewis in the eye for the first time and tucked her hair behind one ear. In fact, she was extremely pretty.

"What size does your husband wear?" Lewis asked.

"Oh, I'm not sure these days," she said. "He's not as tall as you, but he weighs a lot more." She reached out and touched one of the shirts folded in its slot, her fingers lingering on the fabric.

"A bigger man," Lewis said.

"Oh, well, he's gotten fat, if that's what you mean," she said with a louder laugh.

"Happens to some of us," Lewis said, and the woman looked up into Lewis's eyes with a lingering flush of recognition.

"But not you," she said.

"Nor you," Lewis told her.

Lewis glanced over at the nearest cash register. Guy was watching, seemingly with a mix of uncertainty and approval. Lewis, it turned out, had a bit of a gift for the sale. After he'd rung up four shirts for the housewife she lingered at the sales counter for a moment, as though about to say something to Lewis. Then she seemed to remember who she was, and who Lewis was—a *salesman*, for God's sake—and then she left with an uncomfortable half-wave. It was a slightly odd and discordant end to their interaction. It had all been in good fun, hadn't it?

Lewis had lunch with Guy in the Sky Room upstairs: nine bucks for a sandwich and soda, a not-inconsiderable fraction of what he was earning that day. The two men noshed while making small talk about children and real estate. Guy was reasonably bright, in Lewis's estimation, but had a scope of consciousness and awareness about as wide as a cricket's antennae. But Lewis might have been unfair. Life seemed to be working out for Guy Boyle. His kids were apparently not homicidal drug maniacs, he had his home in an inner-ring suburb, a wife he spoke of in complimentary terms. Lewis couldn't account for why he was sitting there stirring a pot of hostility for the man.

No. He knew why. Because there was, if he was honest,

something increasingly wrong with him. He needed a pill to keep from falling into mental anguish and paralyzing fear and guilt. And he had begun to hate everyone, Jay and Ramona excepted.

"You know what I mean?" asked Guy.

"Beg pardon?"

"It's not worth the money." Guy masticated his salad. "I have the money to spend, it's not that. But it's a matter of not spending it on something we don't need. The one we have is every bit as good. Why replace it just because it's a few years old?"

"I'm sure you're right," Lewis said.

Did all of this start with Anna's sickness, or did it predate those awful months? He could blame her; in fact, he *did.* But this feeling went farther back.

"I'm glad we're having lunch today, by the way," Guy said.

"Why?" Lewis asked. "Because you're hungry?"

Guy shot Lewis a look, trying to tell if he was joking. Lewis let him hang there as Guy put down his fork—a sure sign he was serious.

All this responsibility Lewis felt . . . he wished it were possible to talk with someone. Guy was out of the question: too obtuse. There was his neighbor and ostensible friend Stan, but Stan's solution to everything was of the buck-up, could-be-worse school of thought. How to explain this unraveling, this increasingly urgent need to make things right again?

"I don't want to be a jerk, Lewis," Guy was saying. "You know I respect you, and that I think you're a good salesman. And, you know, since we're about the same age, I feel like I can talk to you more directly than the younger guys."

Lewis gripped the edge of the table and tried to breathe. His lungs felt stiff and unresponsive. A cigarette might help, but that would mean going outside and dealing with the chill.

"That woman you sold those shirts to this morning?" Guy asked. "You know the one I mean? The good-looking blonde?"

"There are plenty of good-looking women around here."

"Now you're just being cute," Guy said. "You know the one I mean."

"OK, sure," Lewis said.

"I couldn't help but notice you coming on to her," said Guy.

"What?" Lewis laughed. "It was innocent. If anything, she was coming on to *me.*"

Guy probed the architecture of his teeth with his tongue. "So that's how you saw it."

"Of course!" Lewis said, astonished.

"She looked pretty uncomfortable by the end," Guy said.

Lewis could not believe this conversation. That woman had been bored, obviously unfulfilled, enjoying a little harmless banter with a shirt salesman. There had been an obvious attraction between them, and Lewis had indulged in a little harmless flirting. But now, replaying it in his mind, there were blank spots. He couldn't recall everything he had said. And he remembered touching her back at some point, down low by the tailbone. When exactly had that happened?

"She was uncomfortable," Lewis said.

"She pretty much made a run for it," Guy said. "At least she paid for the shirts first."

"Because of me."

Guy tugged at his tie. "There have been complaints," he said.

"About *me?*"

"I want to keep you working for me." Guy pushed his tray away. "I like you. I feel I can trust you."

Lewis decided for the moment to say nothing. He had no rod with which to check the depths of this exchange.

"It's just that, from time to time, you get a little inappropri-ate."

"Inappropriate."

"A little *intense* with the customers." Guy leaned back, his expression pained. Guy had suggested they eat together. And, apparently, this had been the main item on the agenda.

"Am I about to get fired?" Lewis asked.

"Just be aware. I've been protecting you. But I only have so much sway." With this, Guy evoked the heap-big powers of Nor-man and Gwendolyn, the store managers to whom Guy pledged fealty. Could it be they had been discussing Lewis, crazy old Lewis, and that Guy had had to *intercede* on his behalf?

What had he done? To his mind, he had behaved with im-peccable normality on the job no matter what storms had been raging inside. He tended to *like* his customers. He was effec-tively being told that his social radar was ineffectively cali-brated. Nothing felt right. It was as though his life had ended the night Anna died. The night he . . .

For Christ's sake, that housewife had wanted *him*. Hadn't she?

After his shift was ended, Lewis wandered down to the toy department before catching the bus home. He pledged to him-self not to buy anything but within minutes found himself cap-tivated by an electronic gadget. He began to play with it. It was a book of sorts, shiny and plastic, and it read aloud when you touched it with a stylus.

Ingenious.

This would help Ramona learn how to read, maybe by kindergarten—what an advantage for her. Lewis played with the thing for a good fifteen minutes, touching the pen to the page and listening to it read out words and sentences. There was a nature book, and one that taught geography. He had amassed a pile of the best ones just as a young female clerk came up to him.

"Those are great," she said.

She was a redhead, about twenty-five, wearing one of those sweaters that showed off her breasts without making a big deal of it. She had bright green eyes and wore a long black skirt. Her eyes lingered on his employee name tag.

"They look good," Lewis said. "I mean, I really think these are great."

A little *intense,* Guy had said. Her name tag said Janine. She was just a couple of years older than Jay.

She fixed him with a plastic smile. "Do you already own the main unit?"

"What?" Lewis asked, alarmed. He looked into her eyes, then thought he was coming on too strong. For a horrible second he looked directly at her breasts (a hint of nipple, oh *God*), then looked at the toys in his hands.

"These books," she said. "They plug into a main unit. They don't do anything on their own."

"Oh." Lewis was dumbfounded. "Do we sell that here?"

The girl laughed. "Of course we do." She picked up a big plastic box and held it out. He took it.

"All right then," Lewis said.

They piled all the crap on the counter. Before the girl was finished ringing it all up, Lewis grabbed a stuffed calico cat and put it on the counter. Then a black one. Ramona collected stuffed cats.

"OK, that's a hundred and twelve dollars and sixty-two cents," she said after she had scanned everything. "With your employee discount."

Lewis handed over his credit card. His hands were shaking, and it was hard work to look everywhere but at the girl.

6. IT WAS ALL WELL AND GOOD FOR A DEAD BEARDED GUY.

t was getting colder with alarming speed. Jay dropped Ramona off at day care—enduring a minor emotional squall in the process, after which Ramona's mood shifted with mercurial ease into resentful recalcitrance—and when she walked to her car she began to shiver. The temperature was down around freezing. It was an early frost, but not terribly unusual. About ten years back there had been a legendary Halloween ice storm; everything had been encased in inches of clear frozen rain, with power lines snapping and cars doors sealed shut. Jay had been just entering her teens then, riding out a late-onset puberty that in retrospect was the turning point at which life became impossibly complicated and difficult.

But that was her story—brilliant girl steers ship directly into iceberg of sex. This body she inhabited, which gave her pleasure but which also evoked too many echoes of her mother, had absorbed a single shot of semen and incubated an entirely new human life. Years of sunshine and snow she wouldn't know—she'd become a mother too young.

Jay steered through the sluggish traffic toward work. She'd gotten a late start and was going to be tardy for her shift, which started at the end of brunch and ran through midday—terminating before the lucrative drinks-and-dinner hours. She'd learned that preserving her inner peace (such as it was) was best accomplished by avoiding paranoid speculation about being slighted and steered away from the best shifts. Of course, she suspected she was.

She gunned the engine and shot through a yellow light. A car coming from the other direction blared its horn and nearly ran into her. She had never been the best driver in the world—too many thoughts intruding, too many things to look at. She was more cautious when Ramona was in the backseat.

Ramona's father was named Michael Carmelov, currently of Coos Bay, Oregon, living with his parents, a college dropout like Jay. Michael had come to Minnesota for college because of vague family connections that Jay had never been able to entirely sort out. They hadn't gotten to know each other very well. Jay met Michael at a party early her sophomore year. Michael had been in premed, but his grades weren't good enough to promise much in the way of a medical career, and it was obvious even then that he'd never have the endurance to navigate the years of sacrifice required to actually become a doctor. Jay had been a history major, earning mostly A's. Michael was very good-looking, with wavy hair and delicate features that in repose fell into an approximation of perceptiveness and sensitivity. It was one of those accidents of genetics—the way a face could deceive without trying.

They never even became boyfriend and girlfriend. They went to a couple of all-ages indie-rock shows together at the Seventh Street Entry. They attended several parties that were indistinguishable from the one where they met. Michael wanted to have sex, so did Jay. They practiced the pull-out method, which had worked for Jay with the ten or so partners she had racked up through high school and one year of college. In fact, Jay had started to wonder about her fertility—envisioning a future when she was thirty-five and unable to bear a child. It became one of many amorphous anxieties that plagued her in those days.

It turned out she needn't have worried. She had sex with Michael three or four times, and she got pregnant. What rankled still was that the sex wasn't very good at all. She'd had a lover at sixteen, her second, who with a total lack of carnal training had been better in the sack than Michael. Rookie luck, she supposed. The memory of Michael made her bitter—the way he pawed at her breasts with no recognition of the subtle nerve topography there, the way he seemed not to have heard of the clitoris, the way he mounted her and heaved in a middling fashion that brought neither the satisfaction of the subtle stroke or the aggressive joy of the animal fuck. *He* was the man who had fathered her child.

The restaurant where Jay worked was on a stretch of Lyndale that featured a bike shop, a brewpub, a rug store, and two coffeehouses. Back when Jay was in high school, she used to smoke pot with her friends and walk around this neighborhood. One time they snorted some crystal meth (obtained from a connection to the rural wastes of the Iron Range) and walked miles and miles for hours and hours around Uptown and the Wedge, in widening circles until they were all the way downtown at the doors of the City Center. In the late-morning wind, Jay could taste the methamphetamine in the back of her mouth as, six years after the fact, she prepared for her shift at the Cogito.

She tried to remember what the building had been in earlier incarnations, during her childhood and teenage years. Nothing came to mind. Time passed. Lewis was always going on about the mutability of things and, though she had never really doubted him, she was now seeing for herself. The Cogito had existed less than a year, and would undoubtedly vanish in a few more. Restaurants had their own reality: you leased a place with kitchen facilities, you cooked food, customers showed up and told their friends about a new cutting-edge eatery they had discovered. Maybe a reporter from the newspaper came and did a story. Then, after a while, the restaurant's familiar presence, its reliable solidity, became a perfect excuse for never visiting it. That was when you went out of business. If you weren't totally ruined, you could take a chance and open another one.

Jay went in through the back, hung up her jacket, and said *Buenos días* to Jorge, who washed dishes and chopped food for eight hours a day. He was half of an enthusiastically acrimonious duo with Fowler, the cook, who was short and slight and had perpetually bloodshot eyes. Though Jorge was taller, and stouter, the two men were like a pair of dogs who had established a pecking order in inverse order to their respective sizes. The Cogito's other cook was a middle-aged woman called Giselle, who was pleasant and much easier to deal with than Fowler. It was by virtue of this agreeable personality that she generally got the dinner shifts, though in fact Fowler was the better cook.

Jay paused in the kitchen and took in the smells of garlic and saffron, the sizzle of oil in the pan and the warm, close air.

And then in came Phil, her boss. He was about thirty and so good-looking as to be an improbable heterosexual—though these credentials were firmly established by his constant advances toward Jay, usually couched in nice-guy camaraderie but unmistakable nonetheless. Putting on her apron, she sensed Phil's eyes on her. His attractiveness was no problem—Michael Carmelov had obligingly cured her forever of mistaking good looks for appealing inner qualities—but Phil's look added to a feeling she was coming to hate. She wanted to become invisible, she wanted to be left alone. It was like the look Stephen gave her, and Ramona. These hungry eyes stripped her down. Most of all she resented the one-sidedness of all these looks—when did she get *her* visual feast?

"Morning, Jay," Phil said. "You're a little late."

"I had to drop Ramona off," Jay told him, fixing her hair in the mirror. "Plus I fell into a space-time vortex and had a bitch of a time climbing out."

"Those are nasty," Phil admitted. He gave a brunch order to Fowler—verbally, of course, because Phil took pride in never writing anything down. He had asked Jay to do the same, in the name of some amorphous sense of elegance, but it proved impossible. She'd inevitably forget the order, then be forced to return to the table to take it again. Sometimes when she came back, the customers couldn't remember what they had ordered, and the whole process had to begin again.

"This fish isn't good," Fowler said, pointing with a wooden spoon at a ceramic dish of fillets on the counter.

"Dress it up," Phil said. "Put lemon slices over it."

"Where are we getting this shit?" Fowler's mustache folded with distaste.

"I don't even know," Phil replied. "Talk to Bjorn or Jenny about it if you have a problem."

"Just cook it," Jorge muttered.

"Hey, go *fuck yourself,* Jorge," Phil said over the divider that bisected the kitchen.

"You are bitching too much," Jorge said.

Fowler put his nose close to the fillets. "Smell it," he said to no one in particular. "Someone's going to get sick. If no one else is, *I'm* going to, just from being around this trash. It smells like mercury."

"No one's going to get sick," Phil pronounced, as though he willed it to be so. "Just make sure it's cooked all the way through."

"I know how to cook a fucking fish," Fowler said. "I'm just saying it smells like a garbage barge."

Phil threw up his hands. "Then prove it, Great One. Cook the fucking fish."

"All he does is bitch," said Jorge. "It's making me insane."

Jay had worked her share of crap jobs—clerking in a mall music store, scooping ice cream, ringing up orders in a fast-food joint—all through high school. Since leaving college she'd become a waitress. In her excursions into the service sector, she had come to sort her co-workers into two categories: those who belonged at their level of employment, and those who didn't. Fowler was firmly in the former category—he cooked food, and would presumably do so as long as he was able. Jorge was among the latter—he was unskilled, his English wasn't great, but he had a presence that belied the fact of his menial job. He was probably consigned permanently to such tasks, but there was a *Jorgeness* about him untouched by soap suds, cutting boards, and any future trash cans that would need to be emptied. Phil occupied a special place—he was one of the former who believed himself to be among the latter. He managed the day shift at a small restaurant in south Minneapolis. Within a few years he would have lived more than half his days.

The question, naturally: Of which type was Jay? The youthful-promise thing had worked fine so far. She could schlep pasta and uncork Chianti while polishing the gem of her yet-unlined face and destiny, which surely was to *get it together* and become a viable *adult* with a good job and a household in which Ramona could become one of those self-possessed little genius children rather than a life-scarred ragamuffin.

Right? She wasn't going to be waiting tables in ten years, was she?

Jay liked the first part of any shift best. The dining room looked fresh with its undersized tables, rough floor, and austere lighting. Later the room would seem tawdry and worn out, when she felt the same, and Jay would inevitably wonder when this unadorned decorating thing would go out of style—because, honestly, wasn't rough and raw the same as *ugly,* and when had it become déclassé to want to sit in a comfortable chair or have art on the wall that *represented* something, or to play music with heart and emotion rather than merely a detached manipulation of . . .

Whoa. That sounded exactly like Lewis.

She wore a path between the dining room and the kitchen, bringing forth garnished sandwiches, dressed-up hamburgers, and complicated salads. She got hungry and Fowler made her some scrambled eggs, which she ate standing up.

Not a day passed without Jay pondering her decision to quit college. It was a lot of work, college, despite all the good-times propaganda, but she would have been a graduate by now instead of chewing eggs in a drafty kitchen.

"Good eggs?" Fowler asked, looking up from a Mephistophelean fire that was making his forehead sweat.

"The best," said Jay.

"People put too much spice in 'em," Fowler said. "Fucks them up. Eggs taste good. They don't need help."

With the benefit of a few years' experience in the world, Jay understood that her choice of a history major might have been quixotic. If she didn't complete grad school, her degree would have guaranteed prospects little more appetizing than teaching school or, maybe, writing for some *organization.* She still had the option of returning to school to earn some kind of practical degree—business, or communications. But what then? Work for a corporation? Lewis had done that for decades, and made plenty of money, but he never claimed to like it. The Lewis that Jay saw going off to work Mondays barely resembled the laughing, subversive father of Saturday morning. He turned buttoned-up, stiff, and in some automatic mode in which he killed off part of himself. He seemed happier selling shirts. Well, not *happier*—how to use that word, with a man like Lewis—but at least more *authentic*.

So what was she going to do? When she tried to talk to Stephen, he told her to read Marx. She'd *already* read Marx, back in high school. Sure, we were all alienated from our work—point granted. Capitalism sucks? Sure, why not. It was all well and good for a dead bearded guy. But what about her?

She wished her mother were alive.

At least Anna died at home, which was all she had asked for in her final days. Lewis had called in the morning while Jay was making Ramona her toast and juice, and told her that Anna had died an hour before in the first light of dawn. He waited until Jay came over before calling the paramedics to take the body away.

The way it worked was, you said good-bye to someone, and then you thought about them all the time. You knew they weren't coming back, yet still you held each new event and possibility for them to examine, to comment upon. But they never did. Dead people were stupid, with their stubborn inability to keep up with current events.

Jay had an armload of dishes as she wove through the nearly full dining room. The Cogito was going through its growth phase, too innocent yet to look ahead to its decline. Everyone who came in was rubbing their hands together, blowing their noses, their eyes full of the unexpected cold. The street through the window had that browned-out colorless hue of winter before the snow.

She laid out the plates for a trio next to the window— a woman in black, and two bearded men wearing the earnest earth tones of Unitarians. Jay had pegged them as local theater types, or maybe small-time real-estate entrepreneurs. She knew they had her pegged as a waitress.

"Miss?" said one of the men, kindly eyed through glasses. "Excuse me?"

Jay was halfway gone, and had to stop and turn. "Did I forget something?"

"No, it's just that we didn't order this." His companions looked down at their plates as though they had arrived from another galaxy.

"We haven't ordered anything," said the woman in black. "Can we see some menus?"

Wrong table. Jay picked up the plates again. She sensed everyone in the place looking at her. She wavered for a moment and then decided to brazen it out. The rightful owners of the three dishes looked at them warily, glancing over at the other table as though gauging how much they had contaminated the food during their brief ownership of it. Jay smiled as though nothing had happened.

Only a few more hours to go.

7. THE POINT OF FEAR, BEYOND ITS UTILITY AS A WARNING.

There comes a point at which the sweating man begins to feel a chill rather than the heat of his exertion. It's a nauseating feeling, accompanied by a threat of loosening from the bowels and a general blurring of vision. The whole thing was downright ominous. It made a man think of how he might feel in the final moments before a catastrophic physical breakdown.

Stephen stood panting and dripping, watching a man almost ten years his junior line up for a free throw and, inevitably, miss it. These were, after all, graduate students in the humanities. They could toss around a little Kant and Hegel, but they were hopeless with a basketball in their hands.

The game resumed. Stephen had long since stopped caring about the score, his main ambition now being to keep moving without passing out, or dying, or suffering an involuntary explosion from his innards that would embarrassingly soil the court at the university gym. He jogged across half-court, his knees aching, one arm held up for the ball.

Of course he shouldn't have done *that*. He was the sole faculty member on the court, and the students kept one eye on him at all times—in part to divine whether he favored any of them, also in sheer curiosity over whether he could keep his feet. As soon as he indicated an interest in the ball, it was duly passed to him. And here it was, orange and pimpled, requiring a dismaying amount of arm strength to keep it bouncing.

He was being guarded by Francis, a second-year kid from Brown who went to great pains to convince people how unguarded and guileless he was. Stephen bounced the ball and tried to keep his eyes in focus. Francis was giving him plenty of space, not poking at the ball, for which Stephen was both grateful and abstractly irritated. He took a couple of lateral steps, and Francis followed a step behind. Surely he wasn't going to lay off so much—Stephen was only thirty-two, after all. Did they have him placed in another generation?

Looking around, trying to remember which players were on his team—Tim Rappel? King? That cipher from Urban Planning?—Stephen felt a spasm somewhere in his midsection and half-coughed, half-belched up something that tasted like . . . like . . . *last night's three whiskey and sodas.* He kept the ball bouncing and tried not to think about it. From the waist down he was all pain. Above that was an entire mountain range of trouble, peaks of nausea and valleys of abdominal insubordination. Breaking into a run seemed out of the question.

But it appeared he had to do something. He had been dribbling the ball for a long time. Someone said something about Gary Payton that may or may not have been directed at him. He was too flustered and spent to try passing the ball, so he put his head down and stepped past Francis, who stared in surprise and made little attempt to stop him. A couple of opponents closed in on him now, but moving forward with perhaps the final reserves of his legs and heart, he burst to within about eight feet of the basket and let loose a one-handed floater.

Stephen's momentum carried him into the Urban Planning guy, who shunted him aside torero-style. As he tumbled to the floor, already adoring the sweet relief of lying down, he watched the ball reach the altitude of the basket like a wounded bird. *God,* what an embarrassing shot—he had sort of pitched it up there, like an end-of-the-bench sub in a high-school girls' game. Now, improbably, almost apologetically, it sort of *slid* into the net with barely enough force to make it through. It landed on the floor with an exhausted thud, right next to him.

"Nice one," said Francis, who was going to be attending one of Stephen's critical theory seminars next semester.

"That was George Gervin shit," said the Urban Planning guy in the requisite pseudo-insulting manner in which they all felt compelled to communicate.

"Thank . . . you," Stephen gasped. He glanced at his watch as he peeled himself off the floor, leaving a big sweat stain where he had fallen. They'd been playing for half an hour. But *full-court,* he reminded himself. "And now . . . that I've taken you all *to school* . . . ahg . . . so to speak . . . I have to make . . . a phone call."

Stephen staggered across midcourt to the bench at the other end. There were protests about him leaving his team short-handed, but finally the younger men allowed him to salvage some dignity. His chest burned and his guts growled, but he thought he might be able to ride it out. He fought off an over-powering urge to go outside and curl up in the grass, knowing it was too damn cold for that.

He had said something about making a call. To save face as the game resumed, he rooted around in his jacket for his phone. He dialed Jay's apartment out of reflex. There really wasn't anyone else for him to call, anyway. She answered with a tone of tired self-defense.

"Where are you?" she asked.

"At the gym," he said in an approximation of his usual speaking voice. "Playing basketball with a bunch of students. Trying not to drop dead."

Jay laughed. "Yeah, you're such an old man."

"All evidence points in that direction," Stephen said. "I think I almost passed out."

"Then we may have a problem. I'm not sure how much I want to be your nursemaid."

"How was work?" he asked.

"Fantastic. Brilliant. I cured cancer and healed the Republic. Plus I brokered a peace between the Twin Cities."

"Something's bothering you, then," Stephen said.

"Look, don't start—"

"Because whenever I hear this woe-is-me stuff—"

"Didn't I just say not to—"

"You should listen to yourself," he told her. "You sound like you're under attack. And that can only mean one thing."

"Oh, *fuck*, Stephen."

"How long has it been since you talked to him?"

"I hung up about a minute before you called," Jay said. She was laughing.

"They *do* call me doctor," Stephen told her. "And I *do* love you, Jaybird. I don't like hearing you in these moods."

The Urban Planning guy drove the lane and tossed in a smooth layup. Stephen hadn't made such a graceful shot since his blacktop preteen days.

"You know what?" Jay said, flashing back to her default mode of defensive hostility. "I don't like *being* in a bad mood. But it doesn't help to have it pointed out to me when I'm crabby. *They* call you doctor, Stephen, but I don't."

"OK. Point taken. What did Lewis say?"

"The usual. He nagged me about what school I'm going to try to get Ramona into. He insinuated that I'm wasting my time—which I may be. I certainly spend enough time thinking about the subject."

Jay kept talking, but Stephen was only half-listening. Lewis simply never let up. He probed his daughter's weaknesses, projecting his own pain and uncertainty onto her—thus ensuring that she remained in a state of rattled defense. Lacan's *jouissance* was defined as unbearable suffering that produced satisfaction to unconscious drives—perversity, as Stephen saw it, and Lewis had it in spades.

Stephen pulled back from himself. Of course on some primal level he resented Lewis for being alive. That was the price Lewis had to pay for being the father of the girl Stephen felt illegitimate about fucking. Stephen knew it would serve him best to stay on high ground and not let himself get too drawn into the lunacy of this (go ahead, admit it) messed-up and semicrazy family.

But his loyalties were solidly with Jay. There were higher regions of thought, and in them Stephen simply loved her. If they were going to have a future together, she was going to have to get her head together and escape Lewis's suffocating *mishigas*.

"It's the same old stuff," Stephen said, watching the clumsy ballet on the basketball court. "You just need space from him."

"I know," Jay replied. Stephen detected the exhaustion in her voice. This was the same conversation they'd had a dozen times. It was starting to become difficult to find new ways to formulate old sentiments. Stephen felt his mind begin to multitrack. He was due in a committee meeting in about thirty minutes, followed by office hours. That night he had to review a batch of papers graded by a scatterbrained T.A. whose frequently bleary eyes may or may not have been evidence of a pot habit. And then there was the book Stephen was supposed to be writing, which at the moment was little more than twenty pages of disparate notes and a half-assed outline on his hard drive.

He asked Jay an innocuous question about Ramona, buying time while his mind worked. It took just a moment to shift his consciousness sideways and to utterly objectify his own motives. He occupied a unique position in these people's lives—as a latecomer, he was unencumbered by any prevailing sentiment other than his love/lust for Jay (intertwined, as was healthy) and his affection for her daughter. He wasn't caught up in things and now, thinking hard about it, he suspected that he was an ideal catalyst for positively affecting the family dynamic.

But there was a blockage . . . a vague, diffuse fear: on some level he was frightened of Lewis. And so was Jay. Lewis was physically and mentally strong, and he was utterly self-absorbed even by contemporary standards. Lewis was creepy and a little scary. Well, the point of fear, beyond its utility as a warning system, was that overcoming it was educational.

Which meant that Stephen was going to finally deal with his girlfriend's crazy dad.

"Stephen?" Jay said. "Still there?"

The game was breaking up. Another group was waiting by the side of the court to begin their allotted sign-up period. If there were two things students and professors knew how to do, it was signing forms and waiting for things to begin.

"I'm still here," Stephen replied. "Sorry, I was watching the game. It makes me wonder—have I always been so feeble, or am I really getting old?"

"My old man," Jay said in that husky tone she took, the one that always surprised him. "Experience has been good for you. I'm glad I got the older Stephen. It saved me all the fumbling around."

"Oh, and I did some fumbling."

"You all do," Jay told him. "Believe me. I've been fumbled plenty."

"Hopefully I'm not fumbling anymore."

"You are not fumbling, Dr. Grant."

"That is so gratifying," he said.

"It is for me, too," said Jay.

A part of Stephen empathized with Lewis. Any father would be entranced to the point of obsession by such a daughter.

"I'm going to go," Jay said. "We've wasted enough time."

"Right." He started getting his things together. He was going to have to hurry to get showered and dressed.

"And don't worry so much about Lewis," Jay added with uncharacteristic seriousness.

"I'm worried about *you*," he replied.

"Just let it be," she said. "All of this is like ripples in a pond. It'll settle down before too long."

"OK," he said, unconvinced. "I'll let you work it out."

He knew he was lying to her. He was going to get involved.

"Dad needs me," Jay said. "He thinks he has to protect me. It gives him something to think about other than . . . you know, his loneliness."

Stephen wiped the sweat from his forehead and thought about what she had said.

"Take care of that soul of yours, Jaybird," he said by way of good-bye.

INTERLUDE. SHE WOULD MAKE HERSELF DUMB AND SLEEPY FOREVER.

Ramona listened from around the corner. She stared for a long time at the white paint on Mama's bedroom doorway, loving the way it had chipped and been painted over again, making little valleys and craters in slightly different colors. She put her face to the surface and dared a lick, just a little one, before pulling her face away. Some paint had stuff in it that would make you dumb and sleepy forever. Ramona regretted what she had just done. She blinked, thinking she felt sleepy. Maybe it was starting.

"And don't worry so much about Lewis," Mama said on the phone. Mama was sitting on her bed and looking out the window.

Ramona knew she was talking to Stephen by the way she was laughing, a quiet but constant sound, as though everything he said was funny. A lot of the time Mama acted like *nothing* was funny, except now sometimes she laughed when Ramona said something that wasn't meant to be funny—and now that she thought about it, that made Ramona feel kind of mad.

She licked the doorway again. Maybe she would make herself dumb and sleepy forever. Would everyone like her then? They could laugh all they wanted to, while Ramona would sit in the hospital and watch TV and get treats all day. It didn't sound too bad.

Mama was talking about Grampa. His name was *Lewis*. When Mama and Stephen talked about him, they always sounded worried, or like they were arguing.

One time Ramona had called Mama "Jay," just to see what it was like. Mama had gotten mad and told Ramona never to do it again.

The rules were always changing.

"Dad needs me," Mama said. "He thinks he has to protect me."

Ramona stuck her head around the doorway. Mama was sitting on the edge of the bed in her underpants and a T-shirt. Mama was twirling her hair in her fingers. She didn't know Ramona was there.

Grampa thought he needed to protect Mama—well, that *was* true. Mama needed protecting. A lot of the time, Mama acted like she didn't know what to do. That worried Ramona, because Mama was perfect and it didn't make sense for Mama not to know it. Not perfect like God—that was different. Ramona knew God was perfect, but she didn't talk about it much because Mama didn't believe in God. Grampa didn't, either. But someone had to be keeping the sun in the sky, and making sure the birds came back in the spring.

Grampa made Ramona worry. He came to the apartment the day before with some nice new presents, but when Ramona played with them she felt Grampa watching her. She felt his . . . *stress*. Grampa wanted something from her, and from

Mama, that they couldn't possibly give him. Maybe when God made Grandma Anna come back, she would tell them all what happened when she died and make everything better.

Mama hung up the phone and turned around. It happened so fast that Ramona didn't have time to hide.

"Ramona, how long have you been standing there?" Mama asked.

"I don't know."

"You know what I told you about eavesdropping," Mama said, kind of mad, kind of not.

"I know," said the Perfect Princess. She smiled at the Old Queen, who never stayed mad for long.

The Old Queen smiled back. "What am I going to do with you?" she asked.

"I don't know," said the Perfect Princess, who never did anything wrong, and who always made things right.

"Well, at least come give me a hug, you little spy," said the Old Queen, for whom hugs were food, and for whom the Perfect Princess was always available to lend strength.

8. OF ALL THE THINGS HE NEEDED AT THIS STAGE OF HIS LIFE.

I t was not Lewis's favorite time of day—mid-morning, a compromise between the promise of the early hours and the gradual setbacks and accommodations leading to the end of his work shift. He stood by a rack of ties doing increasingly desperate math: he'd made about seventy-five dollars so far that morning, enough to almost cover the cable bill. If he skipped lunch every day that week, he might make enough in wages and commissions not to have to dip too far into his remaining savings.

Of course, that took for granted that he would continue to ignore the increasingly strident demands from the bill collectors that he make headway on Anna's medical expenses.

Carew had woken Lewis at six for his trip to the park to void his bowels, nipping and straining at the leash, the poor damned thing seeming to feed off of Lewis's anxiety. Lewis had popped his antidepressant and—who cared what he looked like—

donned his winter coat and hat against the chill. He had shivered in the park while Carew did his thing, one hand on the cell phone in his pocket, fighting off the urge to call and wake Jay.

Lewis took a deep breath that caught in his chest. His heart lurched. He pretended to examine the rack of ties while listening to the soft piano music filtering through Men's Wear. The pills made his mouth dry, made his teeth taste bitter. He couldn't really say what effect they were having on his mood. He was not depressed per se. He sensed his heart drifting somewhere above the rest of him, which made him feel calmer than a month before.

His doctor wanted him to visit a therapist. She was a new doctor, packaged with the insurance that came with his job at the department store. She was young, thin, and strangely attractive for all her sternness and obvious anxiety over her legitimacy and authority. Lewis had acknowledged that getting his head examined wasn't the worst idea in the world, but he'd mused out loud to the young doctor—a brunette in black jeans with an uncertain smile—that at this late date in his existence it might be better to leave things alone. He told her about his shortness of breath and the chest pains, and she'd assured him that "almost definitely" his symptoms had psychological origins.

Almost definitely.

The day of Anna's diagnosis had coincided with the nadir of their marriage, from Lewis's point of view. What Anna thought, Lewis couldn't have said. She seemed content, but she had let herself get chubby, which had dulled Lewis's desire for her as his own sexual powers continued their gradual slide. While he thought of sex continually, morning erections had become sporadic, and his ability to get it up wasn't helped by the sight of Anna's white cellulite-laden thighs and expanding waistline. Anna seemed content with whatever carnal attention Lewis could manage, however infrequent, and spent her days out on the sunporch painting—canvases of their garden, nothing else. Her painting was very good. Several of her oils were still propped against the walls of the sunporch. When Lewis looked at them, he saw flowers. He stared at them for long periods of time, as though the blurry images would give him some clue of what she thought, or felt.

For his part, Lewis had been seething with anger nearly all the time. He had mastered his job at American Express, and his daily life amounted to little more than tedious nuisance. When he came home, the place was always a mess—newspapers scattered everywhere, dishes in the sink, unwashed clothes stacked in the bathroom hamper. Anna would be on her daily walk around the lake when Lewis unlocked the door and let himself inside. There were times when Lewis hated her, for confining him and blithely consenting to make him what he had become— a man of routine, of moral timidity, of grasping uncertainty.

He even hated her for his affairs, such as they were.

She hadn't felt well for some time. She had sharp pains in her abdomen. She finally started to lose weight, though not in an attractive way. Her eyes settled in caverns of darkness, and she slept twelve hours a night. After a while she started inexplicably vomiting after meals. Lewis suggested she get to the doctor.

The news came fast, all in one day. Anna went to the doctor in the morning, and by afternoon she was on the phone with Lewis.

"I think you'd better come home," she told him.

"What's wrong?" Lewis asked. He had a four o'clock meeting, he remembered, one that seemed very important.

"I'm . . . *sick*," she said.

"How sick?" Lewis asked. He remembered looking out his corner-office window, peering down at the Foshay Tower and the Metrodome.

"Sick," Anna said. "Sick for real."

"Oh, Christ," Lewis had said.

On the way home that day, Lewis steeled himself for the months to come. Driving down LaSalle through the Phillips neighborhood (brick apartment buildings giving way to run-down multitenant houses in the direction he wasn't going) he realized he had known all along that this was going to happen. Anna had tethered him to a life he had never wanted, and now she was leaving him. The torpor, the lassitude, had been harbingers of her death. He thought he had hated her for what had become of him, but now he realized that he had hated her for her death.

He stopped hating her. By the time he pulled into the driveway he had been desperate to make amends. She met him at the door. They sat down and she described what the tests had revealed: a big, necrotic tumor right in the middle of her. They cried, they said all sorts of things. Lewis apologized for the way he had treated her, all the while trying to make peace with all the hateful thoughts. Anna told him she wanted to fight the cancer, but she knew she would lose. The doctor hadn't wanted to say so, but she had seen it in his face.

When they pulled out of their tearful embrace, Lewis looked at her. In telescoping time, he saw all the ages of Anna at once—sexy young aesthete, devoted mother, detached middle-aged enigma. He was not in love with her, the years had taken care of that. But he understood the sheer weight of all they had put up with from each other, and the degree of devotion it had required. Lewis had cursed his cowardice for going into the twilight, and her for allowing it to happen. Now he saw that twilight as the form and texture of his own particular journey through life—as though, for all they had endured, they had been born for each other.

It was terribly ironic. Of *course* he was going to try to make amends before she died. Only a complete bastard wouldn't. Wasn't this singular epiphany of Anna's worth to him merely what anyone would have felt? Was that how it worked—going through life resentful and petty, then loving it all just before it was snatched away? Was he merely going through a clichéd Stage One of Spousal Grieving, now that it was clear she was lost to him?

Lewis shivered in his antidepressant chill. As though there was a pill for dealing with this shit. He straightened a rack of sport coats. He felt his heart beating faster than it should. He had a momentary image of Carew dead, run down by a car, and remembered that he used to fantasize about Anna's death, long before she took ill.

Someone said his name, and Lewis looked up. In this context, it took him a good five seconds to realize that he was looking into the charming green eyes of Stephen Grant.

"Stephen," Lewis said. "Can I sell you a shirt?"

Stephen smiled indulgently and leaned against a counter. He was wearing a jacket and tie, both of pretty decent quality, and carrying a thick leather briefcase stuffed with papers. His hair was brushed rakishly off his forehead, and he looked almost exactly his age. Lewis felt a flush of jealousy.

"Maybe another time," Stephen said. "I was hoping we could have a chat."

"Have a *chat*," Lewis repeated. He gestured around him. "Maybe you're not aware of the setup here. Let me fill you in. This is a business. I am at my job."

Stephen sighed as though he had known this was going to be difficult and now found himself in a scenario he had foreseen precisely.

Lewis felt his jaw clench involuntarily. He might have even liked this guy, if it hadn't been for the knee-jerk condescension that emanated from him like smoke off a slow-burning fire.

"I thought it would be a good idea to talk on neutral ground," Stephen said. "Look, I'm sorry for surprising you. I had a meeting that got canceled. Can you take a break or something?"

Lewis remembered that he had intended, several days ago, to instigate just such an encounter with Stephen. Whatever the hell was on Stephen's mind, this was a perfect chance for Lewis to impart his concern for Jay and Ramona.

"Actually," he said, "your timing is perfect. Let me get permission from Massa, and we'll go get a cup of coffee."

Lewis led Stephen down to the Starbucks adjacent to the big two-story Barnes & Noble down on street level, tucked beneath the skyways. This was an act of subtle aggression, since Lewis had sat through several dinners during which Stephen regaled his captive audience with his thoughts on corporations, globalism, and consumer consumption. Lewis's tenure with American Express, naturally, loomed beneath the surface of Stephen's crusade to edify the ignorant.

With an involuntary gasp, Lewis registered the chill in the air and folded his arms around himself as they crossed the street. Stephen pulled a face when Lewis headed for the revolving door.

"Uh, Lewis?" Stephen said. "You know, there's a coffee shop half a block from here."

Lewis knew the one Stephen meant—the one with the fashion-plate girls behind the counter and the murals on the wall—the one that was *independently owned.* Christ, the things people found to worry about. Even Jay, who couldn't be bothered to dress like an adult even though she had a daughter about to start kindergarten.

"The thing is," Stephen added, somewhat piously, "I don't usually patronize Starbucks."

Jesus. Lewis liked Starbucks. It was clean. The coffee was good, and it always tasted the same, no matter the time of day.

They had *standards* you could count on. They were even blandly cheerful to Lewis when he stopped in most days. What was wrong with that?

"Well, make an exception—just this one time," Lewis said as he pushed open the door. "Patronize *me,* all right?"

Stephen sighed, hitched up his briefcase, and followed Lewis through the door. They moved through the bookstore, past the racks of magazines and into the coffee shop. There was no line, and Lewis ordered his usual cup of coffee from the usual cute young girl, who dispatched Lewis quite quickly then perked up considerably at the prospect of interacting with Stephen. The girl smiled and seemed to regard Stephen's ordering a latte as an act of admirable discernment. What the hell, Lewis thought. So it was Stephen's turn to be relatively young.

They sat together at a small table by the window, looking out at the pedestrian traffic on Nicollet: young men and women in business clothes mixed with that semisubterranean population for whom downtown was apparently the most interesting place to while away their idleness—those shabby, slightly crazed folk of indeterminate age, many clutching to worn and faded bags from Target or Walgreens, as though these totems of consumerism lent them a tawdry respectability that belied their appearance. Lewis stirred his coffee and turned his attention to Stephen.

"I don't have a lot of time," he said.

"This won't take long," Stephen replied. "I wanted to talk to you about Jay."

"Funny, so did I," said Lewis.

"Really?" Stephen said, sipping his latte through its plastic lid.

"Ramona is very young," Lewis told him. "And she is in a confusing situation, effectively having no father. Do you think it's appropriate for you to be spending the night at Jay's apartment?"

Stephen's features froze. He lowered his coffee.

"I assure you, Lewis—"

"You don't have to assure me of anything," Lewis said. "What goes on between you and Jay is your business. But I have a responsibility to my granddaughter."

The words came out unencumbered by forethought. Lewis felt his resentment growing, a black sentiment that he at once embraced and abhorred. He doubted that Stephen could comprehend the vigor of Lewis's loathing for him in that moment.

"Well, I think that Jay—"

"Jay is overwhelmed," Lewis broke in. "Her mother's death has been quite a blow. And, frankly, so has motherhood. She's put her life on hold. Although, I have to say, she didn't have to."

"Is that right?" Stephen asked. He sat back a little bit, his eyes locked onto Lewis's, scanning, analyzing. Not for the first time Lewis felt a bit intimidated by Stephen's self-possession— and then discarded the feeling. Lewis had fifteen years on Stephen, and he hadn't spent all that time sleeping. He had *seen* things on the wide-open plain of time.

"What, are you disagreeing with me?" Lewis asked.

Stephen fiddled with his watch. "Look, Lewis, I didn't come to have an argument," he said. "We have the same interests at heart. You know I love your daughter."

"OK," Lewis allowed.

"It's that you have this particular narrative," Stephen added.

"OK. Tell me," Lewis said.

"You have this way of creating Jay's life for her," Stephen said. "You're constantly telling her what to think about herself, and everything else for that matter. You say she has been overwhelmed by motherhood, and she behaves as though that's true.

But from what I've been able to piece together—and, granted, I wasn't *there*—you treated her pregnancy like an unrecoverable disaster."

"It was a setback," Lewis said.

"You made her feel like a failure," Stephen said.

Lewis bit his lip and fought off a wide variety of impulses, some of them violent. Of all the things he needed at this stage of his life, among the least desirable was the presence of this hair-splitter questioning the way he behaved with his family. Because, ultimately, wasn't Stephen just *dabbling*? Didn't he have the option of *leaving* without any real repercussions? Jay and Ramona were Lewis's life. They were all he had, and now he understood that Stephen threatened the sanctity of the way he chose to care for them.

"You had better watch yourself," Lewis said.

Stephen visibly blanched. "Lewis, calm down."

"I am calm. Right now I am calm."

Stephen turned away from Lewis and crossed his legs. He glanced back for a moment with an odd gleam in his eyes. Was he actually frightened? Well, good.

"Lewis, honestly," Stephen said. "I think that the amount of time I have spent with Jay and the commitment I've demonstrated to her gives me at least the right to have a frank conversation with you without things devolving into threats."

"I'm not threatening you," Lewis said.

"I think you don't have a full understanding of your impact on Jay," Stephen said.

"OK. Tell me."

"Despite herself, she isn't able to regard you as a fallible human being," Stephen said slowly. "Yes, she puts up resistance, but that's just for show, to keep her self-respect. In fact, she takes everything you tell her with extreme gravity. Each of your phone calls is a major event for her. And since Anna's death, you've been calling several times a day."

There was an unpleasant buzzing in Lewis's ears. He wanted to mess with them, try to rearrange them, but he knew his actions would be mistaken as a sign of mental instability.

"I like to talk to my daughter," Lewis said. "Surely you don't have a problem with that."

"Lewis, please, drop your defenses just for a moment." Stephen sipped at his coffee and looked outside, as though seeking support. "The point I'm making is that you have an inordinate impact on Jay. Her life has been in a state of turmoil since she got pregnant, and I assume yours has, too, to some extent. But as someone who knows your family very well, I've observed that your influence on Jay tends to be disruptive and disturbing a great deal of the time. I don't doubt your love, Lewis, or your good intentions. I'd be a fool to do that, and wrong. But there are times when the weight of your judgments, and your questioning of her, is pressing down and making things far more difficult for her than they need to be. She's brilliant, Lewis. It's absurd for her to be spending her time waiting tables. Yet she's convinced herself that's all she's capable of. And, Lewis, there are times when I worry that she's going to start believing that it's a permanent condition. As soon as she believes that she's a case of lost potential, then she will have crossed a line that I'm not sure I can pull her back from. Does any of this ring true to you, Lewis?"

Lewis sat back in his chair and dropped his chin close to his chest. He could not remember anyone ever speaking to him in this fashion. *Lecturing.*

"What was it you said earlier, that I create stories out of people's lives?" Lewis asked. "Well, if that's not what you're doing, tell me what the fuck it is."

Stephen's mouth puckered. "Sometimes it takes Jay an hour to recover from one of your phone calls. And then, as often as not, you call again."

"And this is your business?" Lewis asked. "Educate me. Give me another sermon. Tell me how many times a day I should be allowed to call my own daughter."

"I wouldn't presume to do that," Stephen said. He touched the knot of his tie, and Lewis imagined grabbing that tie, pulling it up, cutting off Steven's wind and watching him gasp for air.

"Don't look at me like that," Stephen said suddenly.

"Like what?" Lewis asked.

"I'm not going to play your games, Lewis," Stephen replied.

"I don't want you to," Lewis said. "You're not invited."

"You need help."

"Oh, but I'm getting so much help from you," Lewis said. "Stephen, you've dated my daughter for a little while. You've been fairly nice to her. If you hadn't, we would have had a problem long before now. But for you to come to my place of *work* and—"

"I'm worried about Jay," Stephen said.

And he seemed, as far as Lewis could tell, to be speaking the truth. It was tempting to let it all wash into him, to take Stephen's hypothesis at face value and respond to it on its own terms. But, really, what the fuck did Stephen know? Stephen had never slogged through the trenches of twenty-plus years of marriage, had never lived through decades of feeling his very self erode into a clutching little core of emptiness. Stephen had never played nurse to a dying woman who, just months before, he had silently and daily judged as the criminal behind all that besieged him. Stephen had never gone to the doctor and subjected himself to the humiliation of revealing a small fraction of his loneliness, fear, and grief, and been given a small pill to take every morning in the hopes that he could pull himself together enough to care for the two fragile souls who would probably come to a bad end without him.

Hating himself even as it happened, Lewis shivered.

"What's wrong?" Stephen asked.

"Nothing, not a thing," Lewis said. "It's the air-conditioning in this place."

Curiosity passed over Stephen's face, but he said nothing.

"Are you done?" Lewis asked.

"It's not a matter of being *done*." Stephen picked up his latte and looked at it as though it had disappointed him. "I just hoped we could have a civilized conversation about Jay, that's all. I love her, you love her. You're her father. She cares about what you think more than anything else, and I wonder whether that's healthy."

"Speaking of healthy, you never answered my question."

"Which one?" Stephen said warily.

"Whether it's *healthy* for you to be spending the night at Jay's apartment," Lewis said. "Whether or not it's good for Ramona to see you in bed with her mother."

"Lewis—" Stephen paused, giving the impression of a man trying very hard to check his words. "I *did* answer that question. I said that's up to Jay to judge. And believe me, we have the same concerns. We try very hard to be discreet."

"Discreet?"

"For crying out loud, Lewis, *calm down.*"

Lewis looked around. There were about ten people in the place, including the girls behind the counter, and they were all looking at him. Had he been shouting or something? He couldn't be sure. He took the lid off his coffee and watched the vapors of steam curl off its cooling surface.

"I am calm," he said quietly.

"I don't know how I thought this was going to go, but it's gone badly." Stephen picked up his briefcase off the floor. "If I've been presumptuous, I apologize. I don't want to antagonize you, Lewis. I don't see any reason why we shouldn't be friendly. But there are unhealthy things happening between you and Jay, and I felt a duty to try to do something about it. It's the same thing you would do in my place."

"In my place," Lewis mused. "What about my place? What would you *really* do if you were in my place?"

Stephen grimaced. "I don't know what you mean."

"I don't really know, either," Lewis said, and then, surprising himself, he let out a bark of a laugh.

Stephen's sour expression deepened. "I don't find any of this very amusing, Lewis."

"Stick around," Lewis said. "It's going to get hilarious."

"Is that another threat?" Stephen asked, sitting straighter in his chair and holding his briefcase to his chest like a shield.

"Now why would I threaten you?" Lewis asked. "We have so much in common. Hey, we're both runners. Maybe we should go for a *jog* sometime."

"I mean it when I say you need help." Stephen started to get up. "You've changed in the time I've known you."

It was shocking, to hear it put like that. Lewis got up as well and stopped short, his mounting anger defused.

Lewis looked back at the table in the corner of the coffee shop, tucked back behind a planter. Anna was sitting there.

She didn't see him.

Then she was gone. He didn't see her get up and leave, and he didn't witness her vanishing. It was simply that she had been there, and she no longer was.

Lewis put out his hand and grasped the back of a chair. He realized that he had nearly fallen over.

"Lewis, are you all right?" Stephen asked.

"Yes, I'm fine," Lewis replied. He looked back at the table in the corner. No one was sitting there.

"Did something just happen?" Stephen asked.

"I've seen things," Lewis said.

"I don't doubt it," Stephen told him.

"I've done things," Lewis added.

"What do you mean?" Stephen said, his forehead wrinkling.

"Nothing." Lewis chucked his half-finished coffee into a trash can. "Nothing at all. Now, if you'll excuse me, I have to go sell some shirts. They don't sell themselves, apparently."

And, with the consolation of a dramatic exit, Lewis returned to his job. He didn't look back to see Stephen's reaction, and he didn't look back to the table where he had seen his late wife sitting, staring ahead of her, looking for all the world as though she was waiting for something.

9. THE DENUDED TREES, THE BARREN FLOWER BEDS, THE STILLNESS.

In the morning it felt as though some irreversible shift had occurred. Jay had lived in Minneapolis her entire life, and seasonal change had been ingrained in her from her infancy—the moment when the scale tipped, when life became a matter of gradations of cold. There was no question now that the windows would remain sealed until spring, and that spring was a theoretical hope akin to the promise of life after death. She looked out the window at the denuded trees, the barren flower beds, the eerie stillness in things natural and man-made, and decided to put on a sweatshirt and take solace in the music of the Magnetic Fields.

Ramona was in the next room dressing Barbies, luxuriating in an aimless Saturday. Jay had spent the night alone, tucking herself in with a second scotch-and-soda after playing back a couple of voice-mail messages from Stephen, who sounded tense and distant. She supposed she could have invited him over—it would have been the usual thing—but she was exhausted, and didn't want to deal with whatever drama lay behind Stephen's cryptic unease. She loved Stephen, and would follow that love wherever it happened to take her in the drift of time. But a quiet evening with Ramona was too good to pass up. Jay glanced through the doorway at Ramona playing, saw the way her arms had grown slender, her legs lengthening, her face shedding all its babyishness. It was no longer impossible to imagine the day when Ramona would say good-bye to her mother and hide herself in the world.

"What?" Ramona asked, looking up from the complicated task of getting a plastic Barbie shoe to stay on an impossibly small and pointed Barbie foot.

"Nothing," Jay said. "I'm just watching you."

"Well, cut it out," Ramona said with an enigmatic smile.

"All right," Jay told her daughter. "Fair enough."

Jay had never been alone in her entire life. She had been a child, then had a roommate in college, and then Ramona had come. The great paradox, of course, was the crushing loneliness that comprised her emotional terrain. She assiduously tried to protect Ramona from her own despair, having vowed long ago not to become one of those single mothers who treated her child like a sort of surrogate spouse. And she had done a pretty good job. So far.

We are nothing without love, sang the baritone from the CD player. And it made Jay wonder where love had gotten her, and whether she had ever felt it, whether what she took for love was the same for those who claimed to love her.

The door buzzer rang. Ramona screamed at the noise and ran out of the room (strange child) as Jay went to the electric box and pushed the button.

"It's me," said Lewis.

"Come on up," Jay said, pressing the button that unlocked the front door of the building.

Lewis came through the creaking door radiating warmth and relaxation. Jay enjoyed a wave of familiarity—this was weekend Lewis, the indulgent and indulged Dad whose sense of expansive fun almost compensated for his tight and sullen manner when he used to come home from work.

"Sweetpea," Lewis said, kissing Jay on the cheek.

Ramona emerged from her room in a flurry of elbows and knees, running in that way of hers that was essentially a parade of off-kilter hops and lurches, giving a squeal of delight as she leapt up into her grandfather's arms.

"Good to see you, little girl," Lewis said, his face half-buried in Ramona's hair.

"Grampa, you know what? You know what?"

"What, sweetie?"

"When I'm five, Mama said I can get a hamster," Ramona exclaimed. "Or a guinea pig. One of those."

"Well, that's really nice of your mama," Lewis said.

Ramona nestled into Lewis's arms. "Did you bring me a present?" she asked with exaggerated coquettishness.

Lewis laughed. Jay noticed how Lewis strained a little to hold Ramona, adjusting his grip and bunching up his shoulders. Ramona was getting bigger. Lewis was getting older.

"I must have forgot," Lewis said, letting Ramona slide to the floor. "But let me see. Are you still saving money?"

Jay watched Ramona perk up, standing on tiptoe and bringing her fingers together in a cartoon enactment of guileless greed.

"Yesss," she said. Ramona had lately been getting an allowance of fifty cents a week for clearing her place at the table and getting her own drinking water with the assistance of a kitchen step stool. She'd saved five dollars at one point in her Hello Kitty bank and used the money to buy a stuffed animal from the Borders in Calhoun Square. Her cash reserves, as far as Jay knew, now hovered at around a buck-fifty.

Lewis pulled a wad of bills out of his pocket and stared at it for a moment making a little growling sound in the back of his throat that he had made for as long as Jay could remember. Then he peeled off a five and handed it to a stunned Ramona.

"Dad!" Jay said.

Lewis chewed on his lip and looked up at his daughter with a flash of apology. "I am the spirit of indulgence," he said.

"Mama, look, look," Ramona sputtered. "What is it? Is it a million dollars?"

"No, sweetie," Jay said. "It's a five-dollar bill."

"Five dollars?" Ramona said. She tugged at her shirt to cover up her little-girl belly. "That's how much my lion cost! That means I can buy another one. Not another lion, but maybe a . . . a . . ."

"You can think about it," Jay said. "Why don't you go put it in your bank."

"Thank you," Ramona whispered to Lewis in a tone of reverential awe.

"You're welcome, honey," Lewis said. He bent lower to put his face close to hers. "Look, that's a lot of money. Maybe I gave you too much. I know you're really good at saving, so you think about a toy you really want and save up your allowance to get it. OK?"

Ramona looked up at her grandfather, puzzled by his seriousness but aware that something very advantageous had just transpired. Jay had been ready to argue with Lewis over the way he'd shattered the humble frugality of her allowance scheme, but she knew she wouldn't. Lewis and Ramona had just made each other very happy, and there was no good reason for Jay to ruin it.

"Have you had coffee yet?" she asked her father instead.

"Yes, I have," Lewis replied. "But it's so damned cold out there that I'll have another cup, if you're making. Anything to warm me up."

They went into the kitchen together. While she was grinding beans and unfolding the filter, she saw that her father looked pale and delicate.

"What is it?" she asked him.

Lewis leaned back against the counter. "Me?" he said, surprised. "Oh, well, nothing. It's colder than I thought it was going to be. Should have worn a warmer sweater. I was shivering in the car and couldn't stop. I guess, you know, these pills I'm taking make me susceptible to chills."

"You mean the antidepressant?" Jay asked, with the smallest measure of malice. Lewis talked about his SSRIs like they were aspirin. Jay was suspicious of any drug that purported to magically alter brain chemistry and make a person better adjusted. Yes, Lewis had been depressed and withdrawn for quite a while—since before Jay's mother was diagnosed with cancer—but he was a moody man by nature and it might have been best for him to work out his problems on his own.

But didn't the problem lie elsewhere? Something about the notion of Lewis absorbing a pill to help him cope was offensive—the idea that Lewis needed help made Jay feel panicky and anxious, and the reality of a doctor invading his brain with pharmaceuticals made her feel protective and helpless. Glancing at Lewis, Jay realized he was diminished in her eyes, and that was not a comfortable feeling.

"Yes," Lewis said quietly. "The antidepressant."

"I wonder why that is?" Jay rushed to deflect the glancing blow she'd just struck by making Lewis say the name of his helper. "You know, that it would give you a chill."

"Maybe it's just cold outside. Beats me," Lewis said with a laugh.

"Grampa Lewis," Ramona said from the doorway, startling Lewis and Jay, who hadn't realized she was absorbing the arcane substance of their conversation. "I just saw a robin outside."

"What's that?" Lewis said, his forehead wrinkling. Ramona's garbled syntax had made her proclamation a mess of *W*'s and elongated vowels. She would soon grow into her tongue, Jay hoped, but seeing her daughter struggle to be understood always opened a fresh wound.

"A robin," Ramona slurred. "A robin."

"Oh, a *robin*!" Lewis enthused. "You saw a robin! Jeez, kiddo, that little birdie had better gather up his things and head south. Doesn't he know it's about to get real cold?"

"I guess not," Ramona said seriously. "I wish I could tell him. It was a boy, you know."

"How can you tell?" Lewis asked.

"Because of his colors," Ramona said. "The girls are less pretty."

"Now why is it the opposite for people?" Lewis said. "Guys like me are all wrinkly and ugly, while you and your mother are as beautiful as you can be."

"And Grandma," Ramona added.

Lewis gave Ramona a look of surprise.

"And Grandma," Lewis repeated.

Ramona looked up at Lewis with transparent inquisitiveness. The coffeemaker burped and farted.

"Hey, Ramona, would you make me a picture?" Lewis said gently. "I want to talk to your mama about something."

Jay, reaching for coffee cups in the cupboard, stiffened. Lewis's tone contained a warning. Lewis's attention remained fixated on Ramona, who reacted with equanimity at this familiar shunting aside of her concerns in favor of adult matters.

"A picture of what?" she asked.

"A sky, and grass, and butterflies," Lewis said.

"And a cat?" Ramona asked.

"And a cat," Lewis agreed. Ramona strode down the hall with her usual intensity of purpose. Jay poured out the coffee and handed Lewis his cup.

"What is it?" she asked.

Lewis moved closer to the window, away from the hall and Ramona's eavesdropping stratagems. He stared out at the drab stillness between the apartment buildings, the cold breeze stirring up trash that would soon be buried in snow until the thaw. When he spoke, it was in a throaty whisper of confidentiality.

"Stephen came to see me at work yesterday," he said.

"At work?" Jay repeated, somewhat dumbly. Lewis had fallen into a manner she knew well—his saintly forbearance in the face of an offense, with Jay left to guess the precise nature of her role in the wrong that had been committed.

"He wanted to have a talk," Lewis said. "A confidential talk, I suppose. But I'm not going to keep secrets for him."

"Secrets?" Jay said. "What do you—"

"He said that there's a problem between you and me," Lewis said tightly. "Somehow I'm creating problems in your life."

To hear Lewis tell it, Stephen had ambushed him with an absurd supposition and slur on Lewis's character. Jay knew what Stephen had attempted—a clumsy stab at making things right. Probably that was how things were done in Stephen's family: grievances were brought out into the light and promises were made to behave better in the future. But the flip side of Lewis's certainty was a horrible vulnerability, which he had exhibited in flashes for as long as Jay could remember—he tantalized her with horrible glimpses into the abyss that awaited her if she forced Lewis to drop his mask of solidity. It wasn't intentional on his part. But now she looked into her father's eyes and saw the entreaty there: *Agree with me, tell me I'm right. I can't be what he said I am.*

"Stephen thought he was helping," Jay told him, her voice unfamiliar to her. "He means well. He must have thought it was necessary to get involved."

And where was this voice coming from? It had evolved from the little girl's voice she had addressed Lewis with long ago, when he was an overbearing specimen of superiority, such a powerful combination of need and demand. Jay wished Anna were there to help the way she always had—until those final years when Jay got pregnant and Anna receded to the murky sanctuary of her sunroom, painting the same pictures over and over again, engaged in a slow dissolve.

"Well, I don't know," Lewis said. He folded his arms and Jay saw the outlines of a cigarette pack in his shirt pocket.

"You're carrying them around now?" she asked, pointing.

Lewis glanced down. "Well, I can't very well smoke them all day if I don't carry them on me," he said.

"Very funny."

"Look, that was a joke." Lewis put down his coffee cup. "I smoke maybe three a day. Don't worry. Your domineering psychotic dad is going to be around for quite a while yet."

Lewis laughed, but it was a hollow sound. Jay had made the coffee too strong, and it filled her mouth with a dry, acidic taste. She noticed that Lewis hadn't finished his.

"Well, what did Stephen say to you?" she asked.

"He went on with his professor bullshit," Lewis said. "Something about me making a story about your life and keeping you from making your own."

"Dad, you can't get away with playing dumb," Jay said.

Lewis grinned. "Well, darling, he's a big old professor and

I'm just a shirt salesman. You can't expect me to follow everything he says. I think it would have made him more happy if I'd have taken notes."

Jay said nothing, not willing to take the bait and adopt a conspiratorial alliance with Lewis.

"Look, Dad—"

"Mama?"

"It doesn't sound like you had the most constructive—"

"Mama?"

"Yes, Ramona?" Jay said.

"How is it my responsibility to—"

"Do you know where my spongy things are?"

"Just a second, Dad," Jay said. She didn't know how long Ramona had been there, or how much she had heard. She supposed it didn't matter. Ramona was growing up with Jay as a mother, so she was going to see and hear all kinds of things. In another home, she would grow up seeing and hearing all sorts of different things. It was the essential compact between parent and child—the parent pretends certain realities don't exist, and the child plays along. But both are human and understand the unspoken realities.

"What, sweetie?" Jay said.

"My spongy things."

"If I'm ambushed at work and presented with a catalogue of my failings," Lewis said, "I don't understand how I'm supposed to react."

"Just a *second*, Dad," Jay said. "What spongy things, honey? You mean those dinosaurs we got at Target?"

"Yeah," Ramona chirped, her voice the highest note plucked on a celestial harp.

"I actually know the answer to this one," Jay said, kneeling slightly. She did a quick memory scan of the confines of their apartment, from the little carpeted entryway down the hall to

the living room, the kitchen, the bathroom, their twin bedrooms.
"Your bath toys. The spongy dinosaurs are with your bath toys.
You were playing with them the other night."

Ramona cooed with appreciation over her mother's com-
mand of their small universe. She hopped out of the room without a look back.

"God, she's so happy," Lewis said.

"I hope she stays that way," Jay replied.

"You were just like her," said Lewis.

And it was true—Lewis remembered when Jay was Ramona's
age, with Lewis in his late twenties, when they had just bought
the house (what a bargain *that* was) and Jay would play for hours
in the garden in her imaginary universe. Jay had been a precocious child, diligent and serious. Lewis had adored her more
than anything from the very moment of her birth—a moment that
had shocked Lewis with its intensity, when he was overcome
with sheer emotion stronger than any he had felt before or since,
a rent in reality with the enormity that he had fostered a life. And
now, more than two decades later, she stood in a sweatshirt in
her apartment on Emerson Ave. and helped her own daughter locate missing toys. If only he had a way out of this maze of self, if
only he could unzip his skin and step out, embrace his daughter,
make her feel the raw purity of his love for her. She had once
been such a happy little girl. He had once loved his wife. It took
all his powers of optimism to avoid succumbing to the apprehension that they were living in the ashes of those days. For a
second he considered telling Jay about seeing Anna, but it didn't
seem right. He would share everything when the time came.

"Anyway, Stephen told me I was a negative force in your life, in
so many words," Lewis added. "I call you too much on the
phone. I'm too judgmental."

"Dad," Jay said, seeing a flash of strong emotion flare up in her father's features before he could suppress it.

"Look, maybe he has a point," Lewis said. "Christ, I know I'm not the easiest person in the world to get along with."

"Mama?"

"But to have an outsider just come along and tell me that I'm some sort of awful presence—"

"Mama?"

"Dad, I doubt that's what Stephen was trying to—"

"You should have been there," Lewis said. "I mean, this guy takes me out of work and lays into me—"

"Grampa?"

"Yes, sweet thing, what is it?"

"What's different about a goat and a sheep?" Ramona held up a pair of plastic animals.

"Why do you ask?" Lewis said.

"I'm making animal lines in my room," Ramona replied.

"Oh." Lewis looked up at Jay.

"She asked *you*," Jay said with a laugh, enjoying her father's perplexity.

"You mean what are their differences?" Lewis asked. Ramona nodded. "Well, it's easier to say what they have in common. They both have hooves, I suppose. And long heads with sort of pointed chins."

"And wool," Ramona said.

"No, not that." Lewis knelt down to Ramona's level. "Goats don't have wool. They have hair."

"Hair?"

"Yeah, sort of thick sparse stuff," Lewis said, oblivious, Jay saw, to the fact that he was exceeding the limits of Ramona's vocabulary. "And you can milk a goat. Some cheese is made of goat's milk—it's really good. I don't know about milking a sheep. I've never heard of it done."

Jay watched Ramona raptly absorb Lewis's every utterance, a sight providing her with pleasing associations. She would have hated for her father to learn how little she remembered of him as a younger man, and how the vague impressions she carried were of him being tense and brittle, his voice raised in irritation.

"Thank you," Ramona said, and was gone again.

"I'm going to have to go back to school and study zoology to pull off this grandfather trip," Lewis said.

"More coffee?"

Lewis looked into his half-full cup. "Better not," he said, absentmindedly massaging his breastbone.

"What, are you having palpitations or something?" Jay asked.

"Only the metaphysical kind," Lewis replied.

Jay let it slide. Ever since her mother took ill, Lewis had the look of a man haunted by mortality—specifically, his own. Jay suspected it was part of the reason he started taking those pills, but there were areas of her father's life upon which it wouldn't be proper for her to comment.

"Anyway, this Stephen thing doesn't sound like something to get upset about," Jay said.

"Do I look upset?" Lewis asked, his massaging hand splayed open.

"Sort of."

"I don't know what to feel," Lewis said. "I mean, what does Stephen expect me to do? Curl up in a ball and die so that everyone can have a better life without me?"

"Dad, *don't.* Ramona might hear."

"I've reserved comment on some matters surrounding Stephen."

"*Really.*"

Jay leaned back against the sink. It would be preferable if

Lewis didn't call her up to five or six times a day. Couldn't she summon the courage to tell her father *that much*?

"I suppose you know I have my reservations about him spending the night with Ramona around," Lewis said.

In the tentative morning light of season's change, Lewis's broad, handsome features and tucked-in carriage looked like some artist's conception of aging masculinity. At times such as these he was like a wall impervious to eroding waters.

"Dad," Jay said delicately. "You know what I'm going to say."

"Mind my own business." Lewis tried to smile at her.

"That's part of it," Jay said. "Here's the rest: *trust me*. I know it's delicate, having a boyfriend and a little girl at the same time. I'm managing to pull it off. You know, Dad, I have to balance my own interests with Ramona's. I am *conscious* of that. What you don't seem to acknowledge is that I *love* Stephen, and that he's a good man. He's good to me, and he's good to Ramona. He stimulates me intellectually, and he makes me feel loved. I'm a *woman* now, Dad. I'm an adult. I'm dealing with aging and death and disappointment, the same as you."

Lewis hid behind a mask of bland benevolence, nodding slightly as Jay spoke. Where was this coming from, this flow of hidden defiance? It felt *good*. Jay felt in control, capable of restraining the inchoate outbursts of adolescence in which she'd railed and railed against Lewis, once or twice, before dissolving in tears and apology.

"Look, Dad, I wish Stephen hadn't done what he did," she added. "Surprising you at work and critiquing you wasn't the most political thing he could have done. But at least recognize that he was trying, in his clumsy way, to make things better. Because he loves me. And, presumably, because he wants there to be some line of connection between you two, *mano a mano*."

"What about what he said," Lewis asked. "Am I really that bad?"

"Much worse," Jay said. "You are a fiend of monumental proportions."

"I'm a *baaaaad man!*" Lewis bellowed, raising his fists in his age-old Ali impersonation.

"Just don't hold anything against Stephen," Jay said.

Lewis smiled a strange smile. "I have my own opinions about Stephen," he said.

"Dad."

"And they will go unsaid," he said. "Because this is a beautiful cold bastard of a day in Minnesota, and I want to buy ice cream for my daughter and granddaughter."

"Ice cream!" Ramona bleated from beneath them. She had been there for how long? How much had she heard? What would she make of it? *Shit,* Jay thought. She tried to control what her daughter knew about her, but as a censor she was a dismal failure.

Lewis walked out to the car while Jay got Ramona ready to face the chill of the day. The forecast had been for highs in the forties but the temperature hovered around freezing. Lewis zipped his coat up to his chin after sneaking out a cigarette from his shirt pocket and lighting it against the breeze.

A few unraked leaves fluttered at his feet. Jay's building was nothing special, one of a line of brick four-stacks a block from the clogged artery of Hennepin Ave. Jay lived upstairs, on the left. The apartment beneath hers had a hand-lettered "Peace Now" sign stuck in the window. That sounded acceptable to Lewis.

But there was a time for peace and a time for war, as Ecclesiastes said. Lewis was no biblical scholar, but if he were to believe in a God it would be of the Old Testament stripe—wrathful, righteous, protective. Because, really, wasn't that what it took?

A time to be born and a time to die. Like Anna, moaning in her bed that late night, in the hours before he called Jay to come over and visit what had once been her mother for the last time.

Lewis took a deep drag on his cigarette and looked up at the gray sky. A time to die. *Her* time to die.

He felt the most unbearable fucking grief for what he had done.

It seemed perfectly apparent, *in the cold light of day*, that Stephen was trying to drive a wedge between Lewis and Jay. All that talk of constructing harmful narratives—and no, Lewis couldn't play dumb, he knew exactly what Stephen meant by that—was just a roundabout way of saying that Stephen resented the closeness between Lewis and his daughter. He wanted to be the man in Jay's life. Maybe he even harbored daddy fantasies directed at Ramona.

Well, honestly, *fuck that.*

Another drag on the cigarette, so good, the taste of life and death all rolled into one.

Lewis played the game, the one he indulged in only rarely, his guilty secret: he pretended Anna was still alive. She might be painting on the sunporch, or on a walk with a friend, or languorously making lunch—which sometimes took her hours. Lewis would go home, and they would talk about the garden, or whether the roof needed work, or about their child.

He remembered seeing her the day before in Starbucks. There, then gone. He wasn't interested in whether she had really been there or not. Of *course* she hadn't. But she *had.*

Stephen intruded on Lewis's thoughts. Stephen, who dared to confront Lewis and criticize him. Stephen was little more than a latecomer and an interloper who screwed his daughter and rose from her bed armed with arrows of condemnation aimed right at him.

Well, he could aim back, couldn't he?

He stubbed out the cigarette butt on the sidewalk when he saw Jay and Ramona coming out the front door. Ramona looked bundled up and tiny, her coat shiny pink.

"What are you thinking?" Jay asked. "You have a funny look on your face."

"Ice cream," Lewis lied. "I'm thinking about ice cream."

10. HE HAD DEALT WITH HIS SHARE OF JEALOUS FATHERS.

Most of the masks were reasonably comfortable to wear. Older lover to Jay Ingraham—now *that* was one Stephen liked, aside from the difficulty with Lewis, which surely could be resolved through diplomacy. Granted, Jay had avoided him last weekend, claiming she was tired and making a glancing allusion to his encounter with her father, but he knew she loved him. The mask of quasi-father to Ramona—he even liked that one, despite himself. She was a jewel. The mask of son to his parents? More problematic, rife with loyalty tests and coded entreaties. Best to leave California where it was, on the edge of the world, a territory reverting gradually to the wilds of anonymity.

But the best mask of all for Stephen was that of teacher, and now he looked out from behind its comfortable eyeholes at his class rising up in tiered seating above his podium.

"The paradigm of the internal life of the individual in the

West is integration of identity. This is the gold standard of mental health," Stephen told his class.

In front was a girl who had started the morning in a big, bulky sweater, then taken it off to reveal a tight, sleeveless Lycra top that exposed in astonishing detail the outlines of her nipples.

"The ideal under which we live, rarely articulated, is that integration of emotions, motives, and perception are the norm of our existence, and anything outside of that model is a deviation," Stephen added. "But experience proves otherwise, as we all know, on a simple experiential basis of living our lives in modernity."

Two rows back was Stephen's challenger—there was one in every class, usually a male. He didn't take notes, and he affected a skeptical expression, often opening his mouth a fraction as though about to offer a rebuttal. This personality type took the lecture as a reflection on him, with narcissism so deep that he believed he represented all of the students in a state of constant semirevolt against the teacher. He thought he was an intellectual, but in fact he was a natural politician.

"If there even *is* a self, quantifiable and real, it may be that it is very limited and doesn't have much to say. This is one of the core messages we might extract from our reading so far this semester," Stephen said. "As the text of a book is a form of performance by the writer, *for* the reader—the writer *impersonates* a writer during the time of the text's creation—so our lives have the form of drama. The Buddhists explicitly teach this, although they recommend shedding the drama in favor of cosmic authenticity of a very impersonal variety. Here in the West, we tend to *dig* the drama, although it is instructive to recognize the drama for what it is. In our development, we have learned that there isn't much *to* us, just a series of roles we enjoy playing."

This was the best part of teaching: when the subject of his

lecture ran smack into the very real matters he was thinking about in his own private life. This was what was great, actually *teaching* about what he had learned.

The girl in the tight top leaned forward and looked into Stephen's eyes. She was more than a pair of breasts—Stephen remembered her name, and the fact that her midterm essay had been among the top ten percent of her class. But the breasts, compressed, young and perfect, brought Stephen in touch with his animal self, preverbal and grasping, and he enjoyed it very much.

"In our relationships, we are afforded infinite possibility and freedom, but it is our nature to settle upon roles and continually play them for each other," Stephen said. "We settle upon the dramas and scenes we like, and continually reenact them. And it may be that those people who are most at home inside their skins, seemingly the least affected, the most genuine, are in fact the most skilled *actors*. Like the novelist who can suspend disbelief, or the moviemaker who can lead an audience happily into the most engrossing cinematic reality. They lead the way for the rest of us."

Stephen looked out over his students. He suffered vertiginous disorientation if he looked upward in these tiered lecture halls so, like a performer on the stage, he had trained himself to focus only on those students immediately in front of him. There were a few decent minds out there, and some kids were actually trying to absorb what he was saying. It bothered him that some were taking notes on this part of the lecture. This wasn't something that could be *written down;* this had to be lived and experienced. For many of them, at best they might recall some fragmentary impression of his words at a later date, hopefully adding perspective to their own disjointed, incomprehensible experience of being alive.

"That's that," Stephen said. It was nearly eleven in the

morning, and he had gotten through another lecture. He felt burning in his eyes and an ache in his knees. Outside the window the landscaped terrain was flat, all browns and grays as this northern latitude settled into the long dormancy ahead. A couple of students walked past, their young bodies clenching with a sudden burst of wind.

"Make sure you read your Wordsworth before you come back on Wednesday," Stephen added. "Read the poems aloud, try to figure out what they really mean. Remember, you're not doing it to please me. You're doing it for yourself. The text is not a *code* to figure out to pass a *test*. It is part of your life here on earth."

A hand went up. It was Jason Miller, his would-be rival wearing an ironic gas-station jacket bearing another man's name—a relic of a stranger's monotony.

"Yes, Jason?" Stephen said.

"Well, I've listened to what you were saying," Jason said, leaning sideways in his seat, very aware of the attention he was getting. "And it seems . . . well, it's easy to just throw this stuff out, isn't it? But am I supposed to take your word for it? I mean, I feel *real*. You're telling me I'm not. But how can you speak for me?"

Stephen smiled. Most of the students were packing their things, eager to move on.

"When Freud used the workings of his own mind to make a point, he observed that it was reasonable to assume that his own subjective experience was indicative of his species as a whole," Stephen said. "My observations on modernity are based on my own experience, what I've seen in others, and what is manifested in the assumptions that underpin the books we've been reading together."

"Yes, I know," Jason said, a little irritated. "But I feel *real*. I'm convinced I'm real. I don't want to believe I'm just a bit player in some larger drama."

"Well, you're the *star* of your own drama, Jason," Stephen said. "I'm playing a small role in it—the obtuse and self-important professor."

"Well, I guess I can agree with *that*," Jason said with a cock-eyed smile.

Stephen grinned back. "Out of here, all of you," he said. "Come back and ambush me on Wednesday with your revolutionary take on our old friend Wordsworth."

Stephen stuffed his lecture notes into a manila folder and started fussing with his briefcase. There was a relieved flutter of activity as his students assembled their backpacks, notebooks, jackets, and, in a few cases, laptop computers. Stephen glanced up at a couple of girls who had transferred their intellectual excitement into attraction to Stephen, then a few boys who eyed him like baby wolves just starting to sense the Oedipal possibilities of taking him down. It was enough to make him love them all, at least the ones who cared enough to want to fuck or kill him. He imagined a girl's dormitory room, soft and warm, relics from a safe adolescence mingled with the great works of culture, maybe an ashtray and a box of condoms on the dresser. The *small talk* they would make.

The room had cleared out save for a couple of stragglers engaged in conversation and oblivious to Stephen. Stephen latched his briefcase and picked up his empty coffee cup, ready to head to his office. Something caught his eye then, a patch of color up in the remotest outpost of the lecture hall.

"Lewis?" Stephen said, the name coming out like a cough.

Lewis Ingraham sat unsmiling in the back of the hall, his heavy winter coat folded under his arm as he unfolded his tall, lean frame from his chair. He clapped his hands together once, twice, three times, in a jarring mockery of applause. The few remaining students glanced up at him, then at Stephen, but quickly lost interest—this was something going on between individuals of advanced age, something that didn't concern them.

"I didn't see you up there," Stephen said from behind his lectern as Lewis moved down the aisle toward him.

"No, you didn't," Lewis said heavily, his features set in an unreadable masculine solidity. Not for the first time Stephen thought he would like to age as well as Lewis.

"I suppose I should be honored," Stephen said, trying to strike a note of congeniality. "I've managed to coerce an old alum back into auditing a course."

"I was interested in what you had to say," Lewis said, laying his coat over the rail. "After your lecture to me the other day, I thought I'd have a listen to what you're telling your students."

Stephen could not fail to note the acridity in Lewis's tone. His mind flashed over the Jay-free weekend he'd just endured—and it *had* been lonely, and alarming, not to have her near—and deduced that Lewis had played a part in creating it. He had gotten to Jay and made his case without giving Stephen a chance at rebuttal. He had done his divisive thing, and painted Stephen in the most unflattering tones possible. Damn it, Stephen should have known.

"First of all, I didn't *lecture* to you," Stephen said. "I tried to bring some important issues into the open. You turned it into a confrontation."

Lewis put his hands on the lectern. The difference in floor levels put his head at about the height of Stephen's sternum.

"Did you really mean any of that horseshit?" Lewis asked.

"What horseshit, specifically?" asked Stephen.

"Well, there's so much to choose from," Lewis barked, his voice echoing in the artificial acoustics of the room. "You are the *master* of horseshit, Stephen."

"Unlike you, Lewis."

"Oh, no doubt," Lewis said. "But let's stay on the topic of

you. Because you're so *interesting*. There is no self, you say. We're just playing roles. We impersonate ourselves. This is what you teach?"

"I don't expect my observations to be easy to take," Stephen said. "Nor do I set myself up as the avatar of truth. You just heard one lecture among many. I've been developing these ideas in lectures all semester."

Lewis slapped the lectern and Stephen, to his shame, actually flinched.

"I've heard more than one lecture from you," Lewis said. "Remember last week? Now *that* was a good one. 'You make up damaging narratives for your daughter, Lewis. You're a bad man, Lewis.' You've got me all figured out, right?"

Lewis's deadpan expression had suddenly become dynamic, with a simpering tone when he was mouthing Stephen's supposed words. Stephen would have been offended, but this display was too shocking to take on any reasonable level. Lewis, who that morning looked extremely buttoned-down and conservative in shirt and slacks, had a totally spooky gleam in his eye. It was the look he had, on some level, been waiting to see, the uncensored Lewis that he wanted to warn Jay about.

"You've talked to Jay," Stephen said. "That's why she hasn't wanted to see me."

Lewis moved along the railing, toward the steps to the lectern.

"I talked to my daughter, yes," he said, very cool. "I told her about our conversation. I think she agrees with my interpretation of things."

"You mean you browbeat her into not facing what I brought up."

Lewis smiled, his hand on the railing as he took the first step.

"You have a very nasty way of characterizing my relationship with my daughter, Stephen," he said.

Stephen put down his coffee cup and let go of his briefcase. Lewis was still moving toward him, his face again locked into a mask that betrayed no emotion.

"What are you doing?" Stephen asked.

"Maybe someday you'll have a family," Lewis said. "And then you'll understand something about the responsibilities that life places upon a father and a husband."

"Stop it," Stephen said. "I won't be intimidated."

"The responsibilities of life and death," Lewis said, moving closer. "Giving and taking life. I'm talking about life in an uncertain world. I'm talking about protection, easing pain, cancer and perversion and meddlesome *boy*friends who think they can insinuate themselves into a *man's* business."

"Stop right there," Stephen said. "I don't think we should be talking with you in this—"

"This is a *great* time to talk," Lewis said. He was less than ten feet away now, sliding along the rail in shuffling steps, his eyes locked onto Stephen's. "The perfect time. Things are so clear. You obviously like younger girls, Stephen. Why don't you fuck one of your students and leave Jay alone? She's better off without you. *We're* better off without you. Or, what, is Jay getting too old for you? Do you like getting so close so you can see her little daughter in the morning?"

"Lewis!" So far he had been able to rebut the lunacy of Lewis's assertions, but this was too much. He felt guilty and dirtied to have even heard such a thing.

Lewis paused. "Maybe that's it," he said softly to himself.

"Jesus, that you would even *think*—"

"There's all kinds of things I can think, Stephen," Lewis said softly. He took a step closer. Stephen struggled not to back away.

"This is ridiculous, Lewis," he said.

"If we're all just playing roles, what roles do you like playing?" Lewis asked. "Divider of families? Incestuous stepfather? Are our lives just a game to you? Are you some kind of *God*, Stephen?"

"Lewis, this is crossing the line—"

"So now we have *lines* that we can't cross? Because you say so?" Lewis took another step. He was now close enough to reach Stephen. "You're not the only one who has theories, Stephen. Do you want to hear mine?"

They were alone in the hall. There were no witnesses.

"I don't suppose it matters," Stephen muttered. He wanted nothing more than to be out of that room.

"Here's my theory," Lewis said. "You've read too many books. You're spent too much time having these young people fawn over you and listen to your bullshit like it comes from on high. You're self-important, Stephen. You *analyze* me and Jay like characters in some fucking *novel*."

"OK, Lewis," Stephen said. "There may be some validity in what you're saying."

"Let me tell you the difference," Lewis hissed. "Books are not *real*. But I *am*. You told these kids there's no real self, well let me tell you—there is. I *am*. I lived a real life. I had a wife and a job and I lost them both."

"I know it's been a terrible year," Stephen said.

"The job—fuck it," Lewis said, some inner pain narrowing his eyes. "You sat at my table, drank my wine, fucked my daughter, and then basically told me that my life's work was shit. That it didn't mean anything, that I wasn't contributing anything. Guess what? You were right! It was shit!"

"For God's sake, Lewis, please calm down," Stephen said.

"Not that you're saving lives, either, but at least here you're providing harmless entertainment. As for Anna, let's start with one thing. I saw the way you looked at her."

"Lewis, no," Stephen said.

"It's all right. That part's *fine*." Lewis grinned, his lips tight.

"I can hardly keep up with all these accusations, Lewis."

"Don't you know that's why she liked you?" Lewis asked. "That's why she stuck up for you—because you looked at her like she was still attractive. I allowed her that. It's a good feeling. Of course, you didn't have to live with her for twenty years. You didn't have to deal with her *presence* until it suffocated you."

The lecture room would be unused until twelve, which meant that there was no class session to save Stephen. He tried to stand as straight as he could, but Lewis was a few inches taller. Hostility radiated from the older man like heat, and Stephen sensed a fluttering in the center of his chest.

"You didn't see her begging to die," Lewis said from the depths of his throat. "No, you made sure to cut out before then. And now all I have is Jay and Ramona, and you're trying to get between us. It's very simple, Stephen. You have to go."

"I have to—" Stephen let out a sharp laugh. "Let's just stop this right now."

"You can't be allowed to poison Jay against me," Lewis said.

"I want no such thing."

"I have to protect them from you," Lewis said.

Stephen reached up and rubbed his eyes. It was nearly incomprehensible, the things he was hearing from this man. He had dealt with his share of jealous fathers over the years, but Lewis occupied a category completely his own. The worst of it was that Stephen genuinely feared Lewis. A fight between them would lead only to a Pyrrhic victory for one of them, but Lewis was on the verge of rage. Stephen did not have access to rage, and he knew it.

"Please leave me alone," Stephen said. "If you continue to threaten me in this way, I will call the police."

Lewis blinked. "The police?" he said. "Oh, please, Stephen."

Lewis rubbed his chest and his eyes popped wide. He took a deep, ragged breath.

"Lewis, is something wrong?" Stephen asked.

"I've held life and death in these hands," Lewis said, holding them up as evidence, a terrible look on his face that bridged bewilderment and certainty.

"What do you mean?"

"A year ago, I might have let you get away with this," Lewis said. "I might have backed down. But not after Anna."

"After Anna?" Stephen repeated.

"I'm a different person now," Lewis said. "And I will not stand by while you try to destroy me, my daughter, and my granddaughter."

Stephen picked up his briefcase and coffee cup.

"That's it," he said simply. "We're done here."

When he tried to walk around Lewis, Lewis raised a stiff hand, karate-chop style, and pressed it against Stephen's rib cage. His hands full, Stephen was obliged to stop.

"Don't touch me," he said.

Lewis moved his hand back, but left it in the air, blocking Stephen from leaving.

"I trust I've made my point," he said, cocking his head slightly, staring at Stephen.

"You've made a number of points," Stephen told him. "Most of them incoherent and alarmingly threatening. I think at this point I'm fully justified in telling you to go fuck yourself."

Lewis smiled, and Stephen realized that he had been waiting for just such a provocation. The hand returned to Stephen's chest.

"You have a big problem," Lewis said.

"The only one with the problem is *you*," Stephen said, forcing his voice to remain firm. God, couldn't someone come in here? Couldn't he get away from this damned isolation with Lewis?

"My days of having problems are behind me," Lewis said. "Now I have only solutions."

"Enough, enough, *enough*," Stephen said. He pushed easily through Lewis's hand and made for the door.

"I don't want to see you anymore at Jay's apartment," Lewis called out after him.

Stephen did not look back.

"And I'll be watching," Lewis said. "Bet on it."

Stephen shoved open the door and let it close behind him. He turned the corner in the flyer-festooned hallway and leaned against the wall, breathing heavily.

Now what, exactly, was he supposed to do?

Lewis looked out the window in the empty, silent classroom, the stillness punctuated by the sound of his heels thudding softly against the thin carpet. Though Thanksgiving was more than a month away, he saw a crystalline trace of snow in the air, wept by the gray sky.

He had come on stronger than he'd planned, that was for sure. There were indeed lines that shouldn't be crossed—and they hadn't all been invented by Stephen Grant. But Stephen's smug self-assurance, the way he preened and pontificated in front of his students, filled Lewis with loathing. Stephen took the same tone when he spoke to Jay—brilliant, confused Jay, talked down to by her lover as though she were some adolescent imbecile. It was infuriating.

So maybe he had lost his cool. So what?

So he'd better talk to Jay before Stephen did, that's what.

He looked outside, half-expecting to see Anna again.

Lewis had started out wanting to set things right between himself and Stephen, but Stephen had made it impossible with his recalcitrance and air of superiority. Lewis knew he didn't want Ramona to continue to be exposed to such a man.

It was all Lewis could do not to reach out and slap Stephen across the cheek, to grab that peacock's plume of dark wavy hair and yank hard. Lewis did not conceive of himself as violent, but there were limits to what a man could take.

He shuddered and had to grab the windowsill to right himself. His heart raced, and a deep wave of nausea overcame him. He fought it off. This was not a time to be weak. He felt himself on the verge of losing everything, and for once in his life he was going to fight. He had done enough acquiescing, enough witnessing his own life like an outsider.

There were things a man could do to protect his own. He knew this better than anyone.

11. HE WAS THE CENTER OF HIS OWN TRAGIC OPERA.

Jay looked out the glass, barely able to believe spring and summer had gone, that they had come to nothing, and that—look, what a sight—a trace of snow was flaking off from the overcast sky. She stirred the steam in her latte with her breath and watched a parade of cars go past on Lake Street, jostling like farm animals let loose from their pen.

"It's chilly out," said a pleasant voice behind her.

Jay didn't look; she didn't have to. The presence of Andrea Watson was as familiar as the texture of her own childhood and youth. They hadn't been close friends through elementary and junior high, but had cultivated an arm's-length familiarity based on an uncanny tendency to end up in the same classes. The same age, they'd hung out in high school and then started the U. together. One essential difference was that Andrea had graduated. Living an entire life in a town like Minneapolis meant seeing it shrink steadily and annually—Jay could walk down the Nicollet

Mall downtown and see a familiar face every block. In south Minneapolis, in Uptown, at the C.C. Club or Calhoun Square, she was required to become her own biographer, trying to relate people to the varied triumphs and humiliations of her past.

"I wonder how bad it's going to be," Jay said softly.

"The winter?" Andrea asked. It was a question people took seriously in Minnesota. Andrea looked through her black-rimmed glasses out the window, as though a lifetime in a harsh climate had made her able to discern the future based on a psychic appraisal of the breeze, the sky. "Hard to say. We're due for a bad one."

"That's what I think, too," Jay replied.

Andrea installed her tall frame on the stool next to Jay's. They both had the morning off, and Andrea had called Jay and asked her to come to Weird Coffee, a new place that had just opened on the stretch of Lake Street connecting Uptown to the divide between Lake Calhoun and Lake of the Isles. The coffee shops came and went with the same languorous rhythm as the restaurants, and this one was in its rosy infancy. It was nearly full at almost eleven in the morning, with a gallery of sleepy, irritable-looking people who might have been sleeping in the weeds in the alley, waiting for someone to open up a café so they could come inside.

"I'm glad you could make it," Andrea said.

"It was lucky you called today," Jay said. "I'm not working until later."

"How's that going?" Andrea asked. Presumably she meant: How was Jay's job serving food progressing? It was a polite question, but the fact was that food service did not *progress*. It was adamantly static.

"OK," Jay said. "How's your thing?"

"Slow," Andrea said.

Jay let it go at that. Andrea had been writing freelance articles for *City Pages* and doing some white-collar temp work on a PR project with a consulting company. Andrea was bright, cool, pretty, but she had always given off an air of *almost*—almost sexy, almost very smart, almost happy with herself. She had a boyfriend that Jay had met once or twice. The way he had looked at Jay had cemented her opinion of him before he ever said a word.

"How's Ramona?" Andrea asked.

"She's great," Jay said. "She's in day care today. She brought that stuffed cat—you know, the one you gave her."

Andrea rubbed her palms together with happiness. "Oh, really?"

"Yeah, she really loves it," Jay said. "She named it Fifi."

"*Fifi,*" Andrea repeated with delight.

Andrea's subtext in these conversations was her own burgeoning baby-fever—she never seemed to tire of telling Jay how *lucky* she was to have a child. Well, sure, Ramona was a blessing Jay couldn't imagine living without. But motherhood had certainly changed Jay's life in irrevocable ways that the relatively unfettered Andrea could scarcely imagine. Andrea would one day make a good mother. Just the sight of her evoked thoughts of fecundity; she was statuesque, with solid hips and nice legs and—her unavoidable visual trait—truly huge breasts that this morning strained against the wool of her green sweater. Those breasts had filled out in junior high and had always seemed out of place on a girl, then woman, who went through life with such tentative caution. Her breasts were like a lustful scream in a prim moment. Jay had seen them uncovered on occasion and felt flat-chested and boyish in comparison.

"I was over in Northeast with Brad last night," Andrea said. "We saw a band and had too much to drink."

"I put Ramona to bed at nine and passed out by ten," Jay said with a laugh.

"Don't go getting old on me," Andrea said.

"It's too late," Jay told her friend. "The deed is done."

"Oh, come on." Andrea took a slug from her triple mocha. Being born into Minnesota stock came with a Herculean tolerance for caffeine. "You're seeing a great guy. You must have a lot of fun."

"Stephen's a grown-up," Jay said. "We go out to dinner and movies, but he isn't really into getting wasted. And he hates smoke, so that eliminates the bars."

"Well, he's good-looking enough to compensate," Andrea said.

"That is true," Jay admitted. "And it's different when you have a kid. I mean, she's getting up at seven-thirty, whether I like it or not. She's not real sympathetic to Mama's hangover."

"I love the way she says *hamburger*. Remember when we took her to McDonald's?" Andrea said. "She makes it sound like *hangover*."

Jay smiled. She would not be drawn into laughing over Ramona's language difficulties.

Outside the sun was nowhere to be seen. Jay luxuriated in the familiarity of her friend's presence, the sight of Andrea's eyes through the distorting lens of her glasses. This was the best part of her life, this feeling of *belonging*. It was also the most confining. Jay had never lived anyplace else. Lewis had, Stephen had. She wondered if she would ever wake up to the gray sky of another city she had made home.

"Well, as usual I have a motive in wanting to see you," Andrea said.

"What do you mean, as usual?" asked Jay.

"Oh, you know, I'm terrible." Andrea shifted on her stool. "I always want to see Ramona because I wish I had a kid of my own."

"We're young," Jay said. "Don't be in such a hurry."

"I know." Andrea looked into her mocha. "I shouldn't be in such a rush. It's like with my work—I want something to *happen* for me. I want something better."

"Well, welcome to the human condition," Jay told her.

"You're always able to say things like that." Andrea adjusted her glasses. "I think I'm just not as strong as you are, Jay. Not as *something*, anyway. I wake up and I think, what am I going to do today? Anything that *matters*? What if I do *nothing*? Will anyone even notice?"

"After a while they would," Jay said. "They'd disconnect your electricity."

"You *know* what I mean."

"Of course I do," Jay said. "Look, I'm waiting tables, you know. At least you finished school."

Andrea frowned, wrinkling her usually flawless and translucent pale skin, which she set off by dyeing her hair red.

"Maybe you could go back," she said.

"I don't know, I was thinking about doing something easier. Maybe I'll join the Scientologists and hook myself up to an electric jukebox to learn the secrets of the universe."

Andrea laughed, a little nervously.

"Come on," Jay said. "We were talking about you. Does this have something to do with Brad?"

Brad was an unexceptional guy who happened to be in line to make partner at a downtown law firm. He had an arrogance and sense of being impressed with himself that came with his position. Jay, now that she thought about it, couldn't stand him.

Andrea looked sheepishly away. It *was* selfish, the way she engineered social interaction around her needs—and what was wrong with that? Jay didn't mind at all. Andrea lived her life in connection to people she cared about, feeling out friends for opinions, investing herself in their affairs. Jay did the opposite, keeping people at arm's length—except, of course, for Lewis, for whom the concept of *arm's length* was unfathomable.

"Well, yeah, it's Brad," said Andrea. "Or maybe Brad as stand-in for my own issues."

"Maybe you should cancel your subscription," Jay said.

"To what?"

"Your issues," Jay replied.

Andrea pretended to be offended. "But, my dear, what would I have left to talk about?"

"Well, what's the problem?" Jay asked. "Is Brad still too sexy for his shirt?"

"You think he's stuck up," Andrea said.

"I think a lot of things," Jay told her friend. "What do *you* think?"

Outside, the wind whipped up the faint, tentative snow in the air and sent it flying in quasi-horizontal lines to the pavement, where it vanished. The murky sky was dotted with dark, low-lying clouds, like an inverted ocean.

"You always seem to know what you want. Or at least you know what you think about things," Andrea said.

"Seeming is not always reality," Jay replied.

"Well, you know." Andrea paused. "I guess what I'm wondering is whether it's worthwhile to stay with Brad when I can tell he sees me as a temporary thing . . . you know, until something comes along, someone, I mean, who fits in with his image of who he wants to be."

"You're sounding like a first wife," Jay observed.

"Yeah, without the marriage," Andrea said. She folded her arms over her chest, with some effort.

"Well, I don't know," Jay said. "Are you having fun with him?"

"Sometimes."

"You're always talking about marriage and having kids," Jay said. "Didn't you get the newsletter? People our age are supposed to live out their twenties in a state of suspended adolescence. We're supposed to be running *from* responsibility, not *towards* it. Don't you read *Newsweek*?"

"I don't want to fool around," Andrea said. "We're getting older. It's not enough to be with someone because he's fun sometimes."

"Well, you answered your own question," Jay pointed out.

"I know." Andrea took a desultory slug of her mocha. "But what next? I can break up with Brad, but at least he gets me out of the house. I don't want to end up depressed and bitter."

"No, you don't." Jay tasted her lukewarm latte.

"It's ridiculous," Andrea said. "We have all these comforts—we can sit here on a Monday, sipping coffee, with me moaning about my life. But there's no urgency, is there? I mean, maybe I'm just inventing problems for myself. You don't do it, because it's not in your nature. But if we're not *starving*, or in *danger*, then what are we? I can take my life seriously, or not, it doesn't seem to make any difference. I mean, you lost your mother, and now you have to listen to me complain about my boyfriend. It's so unfair. I'm sorry."

"Andrea, don't be sorry," Jay said, putting a hand on her friend's shoulder. Andrea all of a sudden seemed on the verge of tears.

"No, I *am*." She pushed on her glasses. "I mean, how vulgar, really. I broke the rules. We're not supposed to talk about our worthlessness, are we? I mean, what if everyone talked this way? We'd probably all agree to stop being ourselves. It's too much work, the payoff's too small."

"Look at you getting all worked up," Jay said.

Andrea laughed, and Jay saw that she was crying, just a little. "This is why I have to stay friends with you," Andrea said. "Because I can tell you my worst thoughts and you act like we're talking about a new dress at the Gap or something."

"I have my limits," Jay said. "Start talking about the Gap, and you'll really freak me out."

Andrea shook her head. "When is it going to make sense?"

Jay's cell phone, perched on the counter, went off. Jay glanced down: it was Lewis.

"Never, I suspect," Jay said. "Maybe at the end."

"Is that what you think?" Andrea said, seeming awed.

"Maybe." Jay shrugged. "Sometimes I think we're preparing ourselves for our last breath. Then we'll realize it was all a matter of learning how to let go."

"That's dark," Andrea whispered.

The phone rang a third time. Jay considered letting her voice mail pick it up, but Lewis's pull was too strong.

"It's my dad," Jay said, picking up the phone.

"I have to go to the bathroom anyway," Andrea said, getting up. Jay glanced around and saw a couple of guys in the café casting surreptitious glances in Andrea's direction. What did it do to a girl to have such spectacular symbols of sexuality affixed right to her center of gravity? Apparently, she ended up with a guy like Brad. It was for these sorts of ideas, Jay thought, that fate was going to punish her someday.

"Dad," she said, taking the call.

"Jay, how are you?"

"What's wrong, Dad?"

"What do you mean? Everything's fine."

"You sound weird." Jay sat up straighter on the stool. She saw herself half-formed in the glass.

"Well, I guess something has happened."

"Something?" Jay said. "Dad, what's going on?"

"I went to see Stephen," Lewis said somberly.

"Dad, where are you?"

"I'm driving," Lewis replied. "I'm going to drop off my car at home and take the bus to work. I thought I would talk to Stephen, but I had no idea what a disaster it would be."

Jay ran her hand through her hair. "What happened?"

"Well, I sat in on the end of one of his lectures," Lewis said. "I must say—it was very informative."

"Dad, you're being cryptic. Did you guys have an argument?"

"I guess he didn't see me, because he seemed surprised when I came down to say hello after the class." Lewis paused. "Just a second. Some son of a bitch just cut me off."

Lewis had mellowed over the years, but behind the wheel he was still the star of his own tragic opera, betrayed and ill treated by the venality and heedlessness of Minnesota's motorists. It gave Jay a stomachache to remember all the time she spent sitting next to him while he cursed the world.

"Anyway, I wanted to speak with him about the . . . his grievances. I thought it was appropriate. He came to my place of work. Didn't that give me the right to do the same?"

"Dad, I don't know." Jay sighed. "I don't know."

"I have to say that he reacted badly."

"How?" Jay asked.

"Stephen refuses to treat me with any respect," Lewis said. "All I got for trying to reach out was hostility. What have I done to make him dislike me so much?"

Jay shifted the phone to her other ear.

"I don't think it's a matter of him disliking you, Dad," she said.

"You know me—I want to get along," Lewis said. "But he makes it impossible. He's the one who started this. When I tried to bridge the gap, I just got more flak. I don't know what I'm supposed to do now."

Andrea returned to their place by the window. Her red hair was tucked back behind her ears, and she studied her napkin while pretending not to listen to what Jay was saying.

"You don't have to *do* anything, Dad," Jay told him.

"Look, honey, you know the last thing I want to do is cause problems for you," Lewis said through a hiss of static.

"I know that, Dad," Jay told him.

"I don't want to be the stereotypical father who rejects all his daughter's suitors," Lewis said. "I know you're a grown woman. I kept my opinions to myself until Stephen opened up this can of worms."

Stereotypical father—like the time Lewis threatened to drive by himself to Oregon and extract some vaguely defined restitution from Michael Carmelov? That scene had ended with both Jay and Anna in tears, shocked by the depths of Lewis's rage. Only a threat to call the police had kept Lewis in Minneapolis, seething, affronted, and (once or twice) repulsed by the sight of Jay's swelling belly.

"Stephen is a very rational person," Jay said. Andrea glanced her way. "I have a hard time believing he was so confrontational."

"What are you saying?" Lewis asked. "Are you saying I started it?"

"No, but I also know how hard it is for you to back down," Jay said.

"Why should I back down?"

"Dad, don't yell—"

"All I am trying to do is to protect you and Ramona."

"Dad, listen to yourself," Jay said. "Stephen isn't someone we need protection from."

"Maybe you don't think so," Lewis sniffed. "But you didn't see him today. I didn't want to bring this up, but there are aspects of his attitude toward you that are disturbing."

"Dad, I don't—"

"I guess it's occurred to you that you're a very attractive young woman," Lewis added. "And that Stephen is significantly older than you. I see how much he likes how you reflect on him."

"Dad, this is not a conversation—"

"I know, I shouldn't have said that." Lewis paused. "It's just that I'm *worried*, honey. I think all the time about what's best for you. And for Ramona."

"I'm aware of that."

"I'd do anything to protect you and make things right for you."

God, why did he have to *be* like this? All this intensity, all this consuming need to get a reaction from her . . . and now this insistence that she be on *his* side.

When she was alone with Stephen, she could imagine standing up to Lewis. In those moments, full of lucidity and purpose, she could even imagine the sort of person she wanted to become. And yes, she had imagined herself as a professor's wife, wrapped in Stephen's benevolent distraction.

But like a whisper in her ear, she knew that Lewis had given voice to thoughts of her own. Men tired of women, and one day Jay's toned thighs and upturned breasts would lose their allure for Stephen. One day Jay would be thirty, then forty, while Stephen's students would retain their evergreen youth. Could she be sure her appeal to him was based on more than his constantly expressed lust and the magnetism of physical attraction? And could she be certain that Stephen might not be deceiving himself, in addition to her?

"Dad, I'll talk to Stephen," she said.

"Well, all right, you have your own decisions to make," Lewis said. "I just pulled up in the driveway."

"Let's not make too big a deal of this," Jay said.

"It's hard for me to know what to say," Lewis replied. "Stephen is interfering with what means the most to me. It's impossible not to take offense."

"I'll *talk* to him."

"I wish that were enough," Lewis said.

Jay heard the sound of her father getting out of his car. "What does that mean?" she asked.

"Nothing." The front door opened. "I love you, honey. I'll call you later. Have a good day at work."

"I love you, too," Jay said, and hung up the phone.

"What was *that?*" Andrea said, snapping Jay out of the one-second reverie of impossibility into which she had fallen.

"My dad," Jay said. Andrea knew Lewis from elementary-school days. She had once referred to Lewis as *sexy,* a moment that never failed to make Jay feel utterly revolted with every aspect of existence.

"I know it was your dad," Andrea said impatiently. "But that sounded like a really weird conversation. Is there some problem with Stephen?"

"I didn't think there was," Jay said.

"You don't sound so sure," Andrea observed.

"Break up with him," Jay said.

Andrea's round eyes widened behind her angular glasses. "Excuse me?" she said.

"Brad," Jay blurted out. "You asked me what I thought. Break up with him. That's what I think you should do."

"Wow," Andrea said, sliding her hand over Jay's forearm. "That conversation with your dad really freaked you out."

"Life's too short," Jay said. "Look outside. It's getting colder. The freeze is setting in. What more evidence do you need?"

INTERLUDE. NO ONE GOES AWAY, SHE SAID.

Ramona was not having a good morning. First she had not been given toast for breakfast when, as everyone knew, Monday was the day for toast and sugar. Then she had gotten scolded for moving the littler kids out of the big chair in the front room—and hadn't been able to defend herself, because doing so would have meant exposing the identity of the Perfect Princess, which was simply not done.

She had so many worries. In the morning Mama had been crabby and thinking of all the grown-up things that Ramona wasn't supposed to know about. Like being angry, and being in love, and dying.

It would be a really good time for Grandma to come back. Ramona couldn't understand what was taking her so long.

Grampa Lewis was acting weird, and that made Ramona worried. Sure, he had bought her a big ice cream the other day—strawberry, her new favorite—but before that he had been saying weird things to Mama in the kitchen. Things about Stephen.

Ramona liked Stephen, and she didn't like Stephen. Stephen was nice. Stephen was yucky. It was yucky how he kissed Mama, and how they slept in bed together. Ramona used to sleep in bed with Mama, but now she figured she was no longer welcome.

"Ramona?" asked Teresa, one of the day care ladies. "Are you going to be ready for lunch in a few minutes?"

"Sure," Ramona said quietly.

She looked at her hand. It had a new freckle on it that Ramona wasn't sure she liked. Mama said there was nothing to do about it, that she'd get even more freckles as she got older, and that they'd never go away.

It was hard to get used to the idea of things never going away. Because the weird part was that some things *did* go away. Like Grandma. Who was coming back any time.

"Play with me?" said Vanessa, one of the Twins. Ramona knew it was Vanessa, rather than Elaine, because Vanessa always wore a ribbon in her hair. Ramona was jealous of the ribbon because it was very beautiful. The Twins were two years younger than Ramona, and as such occupied a sort of mascot role for the Perfect Princess.

"Not now," said the Perfect Princess. "Later."

"Aww," said Vanessa.

Grampa Lewis was acting really weird. There was nothing wrong with Stephen. Stephen was actually really nice. Ramona didn't like him all the time, but he liked her, and that was a pretty nice way for things to be. Ramona wouldn't like it if Stephen went away.

Ramona wondered if Grampa Lewis was going to make Stephen die, or if Stephen was going to make Grampa Lewis die. It would be good, as long as one of them died and went to get Grandma and brought her back. But what if one of them died and made Ramona wait, the way Grandma did?

Ramona didn't want any more people leaving. She twitched her hand in the air, the one with the freckle, the way she did when she was making magic. *No one goes away*, she said without making a sound.

Grampa Lewis and Stephen were going to have a fight. Ramona just knew it. She didn't understand why, but it had something to do with both of them wanting Mama. The way Ramona had her Bear, and her lamb, and all the other animals who lived in her bed and who she had to tell stories to before they could go to sleep.

"OK, Ramona, come on in," said Teresa from the doorway to the kitchen. "Your lunch is ready. Hey, what are you thinking about? You look so serious."

"Nothing," said the Perfect Princess, ready for her royal meal, moving through the room with the carriage of undying royalty.

12. THEY HAD LEARNED TO PROTECT THEMSELVES FROM DISAPPOINTMENT.

"You're putting a wall around yourself," Stephen said, the phone cradled against his shoulder, both elbows planted on his office desk.

"I'm not, I'm really not," Jay said. "When can you come over?"

"My office hours are over at four, then I have a quick meeting," he replied. "Can I take you out to dinner?"

"I don't feel like going out," Jay said. She spoke to him on a break from her shift at the Cogito. Stephen imagined her standing there in that depressing kitchen. She would be wearing those black pants and one of those classy tight tops that drove him crazy and more than once had compelled him to make her late for work.

"OK, I understand," Stephen replied. "I'll get some takeout and come over. I'll get Vietnamese—dumplings for Ramona."

"I don't know, Stephen," Jay said. "I think maybe I need a night or two to get my head together."

Stephen's pulse sped up. Jay had never before used the conditional language of the distant lover.

"All right," he said uncertainly. "What did Lewis tell you about what happened today? Because it was really—"

"I can't get into it," Jay said in a tone that encompassed the environs from which she spoke. Stephen thought of that preening peacock of a manager there, the guy who was always so chummy with Jay while sizing her up like a piece of exotic pastry.

"I haven't done anything *wrong*, Jay," he pleaded.

"I know."

"I love you, darling."

"I love you, too," Jay said. Thank God she gave him that.

"I don't want to lose you over this." Stephen glanced up. Standing in the doorway was Katrina Mason, the girl from his class he'd been trying so assiduously not to undress with his eyes during that morning's lecture.

"Is this a bad time?" Katrina said.

Oh, she was so perfect. Stephen shifted the phone to his other ear and motioned to the empty chair diagonal to his.

"No, no," he said. "I'll just be a moment."

"Who's that?" Jay asked.

"A student," Stephen replied, looking away from Katrina.

"You have quite a following over there," Jay observed. "Is she pretty?"

"Not at all," Stephen said. "Listen, you have to know I mean every word of what I'm saying."

Stephen spoke in a hushed voice, all too conscious of Katrina's inquisitive presence not five feet from him. From the corner of his eye he caught a glimpse of bare knee as she crossed her legs. Healthy, healthy, he told himself. Pretending not to notice would be the real disorder.

"I . . . I believe you," Jay said. "Look, my break is almost over. I'm going outside for a smoke."

"A smoke?" Stephen said. "You don't smoke anymore."

"I guess things are changing," Jay said. "I bummed one off Fowler."

"I don't like to hear you talk like this," said Stephen.

"Call me tomorrow," Jay said. "We'll try to work all this out."

"Work it out?" Stephen said. "What is there to work out? I won't talk to your father anymore. It's *his* problem."

"I need to think," Jay said quietly. She had no idea, but even her voice was a thing of beauty—husky yet feminine, infused with the wisdom of a woman twice her age.

He couldn't be *losing* her, could he?

He looked up at Katrina, whose innocent features were framed by close-cropped dyed-red hair. She regarded Stephen as though he were a specimen of an extremely rare beast.

I can go, Katrina mouthed.

Stephen shook his head. "Give Ramona a kiss for me, and we'll talk in the morning. OK?"

"Fine," Jay said, with a noticeable lack of enthusiasm.

"I love you," Stephen said.

"I love you, too," Jay said, with a tone Stephen had heard other women use before. She did not particularly mean it. Then she hung up.

"Are you all right?" Katrina asked.

It took a fair amount of self-control not to immediately unburden himself upon his student, whose solicitous body language made clear that she had affixed upon Stephen any number of romantic delusions. But part of his job entailed understanding that attaching herself to him was part of Katrina's intellectual development. Any indulgence of her attraction was tantamount to the abuse always potential in an analyst/patient relationship. He put his fist to his cheek and allowed himself the pleasure of looking at her.

"I'm fine, thanks for asking," Stephen replied while his mind reeled. His attachment to Jay, he admitted to himself, was founded upon a tacit trade-off between her intrinsic qualities of beauty and smarts against his own status and experience. In other words, he had assumed that if anyone was going to tire and seek escape from the relationship, it was going to be him. Now, imagining life without Jay was enough to induce panic. He had more rivals than allies, and no real friends. Being with Jay enabled him to define himself in a way that he liked, and made it possible to get through the day.

"Maybe I should come back another time," Katrina said uncertainly, showing a hint of affront once she realized she was not the center of Stephen's attention.

"No, I'm sorry," Stephen told her. "Please."

"Was that your girlfriend on the phone?" Katrina asked, smiling as though pleasantly scandalized.

"Let's hope so," Stephen said, trying to smile in return.

Lewis unbolted his front door that night while trying to fight off a full-blown shiver induced by the deepening chill and the chemical tang of the pharmaceutical stew coursing through his veins. Carew undulated at his feet, the sound of the lock throwing him into rapture.

Yeah yeah yeah Lewis, Carew said with his eyes and tongue. *Yeah yeah yeah fuckin' yeah.*

"Go on," Lewis told Carew. "Get inside."

The dog had passed the twilight with his shitting and sniffing at the park, off his leash and reveling in his freedom while Lewis smoked a cigarette and shivered. Dogshit Park had once been the place where, a full two decades ago, Lewis had brought the toddler Jay to stagger and reel in the sand while he and Anna marveled over her every utterance and physical breakthrough. Now the slides and climbing apparatus were occupied with other people's children, their squeals and preverbal utterances filling the void of time with memories to sweeten bitter futures.

"What, are you hungry or something?" Lewis said to Carew in the kitchen. Carew sniffed at his empty bowl with anticipation—Lewis realized the dog was trying to condition Lewis, to plant the idea to feed him, which filled Lewis with unexpected appreciation for the beast.

Hungry hungry, Carew said. *Food? Food, Lewis?*

Lewis lived in a big house, though the kitchen was old-fashioned and disproportionately small. Anna had always talked about remodeling it, though they had settled ten years ago on the stopgap measure of installing new cabinetry and painting the walls. Now there was no money for making any improvements, nor was there much motivation. The kitchen would stay as it was, for the foreseeable future.

He had seen her. He looked around at all the familiar places still haunted by her presence. It was as though, if he focused his eyes just right, he would see her again.

But no, nothing.

When Lewis reached under the sink for the bag of dog food, his chest gave a serious lurch. He steadied himself against the counter and tried to keep breathing. The chill filled him like a block of ice in the center of his hollowed-out carcass—it shook his shoulders and made his hands clench against his sternum. What a terrible feeling, he thought. Death pervaded his consciousness like a low-lying cloud—here, predictably, came the tightening in his chest, like a band cinched true.

Lewis, Lewis? Carew said, at his feet. *All right there? Food?*

"I'm getting to it," Lewis muttered as he opened up the bag and willed himself to go on.

With the sound of the dog crunching his meal echoing in the silence, Lewis moved into the dining room and switched on the light. The big table was piled with newspapers and coffee cups. It was low-level bachelor squalor, though the house was cleaner now than when Anna was alive. She had started letting things go long before she ever got sick. She might have been depressed, Lewis couldn't say. Part of his long-term armistice with Anna had been the unspoken agreement that neither was responsible for the other's moods or happiness, either transitory or long-term. It had been an OK arrangement. Gradually they had lost the vocabulary of emotional need when speaking to each other, and they had learned to protect themselves from disappointment. When Lewis wasn't consumed with his petty resentments—and these times admittedly grew fewer and fewer as the years passed—he would enter into a state of bland contentment, if not happiness.

Immediately after she died, he had entertained a fear that her ghost would come back to haunt him, fully aware of all the treacherous thoughts he had harbored over the years.

He had seen her, but she didn't see him. She had been staring straight ahead. But it *had* been her, just for an instant. Her presence was someplace in the house, in the sunporch, the bedrooms, or between the slanted walls of the third story.

Lewis picked up the portable phone and took the creaky stairs to the second floor. His chest felt a little better, enough for him to believe that his rush of sickness was psychosomatic. He got a thick wool sweater out of the closet and pulled it over the fleece he was already wearing. In the mirror he corrected his posture—*don't stoop, old man*—and stuck out his chest. He basically liked what he saw. He wondered if he would ever be with another woman.

"Are you here?" he said to the empty room.

The first time had been on a business trip to San Francisco.

She was a colleague he had met that day and, after too many drinks at his hotel bar, they had gone upstairs together. Lewis could remember the pink silk of her underwear and the smell of cigarettes on her breath. He was reasonably certain she didn't come. Lewis couldn't remember her face, save for a sort of sensual curve to her mouth. He managed to avoid any further trips to that city, and after a couple of phone calls to his office managed to extricate himself from any emotional debt.

Jay was in elementary school at the time. Lewis remembered coming home, playing a game of Candyland with her and thinking, *her father is an adulterer.* There had been the crushing guilt and the terrible anxiety, of course, there was no getting around it. But, at the same time, Lewis had also felt an oddly exhilarating sense of accomplishment, as though he had proven that none of the strictures mattered, that the foundations of his good life were a matter of spirit rather than form, and that if indeed nothing mattered, then he had done nothing wrong.

The second time had been with a mutual friend. It happened twice, and then Lewis had to endure both the guilt and Anna's suspicion when the friend stopped coming around. The third woman, like the first, came from his work world. The fourth, and last, infidelity had happened two years ago, with a friend's wife. It was enough to stop his heart, just thinking about it.

The wind pushed against the storm windows. Lewis looked out at the bare trees, the worn carpet of the backyard. The coming winter was announcing itself in earnest. He turned on the phone and dialed it without looking.

"Hello?" Jay said.

"It's me." Lewis turned on the light in his study. "How are you?"

"Fine, Dad," Jay said. "Me and Ramona just finished dinner."

"Oh. What did you have?"

"Macaroni and cheese with hot dogs." Jay laughed.

"Ah, the gourmet specialty of your youth," Lewis said. "You know, that's all you would eat for about a year."

"And then it was tuna melts," Jay replied.

"The tuna melts, I almost forgot the tuna melts," Lewis said. "You had your mother making them twice a day."

"She was so nice about it," Jay said.

"She was, wasn't she?" Lewis said, surprised by the force of the recollection—Anna at the stove, Jay waiting with an empty plate, her earnest face composed in a child's version of thoughtful anticipation. Lewis settled into his leather chair, surrounded by shelves of books.

"So, listen, I talked to Stephen," Jay said.

"You did."

"I really don't have the energy to broker a truce between you two," Jay said with a note of exhaustion that touched Lewis to the core. There it was again, that hypersensitivity. It felt as though his borders had been opened.

"You don't have to do any such thing," Lewis responded. "This is between Stephen and me."

"But, Dad, you have to understand—I'm caught in the middle. Just a minute, honey."

"Excuse me?" Lewis said.

"It's Ramona." Jay paused. "Do you want to talk to Grandpa, sweetie?"

Lewis heard Ramona's muffled negative reply and his heart sank. Was this strife with Stephen filtering down to the child? Apparently it wasn't enough for Stephen to drive a wedge between Lewis and his daughter—now his painting of Lewis as a villain was filtering through to Ramona's delicate perceptions.

"It's all right," Lewis said. "She doesn't like the phone."

"She was getting better," Jay said uncertainly. "Look, honey, go play in your room. I'll be off in a minute."

"Has Stephen been talking to her?" Lewis asked.

"Who? Ramona?" Jay said. "Well, sure, they talk all the time. But not the way you think. Dad, don't get paranoid."

Lewis settled into his chair. Night had come, and outside the window his back porch light spread shadows under the canopy of the big elm.

"It's not paranoid to notice an outsider making trouble in my family," Lewis said quietly.

"Dad, don't," Jay said. "I don't even know where things stand between me and Stephen right now."

"Has he—"

"It's not him, it's me," Jay interrupted. "I don't know where my life is going. I'm not sure whether or not I want to spend it with him. Maybe I do, I'm not sure. It's hard to think straight with all this—"

"Mama!" Lewis heard Ramona saying.

"What?" Jay said, not hiding her exasperation. Lewis wished he could describe to her the time in her life when she would move the world to hear the plaintive need of her child again.

Ramona said something Lewis couldn't understand. "OK, honey, OK," Jay said. "Just let me talk."

"What is it?" Lewis asked.

"She wants to take a bath," Jay said.

"She *does*?" Lewis said in amazement. "You know, most kids fight to stay out of the tub. You used to *cry* when it was bath time."

"Well, get this—Ramona has started running her own water," Jay said with a tired laugh.

"Amazing." And Ramona was. But in the cascading sadness of Lewis's thoughts, that painful tumble all of his ideas entered into, Ramona's resiliency and self-reliance seemed unspeakably sad. In the sickly light, Ramona's strength seemed im-

posed on her by her lack of a father, by Jay's taxed resources, by Anna's early death. The added pressure of Stephen's divisiveness was too much, a supplemental burden that was too great for a little girl to bear.

"Lewis," Anna said.

Lewis stiffened in his chair, then shot out of it. He looked around. He was alone.

"Anyway, Dad—"

The shadows in the room betrayed nothing.

"Dad, are you still there?"

"Jay, honey, don't worry yourself about it," Lewis said, speaking very fast. "You and Ramona are my treasures, and I don't want you to spend another second worrying about anything."

Silence on the line. He looked around. So now he was hearing things—though he didn't even believe *that*.

"Jay?"

"Dad—"

What was that note in her voice? Was Jay on the verge of *tears*?

"You know, Dad, it's been really hard since Mom died," Jay whispered. "I know it's been hard for you, too. But sometimes . . . sometimes . . ."

"What is it, Jay?" Lewis asked. "Please. Talk to me."

"Sometimes it feels like . . . I don't know, you have so many *expectations* of me." Jay coughed. "Look, Dad, I don't want you to take this the wrong way. It's just that sometimes I feel like I don't have enough *space* in my life. I'm not blaming you. It's like you *need* so much, and I can never give you enough."

"You're a single mother," Lewis said, keeping his voice delicate, unable to deal with the sobbing note in his daughter's voice. "The demands on you are incredible."

Had he *really* heard Anna's voice saying his name?

"I know that, Dad. It's just that—"

"What, honey? Tell me."

"I'm *trying* to, Dad." Jay exhaled sharply. "Dad, can you just let me *talk*?"

"I'm sorry, I'm sorry," Lewis said.

"I just need space," Jay said in a defeated voice. "That's all I can say. I feel like I don't have any space."

"Mama!" Ramona called out.

"What?" Jay yelled.

"Nothing," Lewis heard Ramona say, in a voice of heart-breaking quietness.

Enough, Lewis thought. This had gone too far. Yes, Jay had burdens and pressures, but Lewis had always tried to make things better. Every scraped knee, every bad test score and blow to her ego, even her disastrous pregnancy—hadn't Lewis been there for all of them? Didn't he specialize in being the custodian of Jay Ingraham?

"Dad? Are you there?"

And now Stephen, the master propagandist, had constructed a fairly tale in which Lewis was the big bad wolf. So he could use Jay up, and move on when he became bored. Well, it wasn't going to work.

Right? he asked the empty room.

"Dad?" Jay repeated.

"Yes, honey, I'm here," Lewis said. "Whatever you need, I'm here."

"Dad, don't talk to Stephen anymore."

"I don't know if I can promise that."

"Dad."

"All right, I won't speak to him."

"Good. Thank you."

After they hung up, Lewis went through every room in the house, looked in every closet. He went twice around the backyard and then searched the basement and the third floor, where the detritus of his married life was stacked in unruly piles of boxes. Carew followed his every step, strangely calm and reverential.

Lewis couldn't shake the feeling that Anna was there. It was as though he sensed her around every corner, but as soon as he arrived there she vanished.

"I'm sorry for what I did," he said. "I was trying to help you."

He felt on the verge of finding her, but didn't. Not that night.

Later, lying on the downstairs sofa in the dark of night, he thought about Stephen. He had problems to solve, and he was going to fix things before it was too late. Perhaps only then would he truly find her.

13. THEY HAD RIDDEN THE SWEET WAVE OF LUST; NOW IT WAS OVER.

When Jay got up in the morning she found that her practice of sleeping with the window cracked open had backfired: the first sight of the new day was her breath condensing in a cloud before her eyes. She shivered, got up from under her thick down comforter, and crossed the room. What she saw outside made her gasp.

It had snowed during the night, about four or five inches' worth. Yesterday's dull gray landscape, the color of a sparrow's wings, had turned into a sedate canvas of white. Old forms reduced themselves to vague outlines and gentle curves. Jay shut the window.

Strange, it hadn't been in the forecast, such as it was—weather predictions in Minneapolis resembled the speculative fancies of hardcore paranoiacs. More than once Jay had thought about forecasting the weather herself, off the top of her head, then comparing the results against what really happened. She abandoned the idea as too Lewis-like.

Ramona was ensconced in a cocoon of blankets in her kid-sized bed. Jay paused a moment before turning on the light to admire her daughter. Kids, Jay had learned, went through phases of plumping up before elongating—that was how they grew. Ramona was definitely in a lengthening period; the leg that was thrust out from the bedding was long, lithe, a working model of a woman's.

Five years, ten. Fifteen, and then she would be gone—and hopefully not having babies of her own.

"OK, kiddo, time to wake up," Jay said, switching on the light.

Jay went into the kitchen and started grinding coffee. She was wearing only leggings and a Super Furry Animals T-shirt, and she rubbed her hands together to warm them. She liked being sleepy, and enjoyed the half-dumb state of impairment that came with morning. It was almost as good as being drunk.

Stephen would want to see her today. And she wanted to see him, she supposed. But she had no idea what to tell him.

Jay's memory came back to her; it felt like a scene in some foreign city, where shopkeepers turned on the lights in a row along the lane, and babushkas emerged to sweep the sidewalk with laced-straw brooms. Business was starting in this new day, albeit in a language scarcely comprehensible.

She thought of the night her mother died. It had been so strange. When she remembered it, it was as a series of images, like paintings. There was Lewis opening the door for her and Ramona. There was Ramona going to the porch with Lewis, the little girl unaware (or so she thought at the time, but surely Ramona suspected) of what weighed on the adults. There was Anna Ingraham in her bed, dressed in a robe, flat on her back, her eyes closed and her mouth slightly open. She had been cold, her skin darkening. The room had smelled of air freshener that Lewis must have sprayed.

It was her time, Lewis said at the door. *She barely suffered. I was there. I made sure of it.*

Jay kissed her mother's cold cheek, held her cold hand, illogically adjusted her pillows as though to make her more comfortable.

"Mama?" said Ramona from behind her.

Ramona stood barefoot in her Spongebob Squarepants nightshirt—a gift from Anna last Christmas. Ramona's fine dark hair stuck out at absurd angles from her oversized head, and she rubbed her eyes with her fist.

"Look outside," Jay said. "It snowed."

"Really?" Ramona squealed, pad-padding to the living room, where she gazed at the street with hushed and reverential appreciation.

Jay realized, all at once and with surprise, that she was seriously entertaining breaking up with Stephen. *That* was the feeling she was having—anticipatory loss. It wasn't going to work out, was it? It was out of her control. Their age gap, the different phases of their lives—they had ridden the sweet wave of lust, but now the forces aligned against them were simply too much.

One time Anna had warned Jay against going down this emotional road. She said that Stephen was a good person, someone who could be counted on. Anna said that initial attraction always waned and it was what was left over afterward that mattered. Yet Anna's marriage to Lewis, and the form it took as it endured, was at best a mystery to Jay. As a girl Jay worshiped Anna in the way one adores her creator, a being endowed with untouchable depths and endless aspects. Later Jay had seen Anna as a person who had not realized her potential, a woman whose talents ended up producing little more than plain, bland landscapes of her own backyard.

"You told me not to leave him," Jay said quietly to her mother. "But maybe you were just talking to yourself."

"What, Mama?" said Ramona, who was pulling on a T-shirt.

"Oh, nothing, honey," Jay replied.

"You were talking to Grandma, weren't you?" Ramona said with a gleam. "I do that, too. I can't wait until she comes back and we can talk all the time like we used to."

Jay was certain that Ramona had no idea whatsoever why her mother suddenly went to her and enveloped her in a stifling embrace, nor why Jay wept silent tears into her daughter's hair—tears that would not dry, but would freeze into tiny ice crystals when they went together into the cold of the snowy morning.

When Jay drove to Stephen's apartment building, tucked into a little residential enclave a short walk from the wooded circle of Lake Harriet, she immediately spotted his car parked on the street. It had been a tricky drive, with cars skidding and spinning erratically in the first measurable snow of the season—Lewis always said it amazed him, how people who had lived in Minnesota their entire lives would drive as though they had never seen the white stuff before. This first blanket was always disorienting; familiar landmarks turned into abstract representations of themselves, and the color white suddenly dominated everything in sight. Black was usually assigned as the hue for the void, but its yin-yang opposite sufficed as well—white was a blank, a confounding nothing, like Melville's white whale a screen onto which to project all manner of rage and frustration.

The snow was like that, among other things. But Jay was not angry with Stephen. She was simply resolved that things had to change.

She parked in front of a house whose lone evergreen had been wedding-caked with big clumps of snow with little patches of deep green showing through the thickening white. Jay looked up; the sky was overcast, and more was coming down. The quiet of the morning made her feel as though she were on a stage set, in a dream or a tableau in someone's sleeping imagination. It was not a feeling she liked.

"Come on," she said to herself. "Go talk to him."

Stephen's building was a four-stacker like hers, but it was in a more upscale neighborhood. While he enjoyed the same square footage that Jay was compelled to share with Ramona, his own patch was considerably better maintained—and he was much less likely to have to endure a horde of ballistic punk rockers living downstairs, as had been the case for Jay two years ago.

Jay rang the buzzer. The place was shuttered and shingled, the windows all tidy and immaculate—it was in the small details that class differences emerged. Well, and admittedly some large details as well, such as the hanging gutter that decorated the back of Jay's building and cluttered the view from her bathroom window.

"Yes?" Stephen said through the distortions of the wire.

"It's me. Jay."

"Jay?" Stephen said, somewhat excitedly. "I didn't—"

"I know. I'm sorry I didn't call first."

"Don't apologize. Come on up."

The door clicked open and Jay went inside. She climbed the stairs and Stephen was waiting halfway out in the hall holding the door open. He was dressed in slacks, shoes, and an unbuttoned shirt, and his thick hair fell nicely over his forehead and ears. He *was* a sight that she had enjoyed getting used to seeing.

"This is a nice surprise," he said, putting his arm around her and leading her into his apartment. When he kissed her, she responded out of habit, but she pulled away the moment his hands started to wander. He looked hurt before he managed to raise his defenses behind a smile and folded arms.

"I'm afraid I don't have much time, anyway," he said. "I have to teach a class in forty-five minutes."

"I know," she told him. "I wasn't even sure you were going to be here."

"Why didn't you call, then?" he asked. "It looks pretty treacherous out there."

"You forget—I'm an old hand at the snow," she said.

"Well, give me time," Stephen said with a laugh. "We'll buy a house together, get a snowblower—the works. You can see me into my old age turning into one of those guys wearing a hat with earflaps and those big old boots I won't even bother to lace up."

Jay had to smile at the image. Stephen was so composed, so adept at inhabiting his self, that it was funny to imagine him as a disheveled old man. She slipped off her shoes and wandered across the ornate rug, skirting the sofa and making for the window.

"OK, my not-so-subtle allusion to our future domesticity didn't get the response I was fishing for," he said.

"Stephen, don't," she said, unable to look at him.

"It doesn't have to be a house," he said. "If that's too close to bourgeois splendor, then we'll buy a plot of land in the country and live in a yurt. You know what a yurt is? It's a—"

"I *know* what a yurt is," Jay said.

Stephen's face fell. "Well, anyway, we'll live in one of *those*. We'll have to section it off so Ramona can have some privacy, but it'll be a fortifying experience for her."

She checked out the stack of CDs next to Stephen's stereo: Mahler symphonies, Mozart piano concertos, the most recent

Bob Dylan album, Thelonious Monk. On top was a Pink Floyd compilation, a nod to the stoner past Stephen sought to hide from everyone.

"Jay?" He moved behind her, not touching.

"This isn't easy," she said, looking out the window. The snow was falling harder now.

"What isn't . . . no, we're not going to have that conversation, are we? We can't."

She tried to withstand his handsomeness hovering over her, the comforting lines of his face. It would be so easy to back down from what she'd decided, and to fall into his arms and let him lead her to the bedroom. For it was always in the bedroom that their differences fell away and everything seemed possible—no, probable—and all *good* things seemed a sure bet.

"I'm sorry, Stephen," she said.

He rested his fingers on her elbow. "Jay, you can't let this business with Lewis come between us like this."

"I'm not." Jay moved away. "You have to understand, it's not the stuff with Dad. Maybe it sparked something, I don't know, but—"

"Jay, in one breath you're saying Lewis isn't breaking us up, and in the next you're admitting he is."

"It's not something I want to debate," Jay said. She exhaled hard and leaned back against the sill.

"I agree," Stephen said. He brushed his hair back from his forehead in a fussy, nervous manner. "We shouldn't be debating *anything*. We should be *together*. Jay, please, don't do this."

"I've been thinking. Which, admittedly, is a dangerous thing." Jay laughed, but Stephen remained grave. "Look, we have too many differences. I just don't feel like it's . . . like *we're* going to work out."

Stephen began buttoning up his shirt, looking down at his fingers, shielding his face from her.

"What?" Jay asked. "What are you thinking?"

When he looked up, his eyes were blurry. Jay was startled to see him this way. He looked years younger.

"It's just that—" he paused. "Jay, it's just that, since we've been together, you've been acting on this paradigm—"

"*Stephen,*" Jay interrupted. "Just talk normally."

He looked as though she'd struck him.

"I didn't know you resented me speaking in analytical terms," he said.

"I don't." Jay touched him lightly on the shoulder. "Don't look so beaten down. It's just little old me."

"But that's just it," Stephen said, showing a flash of anger. "There's no 'little old Jay.' That's precisely what I was talking about. You've set things up so that I'm the high-and-mighty professor with you as the naïve little waitress. But it doesn't hold water. You're a formidable person, Jay—you get it from your father. But you've had this attitude that you're lucky to be with me, that all our differences work in my favor. But Jay, you know, I don't want to be without you."

"Stephen—"

"No, let me finish." He folded his arms around himself, his voice strained. "I'm older than you, yes, I can't change that. But I . . . I *love* you, Jay. I want us to build our lives together."

"Oh, shit, Stephen." She had warned herself against this. His emotions were peaking, her own were like water coming to a boil. She didn't want a crying scene. She couldn't take it. How to communicate to him that she had simply *made up her mind*?

"Don't do this," Stephen said. "Come back to me."

"I'm not going to do that," she said.

"*Why not?*" he asked in a high-pitched, unfamiliar voice, the intonation of a little boy denied the thing he wanted most.

Why not? Because she had made up her mind. Of course Stephen was paying for the sins of Michael Carmelov, and

Lewis Ingraham, and Jay Ingraham, as well. It wasn't fair, but it didn't need to be. Stephen knew what was going on—hadn't they once discussed how it was the female human's rightful responsibility to break up, that it was her role to manage the primal core of mate selection behind the confused jumble of what was called a "relationship"?

The sun was up, a blurred suggestion of itself through the thick pack of overcast. It looked like it was going to snow all day.

Jay looked up at Stephen, suddenly aware that she hadn't answered his desperate question.

"I've always been honest with you," she said.

"I know you think that," Stephen said in a low voice.

"What's that mean?" she asked.

"Nothing." Stephen folded his arms and cupped his chin in one hand. "I'm upset. I'm probably going to start saying stupid things. I have to go talk to a bunch of uninterested undergraduates about Walter Benjamin, and it's going to be hard to do because you've just hurled a load of plastic explosives into my life."

"Don't be melodramatic," Jay said.

"I'm not," Stephen replied. "All right, I am. But you don't seem to understand what I'm trying to tell you. I *need* you, Jaybird. I'm all alone. I'm not sure how much I'm enjoying this life I've chosen. You are the bright spot that gets me through."

"Stephen—"

"I mean these things I'm saying to you," he said.

Stephen's tide of emotion evoked a complex reaction within her, as nuanced as a wash of tastes, or smells. First an ephemeral tang of regret and sympathy for him, then a powerful tug of wishing to make him feel better. Which would mean . . . doing what he asked, transforming her reality to match the dictates of his needs. Being with him, being *his*. And this felt like the basis of almost all her interactions, from the unquenchable thirst of Lewis for attention and reaction to the feckless adolescent sexual needs of Michael Carmelov that had left her with . . . and now a blind alley, a place best untouched, but there were the childish demands of Ramona, so hard to meet. The only person who hadn't made Jay feel burdened had been Anna, whose airy presence had always, if nothing else, enveloped Jay in comfort and acceptance.

"I don't want to be with anyone right now," she told Stephen.

"But we can make each other's lives so much better," he said, holding his hands out as though begging.

"Of course I've believed that from the beginning," Jay told him. "But I don't now. Maybe it's bad timing. I'm so sorry to hurt you, Stephen. This is hurting me, too. And it will hurt Ramona. But I'm doing what I think is best for me."

"And there's no room for discussion," Stephen said.

"No, there really isn't."

"Then get out."

"Yes, I understand."

"Please get out of here right now," Stephen said, turning away. He worked at tucking in his shirt and moved to his desk, where notes and books were piled beside his briefcase.

"We can talk later if you want," Jay offered, suddenly feeling a landslide of panic over the suddenness of what had happened.

"Maybe, I don't know," Stephen said, occupied with his things. "Just get out. Leave me alone."

"All right, I'm—"

"Can you just do what I'm fucking asking?" he shouted, still looking away. "Get out, Jay! *Leave!*"

"Yes, all right," she whispered, suddenly frightened of him.

She went out to the hall and gently closed the door behind her. Just as she started to walk down the stairs, she heard a crash from somewhere inside Stephen's apartment.

What had she just done?

The snow was falling on the street outside, filling the dead flower beds, piling on window ledges, flicked in clumps from monotonous windshield wipers. Jay walked to her car quickly, almost furtively, for reasons she couldn't quite define. She had gotten what she wanted. She was a degree more free.

14. HIDEBOUND, EARTH-LADEN, AND FINALLY FREE.

t had been appallingly apparent to Lewis from the moment of waking that something was wrong. It was an embarrassment to feel stable consciousness so out of reach, to sense the pull of memory as strong as perceptions of the present moment.

But that's the way it was.

He saw Anna in her last night alive on planet Earth, on her back in bed, out of her mind on drugs and muttering things that made no sense. Her sick smell pervaded the room, her once-beautiful face had transformed into a gaunt, unrecognizable mask. One moment she seemed to notice him there, in the next she was half-gone, struggling to project herself into wherever it was that she was going. He had played Pablo Casals on the stereo, her favorite, the strings of the cello luring her into a sweet and welcome nothingness of sleep.

Sleep. It was like she was trying to go to sleep, but couldn't. She had lived two months longer than the doctors said she would.

Lewis had tried to assist her in making a world in which she could enjoy living. The house she loved, their daughter, the garden—he had made them possible. And though she had traded the ephemeral promise of her youth for these things—and it was undeniably true that of this husband and wife, she was the only one who possessed any talent or contact with the transcendent—she had long seemed content to have made the trade, to have accepted the morning light through the kitchen windows and the idle hours on the sunporch. She had made herself content, sometimes happy, in the world that Lewis had made for her. He loved her for it, if it had taken her dying for him to realize it.

Snap back.

Oh, what a shitty morning—Carew French-kissing him was his first waking perception. Then the pills, and the shakes, in the bathroom. The front door was stubborn and didn't want to open, and when Lewis nearly performed a pratfall onto his porch, it was to the sight of inches of powdery snow up and down the quiet street. Bundled up like an Eskimo, Lewis took Carew to Dogshit Park, which had overnight turned itself into an Arctic Refuge. Lewis looked up and saw a squirrel perched on a power line, shivering, staring out at the world with a stunned expression. It had all changed, things were fucked up. Carew, with his indefatigable good humor, sniffed and dug and danced as though it was Christmas morning.

And now he sat in the driver's seat of his car, watching his daughter leave Stephen Grant's apartment building. He was parked down the block, where there was little chance of her spotting him. He didn't know what he would say if she did—because he had little idea why he had come to Stephen's. He simply had. And he had parked and waited when he saw Jay's little blue sedan parked in front.

He looked around for Anna. She *would* come back again, if

he were vigilant. And he sensed that whatever he was doing would speed the process of bringing her back to him.

Lewis owned a gun. It was funny how he had managed to hide that fact even from his own wife. It hadn't been too hard—early in their marriage they had established that looking through each other's things was bad form. Lewis had voted for Jimmy Carter, for Bill Clinton twice, he had opposed both Iraq wars and had made sport many times of Charlton Heston's Moses-at-the-firing-range posturing. Yet one day, about ten years ago, Lewis had gone to a gun shop and bought a .38, then snuck off to a firing range and learned how to fire it. He hadn't seen Moses there, or the Omega Man, but it sure felt good to make explosions come out of his hand and to watch paper targets fall into shreds.

Now he had the .38 in his pocket. Who would expect old Lewis Ingraham to be packing a gun? He had a permit for it. The state had given him permission to arm himself. What a great country.

Jay was unlocking her car. She looked upset. What had Stephen said, to make her look up with such obvious distress at his upstairs window, to struggle with her keys, to pull out so quickly?

Nothing was right. Everything looked ugly, as though trying to tell Lewis something. The tightness in his chest, the foreboding of death, had set in early. He also had a pain in his guts that had started up just before sleep. And the sleep—it was an unwarranted courtesy to call it anything resembling rest. He had woken almost every hour, thinking that someone was in the room with him (Anna?), plunging in and out of a series of dreams that drew upon the worst of his life for source material: deadline anxieties from school days, humiliations at the office, even an evocation of childhood terror, a memory of feeling that he was to blame for the strife between his parents.

He cleared his windshield and watched Jay's taillights flash as she turned the corner. The wipers beat out a rudimentary 2/4 beat, an idiot thud to match the monotonous rhythm in his aching chest.

Stephen's door opened again. From it, toting his briefcase, came the man of the hour. Stephen had on a long black wool coat and, Lewis could hardly believe it, *earmuffs.*

Lewis got out of his car.

Stephen opened up the door of his prim little Volkswagen and tossed his briefcase inside. His breath condensed around his face. Lewis started toward him, staying to the street rather than the sidewalk, his shoes crunching in the trenches carved out by cars through the snow.

He felt dizzy, he felt not right. He felt as if he were about to fall. As he walked, he sensed himself about to flinch from real or imagined dangers. His entire nervous system was overtuned and irritated. He had no idea what he was about to do.

"Lewis?" Stephen said, looking up from his car. "What in the world?"

Lewis pulled his coat tight around his neck and tried to will away the chill that threatened to take possession of his fragile form. His hand in his pocket, he felt the metal of the gun grow colder with exposure to the elements.

"Lewis," Stephen said. "What's wrong?"

There was an urgent manner that required addressing. Lewis had promised Jay he wouldn't talk to Stephen. But he hadn't yet, had he?

"Aren't you going to say anything?" Stephen asked.

Stephen looked red-eyed and haunted, which was a surprise. Apparently he had some sort of conscience.

The snow fell in big fluffy clumps.

Lewis was aware that there was once a time when he felt differently, when the vivid discomfort of existence did not press upon him with such force. But events and the particular bent of his nature had led him to this point—hidebound, earth-laden, finally free and entirely lacking any idea what to do next.

Would shooting Stephen bring Anna back? Was that what she wanted?

"If it makes you happy," Stephen was saying from across a great distance, "your daughter just terminated our relationship. You have been successful. You won."

With great effort, Lewis focused on what Stephen was saying—more accusations, more recrimination.

"What do you *want*, man?" Stephen barked. "Are you stalking me or something?"

Well, maybe he was. It was a question that merited some sort of reply, wasn't it?

Lewis pulled his right hand from out of his coat pocket. In it he held the gun.

Stephen, for an instant, tried to assume a look of sardonic disapproval and mockery. But it couldn't last. There was only so long you could sneer at a firearm, no matter how much academic theory you were armed with. The gun was heavy and cold in Lewis's ungloved hand. Without giving much thought to what he was doing, he switched the safety off.

"Lewis, come on," Stephen said, reaching out for his car to hold him up as his knees started to buckle. "Don't be foolish."

Allegations of foolishness were perhaps not the optimal strategy for a man in Stephen's position. Lewis sensed the precipice at which he now stood, and he intuited the manifold paths that his reality could now take—and so many of them were unfavorable.

It was going to be very hard to go back to selling shirts, wasn't it? Lewis thought he wasn't going to be returning to the department store. That stopgap attempt at normality was closed and sealed.

"Please," Stephen was saying as he looked around the empty street. "Haven't you done enough?"

Lewis flipped the cold metal safety back on the gun and returned it to his pocket. He took out a cigarette and lit it, shielding his lighter from the light breeze and the snow. Stephen suddenly seemed quite irrelevant.

"I can't believe you did that," Stephen said.

After marshaling such restraint, it would be pointless to engage Stephen in any kind of debate at this point—and, Lewis reminded himself, he had managed not to break his pledge to Jay. He puffed on his cigarette as though it was his first, or his last, then closed the distance between himself and Stephen and clapped the younger man lightly on the shoulder. He turned and started walking back to his car.

Though he couldn't remember feeling worse, physically, his spirit enjoyed a strange and unfamiliar ebullience. He played his little game and pretended that Anna was at home waiting for him. She would nag him about shoveling the walk, and he would pretend to be irritated. They would act out their little patterns, so secure in the roles they had defined for each other: *you be you, and I'll be me.* It was such a comfort to imagine, just for a little while, that it was still possible.

Stephen watched Lewis's Lexus disappear into the fogged morning. He leaned against his car. There were a couple of kids walking to school, a neighbor across the street preparing to fire up his snowblower. Where were they a few minutes ago, when Lewis Ingraham drew a gun on him in the stark light of day?

Once inside the car, with the engine running, Stephen tuned in to the motor's rhythm and realized that his own heart was beating extraordinarily fast. His hands were cold and numb. He gripped the steering wheel and stared through the windshield.

It was going to be hard to get to class on time. Of course he had a perfectly acceptable explanation: *Sorry I'm late, students, but I had to get my heart ripped out by my lover and receive a silent death threat from her father before I could make my way over to campus.*

It was true that Stephen had a tendency to view the events of his life in literary and analytic terms—every neck ache was a manifestation of unresolved conflict, each sin of omission was a veiled statement of intent, yes, yes, guilty as charged. He saw the unfolding of life's events as interconnected nodes in a great pattern that he could understand if only he *thought* about it hard enough. Jay used to laugh at him in their early days together, when they were still in the initial process of unveiling themselves to each other. She was positively tickled that Stephen found it impossible to admit that some things just *happened;* she had claimed that, in his way, Stephen was every bit as superstitious and portent-seeking as a medieval villager hiding inside his hut at the sight of a shooting star.

No one understood him the way Jay did. Stephen steered his car through the slow-moving herd, feeling the wheels slide under him as he made a turn. He pulled his earmuffs down around his neck—they were a concession to the cold that didn't require matting down his hair under a hat. The snow was engulfing everything, daubing big blots of white silence over the city. He would never get used to it.

He had to slam on his brakes at the final stoplight before the Lyndale entrance to 94. His car slid out and its nose protruded rudely into the crosswalk. People gave him dirty looks as they walked around him.

This was the first drive to work in the post-Jay era. He would come home alone that night, eat alone, grade papers alone. There would be no one there in the morning. He would most likely never again see the supple curve of her back, the perfect spheres of her breasts, or her eyes closed in transport as he lost himself within her. Jay was, for all her aimlessness, extraordinarily sure once she actually got down to the business of deciding on something.

So that was that. Stephen merged onto the freeway, checked the clock on the dashboard and saw that he was going to be late for his own lecture. He'd gone and fallen in love—after years of trying to perfect an impenetrable core that couldn't be budged by hurt or dependence—and now she'd left him. He felt, strangely enough, as though nothing at all was happening.

And now the memory of the gun. Stephen had stared down the barrel, the way detective novels described it, and seen down into a black void of darkness. He wondered how close Lewis had been to pulling the trigger. It looked like a big gun, and it might have killed him—Stephen had read once that the impact alone from a bullet is often enough to disrupt the heart's rhythm and induce death. He imagined the red of his blood on the white snow, the cloud of scorched gunpowder in the crisp morning air.

He supposed something had to be done about Lewis, but he wasn't sure what. Stephen wasn't inclined to respond to violence in kind, and Lewis hadn't actually *done* anything. He suspected the old boy had engaged in a little old-fashioned angry-father terrorism.

Which brought him back to Jay. He had lost her.

Stephen pulled his car into one of the last spaces in the ramp nearest the lecture hall. He switched off the motor and looked at himself in the mirror under the sun visor, trying to get into character for his students. He worked harder than usual to locate his inner professor that morning, because it surely wasn't much fun at the moment being plain old Stephen Grant.

INTERLUDE. FEEDING THE PENGUINS AND MAKING SURE THEIR BABIES WERE SAFE.

In Antarctica it was cold *all* the time. Sometimes you couldn't even go outside because your nose and your toes and your fingers would freeze and fall off. And the doctors wouldn't be able to put them back on again. You'd lose them *forever*.

The Perfect Princess had left her throne unoccupied for a time (always a dangerous prospect—there were would-be usurpers everywhere) in order to mount an expedition to Antarctica to look for her Grandma Anna. She had with her a team of royal assistants who helped her in her terrible struggle, and who lived to tend to her every terrible whim.

"Bring me some hot tea," the Princess said to Milo.

"Got a ball!" Milo said, tossing a basketball into the snow, then running after it and falling down.

A princess had to understand that, at times, her royal retainers might not understand her requests. She took a step into the deep snow of Antarctica, enjoying the crunch of her boots on the frozen soil and the feel of her furry hood on her cheeks.

Grandma Anna (and how she loved just saying the name) was out there somewhere, maybe feeding the penguins and making sure their babies were safe and warm. Grandma Anna was like that. She liked taking care of things, especially people.

Mama had been sad in the morning, and Ramona knew it had something to do with Stephen. And Grampa Lewis. Ramona's grampa had a weird look in his eyes sometimes these days. She knew he loved her, and that he would never hurt her. But he might hurt someone else, maybe without meaning to. He was that strong.

"Want to come with me?" said Ashleigh, the only girl at day care older than Ramona; she gestured into the wilds of the backyard, over by the swing set.

"No, thank you," Ramona said quietly. She preferred the company of the younger kids, who played compliant parts in her make-believe and who never made fun of the way she talked. Ashleigh was wild, and brave, a runner and a climber.

"Time to come inside!" called Janet from the doorway. Janet was a grown-up. Janet was always trying to help Ramona talk better, which was nice in a way, but Ramona hadn't figured out yet how to tell Janet that she would rather be left alone.

"Ashleigh! Milo! Danny! Ramona!" Janet said. "Come on in! It's getting colder!"

Slowly, one by one, the children broke off from their exploration and started the long trudge to the door—and quite a slog it was, weighted down with boots, coats, mittens, scarves. Ramona thought about the hot chocolate and the warm chair that waited for her inside. With any luck it would soon be TV time. And then everything would be perfect.

The snow swirled in a gust of wind, and Ramona was the last child standing in the wilderness of the yard. The Perfect

Princess prepared to warm herself in her Antarctic camp, with her faithful and loyal servants all around.

But then she saw a figure through the mist of heavy snow, a small adult dressed in regular clothes, with no coat or hat. That wasn't right. There weren't supposed to be any grown-ups in the yard.

"Ramona!" Janet called out, her voice sounding very far away.

The Perfect Princess took a step toward the person, who was clearly a woman. Ramona was a little scared, but she had a feeling that this was the right thing to do.

"Ramona!" Janet said. "Where are you going? Come inside."

Ramona took a few more steps through the snow and there, over by the basketball hoop, was the face she had been waiting to see.

It was Grandma Anna.

"You came back," Ramona whispered to her.

Grandma Anna looked the way she used to before she got sick. She was wearing old jeans, a man's shirt, and sandals. She smiled at Ramona, and Ramona felt a shiver that was both happy and sad.

"Are you staying?" Ramona asked.

"Ramona!" Janet called.

Grandma Anna nodded and smiled. She put a finger over her lips the way she used to, when she thought something was so special that she and Ramona would keep it between them like a secret treasure.

"Mama really wants to see you," Ramona told her.

Grandma Anna nodded, one hand resting on her cheek, and she looked at Ramona in the way that always made Ramona feel extra-special, like there was something about Ramona that made her grandma happier than anything else in the world.

"Will you come with me?" Ramona asked.

"Ramona! Now!" yelled Janet through the veil of snow.

Now Grandma Anna pointed to the door, as though to say that Ramona should be a good girl and do as Janet said. And that was true. Grandma Anna always knew the right thing to do.

"OK, but come back," Ramona said.

I love you, Grandma Anna mouthed silently, and when Ramona turned away and looked back again, she was gone.

15. EITHER EMBRACE HIM OR THROW HIM OUT IN THE SNOW.

Lewis went to work after all. It turned out to be easier than he thought to threaten a man at gunpoint, then put in a shift on the sales floor. If anything, he felt better than usual. His inexplicable (to him) actions had made him feel years younger. While he still felt a sick vibration inside, his knees and hip were free of aches, and after he got home he treated himself to a pain-free run in the snow around Lake of the Isles, where he passed the small lagoon where he once deposited the ashes of his late wife.

By the next afternoon he gave little thought at all to the loaded pistol that rested on the sideboard in the dining room, next to that day's *Star Tribune*. He did a round of push-ups in his underwear and drank two cups of coffee. The snow had stopped falling for the moment but the temperature was plunging, making it necessary for him to crank the thermostat. The hell with the gas bill. He wasn't going to freeze in his own house. He put on a Frank Zappa record and padded around tidying, suddenly inspired with ideas of order.

When the doorbell rang Lewis took it at first as a sound effect on the record, which was percolating with a lewd, dense quasi-funk. But then he spotted the shadow on the other side of the front door, and jogged into the dining room to toss the newspaper over the gun. When the bell kept ringing he made for the door, cursing under his breath. It was probably the mailman hand-delivering the latest stack of bills.

It wasn't the mailman. When Lewis threw open the door he felt a flash of warmth at the sight of his neighbor and friend Stan Garabaldi. He couldn't remember the last time he'd had a visitor other than Ramona and Jay.

"What the hell do *you* want?" Lewis barked.

"I came over to see if you're holding," Stan said, stone-faced. "I'm jonesing, Louie."

"If I was, I wouldn't share it with you," Lewis told him. "I'd lock the doors and get *wasted*, man."

"You gonna have me in," Stan said, "or am I gonna stand here with icicles hanging off my dick?"

Lewis chuckled and held the door open for Stan. He'd known the older man since Jay was a baby. In that time, Stan had gone to fat and lost his hair, divorced one wife and married another, and now had a son in high school. He'd also developed a heart condition and retired early from his marriage-counseling practice, letting his younger wife deal with the working world while he occasionally took odd jobs.

Stan wheezed and complained as he undertook the Minnesota visitor's ritual—divesting himself of his outerwear and heavy boots, depositing thick clumps of icy detritus all over and around the thick wooly mat in the entryway. When he was done he stood, a head shorter than Lewis, flushed and red in his zipped-up fleece jacket.

"So what're you up to?" he asked in his gravelly baritone. "Didn't even know if I was going to catch you home."

"I don't work today," Lewis told him. "The sales of silk ties and mid-price shirts have fallen on lesser lights for the moment."

Stan padded across the living room in his socks. "Listen to this shit," he said, motioning at the stereo. "Don't you even have a CD player?"

"I have become a dinosaur," Lewis admitted.

"No shit." Stan picked up the record cover and looked at it with begrudging approval. "I remember this one. It's got that song about it hurting when you pee. I've been there."

"Two-plus decades of monogamy had their drawbacks," Lewis said. "But at least I never got the clap."

Stan laughed loudly. "There's still time," he said.

Lewis smiled ruefully. He had to give Stan credit—he never pussyfooted around the topic of Anna. He was one of the few people who managed not to treat Lewis as though *he* had some terrible disease.

"You want something?" Lewis asked. "Coffee? Bourbon?"

"No, no." Stan glanced around the place, resting his big hairy hand on the back of a chair. "I'm just checking in on you. Checking *up* on you, I guess I should say."

"Checking up?" Lewis said. "Fuck, Stan. You know I'm fine. You're not going to be like everyone else, worrying about how I'm *doing*, are you?"

"Well, Lewis, I know you have about ten layers of crust on you—"

"More like twenty," Lewis interrupted.

"I saw Jay yesterday," Stan said, more serious now. "Actually I took a client to that restaurant she works at. I forgot she was even working there until she came to take my order."

"The Cogito?" Lewis said.

"Yeah. The Cogito."

Lewis glanced into the dining room and saw he hadn't done a good enough job of covering the gun—a little flash of metal was visible from where he stood. He moved his body to block Stan's view. Stan glanced over Lewis's shoulder, too perceptive not to notice Lewis's sudden unrest.

"Anyway, she looked kind of stressed out," Stan said. "She's such a good kid. Smart. When I asked her how you were doing, she got kind of weird with me. So I decided to come see what was up."

"Stressed out?" Lewis said. "How do you mean?"

"Come on, Lewis. Don't get cute with me." Stan frowned, which entailed a reorganization of his bushy eyebrows and a shortening of his bulldog neck. "Stressed. Unhappy. Showing outward signs of strain. You and her have always been the same in some ways—neither of you are real chipper-sunshine types. But I was a little worried about her, and I got the feeling it was something to do with you."

"Aside from the obvious shit," Lewis said, "I'm doing fine."

Stan shrugged. He knew this was how it was going to go.

"Seriously, Stan," Lewis said. "I'm glad you stopped by. I appreciate your concern. But I'm as well as I can be."

"Yeah, well," Stan's voice trailed off, and he rubbed his big belly. He'd put on about fifty pounds since Lewis had known him, slow and steady, and now looked to be about fifteen years older than Lewis rather than five.

"I'm a little nervous," Lewis admitted.

"Yeah?" Stan gave him a look of commiseration. "They got you on pills?"

"They do," Lewis said.

"They working?" Stan asked.

"A little bit," Lewis said.

Lewis considered telling Stan about Anna, about his growing conviction that her piecemeal revealing of herself was leading up to something big. But he knew how that would sound.

"Well, it's a start," Stan said. He folded his arms and leveled Lewis with a look of warm frustration. "You know, it wouldn't be the biggest failure in the history of the human race for you to admit that you've gone through some major setbacks and that you need people."

"I admit that freely," Lewis said, throwing open his arms.

"Why don't you come over for dinner Friday night?" asked Stan. "Celia can make something nice. You don't want me cooking."

"No, I don't," Lewis said. "And let's say maybe. I'll call you."

Stan let out a long sigh that arrested itself somewhere toward its end. In the past few years Stan had taken on a kind of somber authority, having lived through the ugly meltdown of his first marriage to Katherine, a wisp-thin woman who had turned out to be harboring a seething rage toward Stan which she manifested in the form of an ugly legal battle which ended in Stan keeping their house but paying dearly for it in the form of cash, present and future, and the souring of his relations with his son. Then had come the discovery of the blockage, and the bypass, a real danger to his existence that trumped all of Lewis's pains and fears. With his burly mass and bloated-up, boyish face, he seemed to have reached a sort of uneasy accord with himself and his fate. He also seemed to understand Lewis on some fraternal level that made Lewis want to either embrace him or throw him out into the snow.

"And what're you planning to do with *that*?" Stan asked, nodding over Lewis's shoulder.

"With what?" asked Lewis.

"You're being cute again," Stan said. "I'm referring to that firearm you've tried to hide under the paper."

"Oh, *that*," Lewis smiled. The record ended, and the tone-arm came to rest with a thump. "I was cleaning it."

"You were cleaning it," Stan repeated.

"Look, Stan, it's legal," Lewis said. "I live alone. I have a right."

"Hey, I have *two*," Stan said. "But I don't leave them sitting out."

"I don't have to explain myself," Lewis said.

"No, you don't." Stan gave a long, ponderous nod of agreement. "So how are you getting along with the boyfriend?"

"My boyfriend or yours?" Lewis asked.

"Very funny." Stan shook his head. "Come on, Lewis. How long have we known each other?"

A long time indeed. Stan had been a stalwart ally during Anna's illness, bringing her food and books, more than once spending an afternoon with her and sending Lewis out to the movies for the sake of his sanity. Lewis owed Stan a debt.

"There's no problem with Stephen."

"Stephen." Stan snapped his fingers. "That's his name. You know what? I don't believe you."

"Why—"

"Because the last time I talked to you, you were complaining about him." Stan winced as though his words pained him. "You said he was bad for Jay. You remember? Now she's miserable, you're evasive, and you practically twitched when I asked about him. I know how you get, Lewis. If you don't like one of Jay's boyfriends, there's trouble."

"You're off base on this one, Stan," Lewis said. "Apparently Jay and Stephen have broken up, but I had nothing to do—"

"Oh, Lewis," Stan said sadly.

"What?" Lewis exploded, about to tell Stan to mind his own business, when the doorbell rang. Lewis looked up and saw another shadow beyond the door.

"Fucking Grand Central," he muttered, leaving Stan in the living room. He opened the door to a young man in a suit.

"Lewis Ingraham here?" the kid asked. He was scrubbed and broad-chested, like one of the kids who worked under him at AmEx.

"Yeah?" Lewis barked. "What do you want?"

The kid pressed a manila envelope to Lewis's chest.

"You're being served," the kid said with a trace of satisfaction. "Hennepin County Court."

Lewis took the envelope but didn't open it.

"What the hell—"

"Restraining order," the kid said. "You have a hearing in ten days. Until then, do not contact or get within five hundred yards of Stephen Grant."

"You're out of—"

"Do you understand?" the kid interrupted.

"Yes, yes."

"Thank you and have a good day," the kid said, then made for his car. Despite the cold, he wore only a suit jacket. He was obviously made of hardier stuff than Lewis, who shivered as he slammed the door shut.

When he turned around, Stan was emptying the bullets from the gun and putting them in his pocket.

"That's *mine*," Lewis said.

"I've seen enough," Stan said. "Talk to me in a couple of weeks, and if you're making sense, I'll give this back to you."

Stan stuffed the .38 into the pocket of his jeans.

"Fuck you, Stan."

Stan shook his head, sadder than before.

"I'm just being your friend, Lewis."

"I mean it," Lewis said, caressing his sternum with his free hand. "*Fuck you*, Stan."

"You should step back and look at yourself, Lewis," Stan said. "This isn't right. This isn't you."

"I'm more myself than I've ever been."

"Think of Anna," Stan said. "Think of how she would take this craziness. It would break her heart."

"Anna's *gone*!" Lewis shouted. "She made me—"

"What?" Stan said, eyes widening with curiosity. "She made you *what*?"

"Nothing," Lewis whispered. "Just go. Get out."

"Will do," Stan replied. "Just one thing."

"*What?*"

"You do what that shithead said," Stan told him. "Stay away from that boyfriend. Don't get yourself in trouble."

"I don't—"

"Just *stay away*," Stan hissed. "You have a weird look in your eyes, Lewis. Don't fuck your life up."

Lewis let his head drop and motioned Stan to the door. *Don't fuck your life up.* As though it was anything other than fucked already.

16. BECAUSE SHE WAS A LOT LIKE HER FATHER.

By rough count, Jay served forty-five people food, drinks, and desserts in a thirty-six-hour period—not counting Ramona, who consumed her usual ration of macaroni, snack chips, whole milk, and sliced fruit. It was routine, it was monotony, it wasn't all bad. Jay felt infinitely thankful to Ramona for being who she was: the one person whom Jay would never think badly of, and who (hopefully) would never think badly of her.

Now the day's work was done, and an unusual silence reigned over her apartment. Ramona was in her room playing a game on the machine Lewis had bought for her—weird tinny song snippets and demented voices burbled steadily into the hall. And, strangely enough, the phone was not ringing. She was a little surprised that Stephen hadn't called since she'd broken up with him, although prideful silence wasn't an unfathomable reaction on his part. What was odder was Lewis's sudden lack of communication. Jay hadn't heard from him since early the day before, which meant he was about six or eight phone calls behind. It surprised her to feel the omission of hearing about Carew's latest transgression against dignity, or the most recent bout of fear and loathing Lewis had experienced at Marshall Field's.

It occurred to Jay to call Lewis, but she decided to enjoy the respite—one that was bound to be temporary. If this was to be the feel of life without the pressures imposed by Lewis and Stephen, well, so be it. She mixed herself a weak gin and tonic in the kitchen, looking out over the snow and the fading light of day. It was going to be a terrible winter. Thanksgiving was still a long stone's throw away, and already it felt as though the cold had locked in, the feedback loop of frigidity set and immutable. Steam vented from the smokestack on top of the apartment building across the way, and through the storm windows she could hear the lonely scrape of a snow shovel against the pavement.

The harsh rhythms of winter had shaped Jay's temperament since she was a little girl. Lewis always tried to soften the terrifying reality of the natural world dying off and frozen stasis setting in—he would extol the bright blue skies, and make sport of the very coldest days by performing physics stunts such as tossing pots of warm water into the yard to make weird abstract ice sculptures. But even in her most innocent childhood she knew this was Lewis's equivalent of whistling past the graveyard—in fact, she understood how much of Lewis's behavior was a variation on this theme.

She took a sip of her drink and was glad she'd taken the time to slice a lime. In the next room a computer cat was singing a song about being a real cat. The windows gave a little rattle to commemorate a gust of wind.

Jay knew she couldn't complain—not without being churlish, nor without failing to recognize the incredible good luck she enjoyed to be who she was. There were people being bombed and blasted, people starving. Yes, she knew all this. But she knew her nature—several senses, a mind and memory, a hunger for evaluation. It might have been rational to keep on serving food and paying the rent and reading the occasional book, and calling that a good life—though, among other ironies, those who knew her would regard her as a defeated failure. But there were worse things than self-determined resignation. Maybe it was simply a matter of *deciding* to be content. She still had the bulk of her twenties ahead of her; maybe the key was simply to quit worrying so much.

But that wasn't going to happen, was it? Maybe she had too much Lewis in her, too much of an impulse to hold everything up to the light, too strong an impulse to ask what was wrong. Her mother hadn't been like that, but then Anna was in many ways a mystery to her daughter—she was a source of comfort, a calm voice of compassionate reason, yet Jay could never claim to understand her. A mother could never know herself the way her daughter knows her, Jay thought, but if she was unable to define Anna, how then did Anna define herself?

In the weeks before she died, when everyone including Anna knew that her time was drawing short, she began saying strange things. In a half-lucid state, her face bathed in sweat and her eyes filmy, she talked of planes and trains. She talked about looking down from the peak of Mount Kilimanjaro, and walking the streets of Rome. She described going to Detroit and looking in on her brother's family.

Don't be ridiculous, Anna said when Jay questioned her about these journeys after Anna had come fully awake. *I never said anything like that. If I did, I'm even crazier than I thought.*

"Hey, Peanut," Jay said, looking into Ramona's room. Ramona was partly perched on the chair in front of her desk, one foot on the floor, the other leg folded beneath her.

"Hi, Mama," Ramona said without looking up from the toy screen. Her hand twitched with mouse-clicks.

"You want something to eat?" Jay asked.

Ramona blinked. "Maybe," she said. "Can I have some of those cheesy things?"

"Um, you mean Cheetos?"

"Yeah," Ramona said with a glimmer of enthusiasm. "Those."

"Well, you can have the ones that are left," Jay said, never enthusiastic about feeding Ramona processed snack food, but also willing to admit that small pleasures were not to be underestimated. "But there's no way I'm going to let you eat them in your room. All that cheese dust would clog up that keyboard."

"Oh." Ramona sagged a little.

"Wait until you're done," Jay suggested, taking a sip of her drink.

"All right." Ramona stared ahead for another moment, then looked up. "Oh. Mama."

"Yes?"

"I saw Grandma Anna the other day," she said, raising her arms in one of her favorite gestures of happy triumph.

Jay felt a chill. "What do you mean, Peanut?" she asked. "Do you mean like in a dream or something?"

"Kind of like a dream," Ramona said in a far-off voice. "Kind of like real."

Jay leaned against the doorway. She took a deep breath and let it go. "You know Grandma Anna is gone, right?"

"Well, she's not here," Ramona said, looking up from the machine. "Is that what you mean?"

Jay didn't know what to say. Ramona had seen Anna's dead body after Jay's final time alone with her. Ramona had kissed

Anna's forehead and burst into tears. Later that day, when Ramona asked what happened to things when they died, Jay had told her the truth. She had said that she didn't know. No one did.

"Kind of not here," Ramona said. "Kind of like here. Sometimes."

Ramona's voice trailed off into uncertainty. She looked up at Jay in that new, guarded way she had—totally open to her mother's appraisal and judgment, yet now only recently holding something back, some apprehension entirely her own.

"You're not worried, are you, Peanut?" Jay asked.

"What?" Ramona replied, as though the concept was entirely foreign to her.

"Nothing," Jay said. "You go on and play your game."

"Mama?"

"Yes, Ramona?"

"Are *you* worried?"

Ramona absentmindedly chewed on a long strand of hair that fell to one side of her face. Her arm holding the mouse was long, pale, unblemished—its supple forearm elongated and no longer showing the rounded curves that harkened back to her babyhood.

"About what?" Jay asked.

"I don't know." Ramona adjusted the stuffed animals in her lap. "About Grandma?"

"Peanut, I'm not worried," Jay said. "I mean, I'm a grown-up, so there are some things I worry about. But nothing big. Nothing *you* need to be worried about."

"But I'm not worried," Ramona said.

"Well, good."

Ramona turned her face back to the computer screen. "And I *did* see Grandma the other day. She smiled at me."

Jay lingered awhile in the doorway, waiting for some other

clue to understand what her daughter was talking about. But none came. Ramona was starting to learn to seal off her secret world. Probably, in the end, it was healthy for her.

Jay stretched out on the sofa in the living room, vaguely taking in the clutter all around her but too tired, really, to even consider dealing with any of it. It would wait until tomorrow. Tomorrow: the time when all problems would be solved.

It had been such a short time since she broke up with Stephen, and though she felt his absence like the ghost of a severed limb, she didn't regret what she had done. She realized all at once that she had broken up with Stephen because she could not break up with Lewis. It wasn't Stephen's fault that he was older, that he wanted his love to make her better. She simply needed to make her way through the thickets of these days alone.

Poor Stephen.

Still no call from Lewis. A remote sector of her consciousness sent up a flare indicating that she should be worried about him. He seemed completely healthy, physically. Jay had of course noticed his nervous tic of rubbing his chest, and the pallor of his complexion, but he was on medication and probably, now that she thought about it, suffering from hypochondriac anxiety after months spent with the dying Anna. Lewis never took anything easy. For someone like him, a big rupture in his life was an event of monstrous proportions. And how did Jay know all this? Because she was a lot like her father.

Stephen had said so. Of course Stephen rarely spoke to his parents, so Jay had never enjoyed the luxury of meeting them and pointing out his flaws by dissecting their failings. Her life had been lived all in one place. She was easy to read. She could barely walk down the street without being flooded with memories.

And maybe that was the problem. Jay rested her drink between her breasts, enjoying the cold through her long-underwear top. She pushed out her heels, stretching her hamstrings. There was something to this train of thought—she had long felt constrained and ill served by being locked into this body of hers. But it was possible that her body wasn't the problem at all. Maybe it was the city. It could be that she was at such an impasse because she had exhausted the possibilities of Uptown, of the windy streets below the downtown skyline, of the motley architecture of South Minneapolis.

Granted, she wouldn't be the first to run away from her problems. But why should that stop her? A new city, she thought, a place where no one knew her, and where she could define herself any way she saw fit.

Ramona might have a hard time. She would miss Lewis. But she hadn't started school yet, and when she did there would be a new cast of characters in which to immerse herself. It would be better for Ramona if Jay were happy. It was a source of unending guilt to Jay to think that Ramona might be growing up with an unhappy and unfulfilled mother.

But where? Chicago, maybe, though that city's vastness had always been daunting. Madison? No, too small, worse than Minneapolis and with the same weather. Milwaukee? *Please.*

Jay surprised herself by laughing, alone in the fading light, at herself for devising a way out of her maze—and for having the temerity to dismiss a city she'd never even seen, all its inhabitants and secret corners rejected as though she was some sort of princess.

"Hey, Mama," Ramona said, coming into the room rubbing her eyes. "I'm done playing."

"Come here," Jay said, holding out an arm but not getting up.

"What are you doing?"

"Just thinking," Jay said.

"About what?"

"You know, you're talking so well these days," Jay said. "I don't think you're going to need to see that speech therapist they were talking about when I brought you in to get tested."

Ramona pondered this. She sort of shrugged. She was not particularly adept at accepting praise.

"Mama," Ramona chirped. "Where's Grampa? And Stephen?"

Jay ran her hand over her daughter's fine brown hair. Ramona was standing over her, and unconsciously pressed the side of her body against her mother's.

"Honey, I don't think we'll be seeing Stephen anymore."

Ramona's thumb thrust up into her mouth, and she turned away while pressing harder into Jay.

"Honey, are you all right?" Jay asked, startled.

And here came the tears. Ramona cried these days as though she was ashamed of herself for doing it. But this was unexpected. Ramona's standoffishness to Stephen had been unremitting. Jay realized now that she had underestimated the depth of Ramona's feelings. She sat up, put her drink on the table, and took Ramona in her arms.

"Oh, sweetie, I'm sorry," she whispered. "I love Stephen, too. It's just that it wasn't going to work out with me and him. It's messy grown-up stuff, honey. I'm so sorry."

"Can I see him sometime?" Ramona blurted out, holding her wet thumb in front of her tear-streaked face.

"Of course, honey," Jay said. "I promise. Stephen really loves you. We'll wait a little while, and then I'll call him. I'll bet he'd love to take you to a movie or something."

"With popcorn and soda pop?" Ramona said, calming down.

"All you want," Jay said.

"OK," Ramona allowed, slumping as though absorbing another in a long series of defeats.

"Hey, honey, what would you think about living someplace else?" Jay said, keeping her voice as soothing as she could.

"Like where?" Ramona asked, the thumb shooting back into her mouth.

"I don't know for sure," Jay said. "Maybe another city."

Ramona's eyes widened. "What about Grampa Lewis?"

"I'm not sure," said Jay. "I'm just thinking."

"He'd be OK," Ramona said.

Jay rubbed Ramona's shoulder. Another surprise—how easily the idea of being away from Lewis passed through Ramona's mind.

"But would Grandma Anna be able to find us?" Ramona asked gravely.

"What do you mean?" Jay asked.

"She would," Ramona said confidently. She rubbed at her eyes. "Grandma Anna will find us wherever we are."

17. THE VOID WAS REACHING OUT AND CREATING A MONUMENT.

In the morning it was snowing again. By rights, it was the time of year in which a big fluffy snow like that of the days before might be expected to melt before the prolonged freeze set in. But this wasn't going to be one of those years. Stephen hadn't been in Minnesota long, but he recognized the beginnings of an epochal winter when he saw one.

He had completed his morning office hours without doing anything stupid—such as arguing with one of his male challengers or reaching out and caressing the hair of one of his young would-be suitors. To his students he was a blank slate onto which they projected their first tentative outpourings of independence. He had a knack for being taken as an appropriate post-Daddy figure—and he was the age most of their daddies were when they were children and beginning to compile all the tendencies of their particular personalities. Their responses were so transparent: fight, fuck, destroy, captivate, curry favor.

The problem was that he wanted to do all those things as well, and if he became weak he was going to fall in love with some brilliant, fresh-faced girl one of these days. He knew he wasn't immune to doing something precisely because it was a very bad idea.

But he had gotten through, stayed cool and untouchable even though he had woken in the morning feeling as though he rose from the ashes of a smoking ruin. The woman he loved had cut off his prick—metaphor, metaphor—and he'd had to get drunk by himself in front of the television. He'd scoured his brain and could think of no one with whom to telephone and share his misery. He'd never been close with his father, who despite the accident of having a family only wanted to be left to his pot pipe and basement wood shop. Stephen hadn't talked to his brother in more than five years. The few friends who might be candidates for commiseration were scattered around the country, mostly with families, and he knew from experience that the unfamiliar sound of their voices on the phone line would preclude any hope of intimacy.

Face it—intimacy is vastly overrated. Stephen could have found *someone* to listen to his tale of woe, even a friendly bartender. But was it even worth telling? Man gets girl, girl loses heart. Girl's father pulls gun. Man files for restraining order.

Stephen closed his office door and stripped off his clothes. He folded his slacks and laid them over the chair along with his shirt and tie. He began pulling on his black running tights, a laborious exercise made worse by the close confines of the room.

The restraining order had been a spur-of-the-moment thing—Stephen had actually been downtown at the Government Center renewing the tags on his car when it occurred to him that he could legally order Lewis to lay off. He briefly considered finding a police desk and asking about filing charges, but that seemed too vindictive. When Lewis had silently approached and flashed the gun, he had seemed pretty lost and befuddled—a man unraveling, if Stephen was any judge. So Stephen found the right office, filled out the paperwork, and had Lewis served with papers. Hopefully it had been enough to shock Lewis out of his funk of weirdness. While it was of course impossible for Stephen and Lewis to reach any sort of accord, Stephen had a sort of residual fondness for the old boy, and a muted respect. Now that he never had to deal with him again, Stephen realized that he sort of *liked* Lewis, and would miss him.

"That might be going too far," Stephen muttered to his own Greek chorus, bent over the laces of his running shoes. He slipped on his reflective tunic, a hat and gloves, and opened the door to his office.

He stopped in the hallway to view himself in the mirror. He looked preposterous. His hat made his hair flare out around his ears like a pair of wings, and his ridiculous getup combined the worst elements of a football uniform with a ballet outfit. But damn it, he was going on a *run*. He had to defy the snow, and Jay, and Lewis, and English Literature, and the crushing reality of his own incarnation. He wasn't going to recoil from the snow and the cold like every molecule of his California-reared body demanded. No, he would go out and *enjoy* the weather, and his life.

"You are not dressed like that," said Sonia Wiley, walking down the hall with a pile of folders under her arm.

"Your eyes do not lie," Stephen replied.

Sonia was a secretary in the department, a few years older than Stephen and married with two small children. She was compact and wiry and, though she seemed perfectly content with her family life, Stephen found her extraordinarily attractive. Not least among her many virtues were a pair of perspicacious brown eyes set in the flawless skin of her face, eyes that bespoke a radiant nuance of perception that made her sarcasm and casual ribbing all the more provocative.

"Well, your legs sort of look good in those tights," Sonia said.

"My God," Stephen said. "The first compliment I've heard in ages."

"Yeah, like I believe *that*," Sonia said, brushing her dark hair from her forehead.

Students were passing by—thankfully, none of them Stephen's. He didn't want *this* interrupted.

"No, I mean it," he said. "Your small kindness is going to buoy me for the rest of the day."

"Oh, you are so full of shit." Sonia adjusted her load of folders. "But really, come on—you're going out running? Today? Have you noticed the weather?"

"Clear and sunny," said Stephen. He tapped his forehead. "The weather's all a state of mind."

"Your state of mind is *crazy*." Sonia laughed. "No kidding, Stephen. Where do you think you're going?"

"I run on the path by the river," he said, feeling his confidence in his endeavor begin to wane. It *was* snowing like hell—he could see that through a window at the far end of the hall. But what was he to do? He was already wearing his silly costume.

"*Stephen*," Sonia said, with a tone she must have reserved for her children. "Seriously. You could slip and hurt yourself."

"Oh, I'm too nimble for that." He laughed. "See, you don't know that about me. I have many talents."

Sonia smiled an enigmatic smile. "So you say."

"Well, anyway." Stephen scuffed his shoes against the floor, feeling very intimidated by the depths and confidence he sensed in Sonia's sexuality. That was the thing about flirting—he wasn't particularly good at it. Sonia, if she chose, could probably turn Stephen into an intemperate lunatic. She was the kind of woman who understood this and found it amusing. She was far more sensible than Stephen, and at the end of the day would go home to her husband and children—the life *she* had chosen, the one that suited her. Stephen, like most men, was a penis on legs careening from one opportunity to the next. Some men, he supposed, had the skill and audacity to go around choosing partners, but he was not one of them. He was always the one who got *chosen*. And Sonia, if she wanted, could choose him.

But she wasn't going to.

"Don't do it," she said in a stern voice. "Change back into your regular clothes. Have a cup of coffee. If you have to run, there are treadmills at the fitness center."

"I want to be outside," Stephen said. "I have things to work through."

"Your girlfriend," Sonia said, flashing a galaxy of comprehension.

"*Ex*-girlfriend," Stephen corrected.

Sonia nodded, a little sadly, as though in pity for those who hadn't sorted their lives out.

"Just be careful," she said. "It's cold. It's snowing hard. There's a lot of ice out there."

"I'll be back in about half an hour," Stephen said.

"It's your funeral," Sonia said over her shoulder, making her way back to her office.

My funeral. The great dream—attending one's own memorial. The way things were going, there wouldn't be too much trouble arranging a sufficient number of chairs.

When he got out of the department and started jogging down the path toward the river, Stephen labored to breathe until he felt his lungs reach an uneasy accord with the cold, dense air. The sky was gray and glowing with the sun's radiance diffused through the clouds, and the snow, which was falling quite heavily. There were far fewer cars than usual on the road, and the campus had an about-to-shut-down quality. But Stephen knew better. It was going to take more than a foot of snow to close down an institution in Minnesota. Soon the plows would be at work, the shovels would be scraping, it would be as though nothing had happened.

Quickly the campus began to thin out and the path branched off. The snow fell in heavy clumps and his breath condensed in a fog around his head. Stephen followed a fork over a rise into a patch of woods. His legs ached—it had been more than a week since his last run—and his eyes watered in the cold and his nose began to fill up.

But then he took a bend in the road and everything changed. He was alone on a pathway that threaded along the Mississippi—the actual river was far below, at the bottom of a small canyon it had carved out over the millennia. Here, in the heavy snowfall, in some of the coldest air he had ever sensed, Stephen had lucked onto perfection.

There was next to no sound save for the cushioned impact of his running shoes. The snow was falling hard enough to create a shimmering curtain over all things, and the sky was shining with that strange diffuse luminosity—it made Stephen think of the long adagio in Rachmaninoff's Second Symphony.

"Good lord," Stephen whispered to himself as he ran. And this was no appeal to a Christian God, or to secular reason, but to the view itself. If it was possible to pray to the force he was witnessing, that was what he wanted to do.

The landscape wound in gentle curves. The tree-lined edge of the land gave way to a slope; below was the river, silent and white. On the other side the land rose again in birches and elms. All was white. It fell from the sky, it accumulated at his feet, and it covered every branch and shrub. It was as though the void was reaching out and creating a monument to itself, a crystalline, bleached, padded, silent cathedral in which Stephen was the sole worshiper. His pulse rose, and he no longer even felt the cold as anything other than refreshing ambience. He could see not a single other person. *Fools.* They were inside? Missing this?

He ran down a small depression, feet skidding a little, the weight of all the snow in the air overwhelming him. Problems? He had no problems. This experience, he felt without irony, would be enough to get him by for weeks. It was snowing so heavily that it looked as if the flakes were *rising* up from the ground and ascending into the sky.

It was enough to make him laugh out loud. It was snowing so heavily that Stephen wanted to walk upon it, to rise in its midst, to take it like a staircase into the sky. And the sky was so close, close enough that he could almost jump up and touch it.

Then he was no longer alone. The figure that stepped from the trees was tall, wearing a hat and scarf, and it moved from the woods into the center of the path, on an interception course.

Lewis?

Lewis stood blinking snowflakes out of his eyes, looking shocked and surprised as though it was Stephen who had appeared out of nowhere like an apparition.

Stephen stopped running as he neared Lewis, slowing to a jog then halting. He stood panting, reaching down to rub his hamstrings.

"What is this?" he asked, his voice sounding odd as he panted to catch his breath.

"We can't go on the way we have been," Lewis said, his voice thick and cold as the air. His strong features were composed into a visage of decision.

"What are you—" Stephen paused, moving around Lewis in a half-circle. "Didn't you hear? Jay broke up with me. She *walked out.* You got what you wanted, all right? Just fuck off and leave me alone."

"Nothing's right," Lewis said, reaching up to caress his chest through his coat. "Can't you feel it?"

"Lewis, I filed a restraining order against you," Stephen said. "What you're doing is *illegal.*"

"None of this is right," Lewis said.

Stephen understood that the man had actually gone off the rails. Lewis was distracted, as though taking in more than one level of reality at the same time. He was talking to Stephen in the oddest fashion, with a complete absence of social inference or any of the little habits and markers that people utilize in their efforts to be understood. It was as though Lewis was talking to himself in a dream.

"No, no," Lewis said. "You've created far too many problems. You're behind this."

"I'm going to complete my run," Stephen said. "You're going to go home. And I'm never going to see you again. Do you follow me?"

Lewis looked up at Stephen with a chilling emptiness in his eyes.

"It's all coming to an end," he declared. "But it isn't over yet. I'm going to fight this. I'm going to find her."

He closed the distance between himself and Stephen, and before Stephen could begin to comprehend what was happening, they began to struggle. Lewis was alarmingly strong, and Stephen's sneakers slipped and skidded on the icy pavement. Lewis was working his hands up toward Stephen's throat, and Stephen managed to hack them away and plant a decent openhanded slap onto the thick wool of Lewis's hat. Stephen stumbled a couple of steps, and considered whether it would be a humiliation to run for it.

He glanced up and down the path. *No one.* There was no one to witness what was happening.

In that instant, when he looked away from Lewis, the old boy decided to change his tactic. He lowered his shoulder and drove himself into Stephen—how strange it was to be lifted off his feet.

Lewis propelled Stephen off the path and over the snow that separated it from the drop to the river. Stephen felt as though he was flying through the snow with the sky close enough to touch. He almost enjoyed the experience until he realized what was happening.

He grabbed at Lewis as balance totally left him, desperate to cling to the earth, terrified of leaving it—but then the fight was lost. He tumbled over the edge. He fell and fell, and could not stop himself.

His mind was in a riot as he felt his body breaking. The cold was no longer a friend, and no one, it seemed, was going to save him.

Lewis watched Stephen go over the edge. His own body gave a huge convulsive jerk, as though it was he who was doing the falling, and he planted his feet hard in the snow and gasped like he was waking up from a dream. He took a couple of steps forward and looked down to see Stephen tumbling, twisting, moving downward and tossing up snow as he went.

Lewis had woken that morning feeling sure of himself, though filled with strangeness—it was as if he was slipping away and had to do something to set things right. He had swallowed his pills at the kitchen sink with Carew at his feet, the dog nervous and unsettled, sensing the veil of insubstantial breaking-up his master was suffering. Lewis remembered putting his hand on the dog, trying to be reassuring; despite the drifting away in his spirit, Lewis *did* feel sure of himself. He knew this was going to be a day in which everything changed.

He looked around. She wasn't there.

Stephen had gone limp about halfway down the slope and rolled the final dozen feet or so through a snow-covered thicket and—could it be? was it possible?—into the water. Lewis watched in rapt fascination as Stephen broke through the ice and sank slowly into the shallow water. He must have been hurt, because he surely could have simply *sat up* and saved himself.

But he didn't. He sank. His face, looking up to the gray sky, disappeared under the black water.

Lewis looked around again. There was no one on the path. No one had seen what had taken place.

Was the situation redeemable? *I just wanted to talk. He started the fight. It was an accident that he went over the edge. The restraining order he filed against me? Hysteria. I was trying to explain why it was unnecessary.*

Of course the *point* of restraining orders was that the time for explaining was past.

Cars crossed the bridge. No one seemed to be slowing. Lewis could see Stephen's knees poking out of the water's surface, but his head remained submerged.

Got to go down there! a voice screamed inside Lewis's head. *Got to save him! For God's sake, don't let this happen!*

He took a step toward the edge. He could be down there in thirty seconds. He could pull Stephen from the water and haul him to a doctor. No, no: the cell phone. He turned it on.

He could dial 911 and put a stop to this. He could simply tell the truth: that he had found Stephen's office door unlocked and saw his clothes inside, deduced that Stephen had gone running, remembered that the path along the river was his route of choice. He wasn't armed. He hadn't premeditated murder.

And murder was what this was becoming. Another murder.

Lewis felt someone present, watching him, but he remained alone amid the heavy snow and the trees and the crushing silence. His hands shook and his chest burned. The seconds were passing, telescoping, and still he hadn't gone down there to help Stephen.

His head swiveled. *There.* Back the way he had come, walking away. It was her. He caught a faint glimpse of her hair pulled back from her face.

Lewis sprinted through the trees. He caught one more glimpse of her in the snow, moving past an old tangled elm. But when he reached the top, she was gone again.

"Don't go," he said, but in reply he had only the cold and the wetness of falling snow against his face.

It was the end and he knew it. He drew his coat tight around his neck as he felt the temperature drop.

In the car, the public radio was prattling on as though nothing had happened. Lewis took the streets back to his house.

"There's a travelers' advisory for greater Minnesota covering the rest of the afternoon and through the night," intoned Gary Eichten, the afternoon host. "We're looking at about a foot more snow on top of what we already have, then there's a front of arctic air moving in by morning—right now, the forecast is for temperatures well below zero."

Lewis steered his car through South Minneapolis, past the cottages and four-stackers, the odd turrets, add-ons, the decaying apartments. All was covered in white, as though hiding from him as he steered in a great bubble of silence.

18. EVERY FEW YEARS A REAL CLIMATOLOGICAL HORROR CAME ALONG.

J ay parked her car, sort of—she sailed it into a great fluffy
mound of snow, her front tires grinding when they made
contact with the curb. She switched off the engine and sat
there for a minute, letting her breath fog up the windshield.

This was turning out to be a vengeful witch of a snowstorm.
Car headlights shone feebly through the white blanket that
comprised the lower atmosphere. The awnings in front of the
shops sagged. Every so often the wind whipped up, rearranging
the drifts and creating a complete whiteout. A couple of doors
down from where Jay was parked, an old guy was quixotically
shoveling the path in front of his hardware store. As soon as he
scraped the concrete, it was covered anew.

No one was going to pay her for sitting in her car all morning, so Jay got out—just in time to have her door nearly lopped
off by a passing bus. She hugged her car until the thing passed,

racing hard as though it knew of a warmer place just over the curve of the horizon.

Inside the Cogito (she was supposed, she recalled fleetingly, to refer to the place as just *Cogito,* but found it impossible) the lights were on but the place was silent and shadowy. Snow was piling up on the windows and blocking out the light.

Phil, Jorge, and Fowler were in the kitchen, each trying scrupulously to pretend that the other two did not exist. Fowler was tossing some meat into a sizzling pan, and Jorge was making a desultory effort at slicing some carrots and onions. Phil was looking at the business section of the *Star-Tribune.*

"Howdy, kid," said Fowler.

"This is a cheerful scene," said Jay as she began to extricate herself from her snow-covered boots. She was creating a small lake of water over by the manager's desk, but it was bad form for anyone to complain about such things given the circumstances.

"Hey, I get paid the same," said Fowler, staring at the cooking meat. "But we're not gonna get anyone in here today. I was just done explaining that to Boss Wonderboy over there."

Phil stared at the newspaper as if he hadn't heard.

"You people are crazy," Jorge said, a little sadly. "Going out in this weather? Expecting people to come to a *restaurant?*"

"The boss said to stay open for a couple of hours," Phil said, his voice Wizard-of-Oz-like from behind the headlines. "I don't see why you want to go home. You don't get paid if you go home."

"I'm just talking fucking common sense," Fowler said.

"Last time I checked," Phil said calmly, "it was impossible to fuck common sense. Might be nice to try, though."

"They are both insane," Jorge said to Jay, as though she was the only one left who hadn't taken total leave of rationality.

Jay had indeed thought about not coming to work, when she woke and saw the snow piling up to obscure the curbs and almost reach the wheel wells of cars. But that wasn't the way things were done in Minnesota. It would take worse to keep everyone indoors.

"There aren't too many people out there," Jay said, peeling off one of her two sweaters and instinctively turning away from Phil, who suddenly took a lot less interest in the paper.

"I know that," he said, sitting on his desk. "I'll be surprised if we get a single customer. We'll give it an hour and a half, then the boss won't be able to give us shit. It's only going to get worse with that cold snap coming in overnight."

"Cold snap?" Jay asked.

"Don't you have a radio, kid?" Fowler asked with his familiar gruff kindness.

"Didn't turn it on," Jay admitted.

"It's gonna get cold, *chica*," said Jorge, stabbing the air with his knife.

"Colder than *this*?" Jay said.

"Try subzero," said Phil. "Major Canadian air mass."

"*Cruel* cold," Fowler said, with more than a trace of relish. "We're going to be locked in for days."

Jay had received news of this kind many times throughout her life. One did not live in Minnesota without acquiring an intimate knowledge of the variations and many permutations of extreme cold and the things it did to water, air, and the human body. But it was only every few years that a real climatological horror came along—the kind of atmospheric bad luck streak that evoked a very real and pragmatic fear of freezing to death. It was always the same: the air pulled down by chance from the Arctic, the ballooning shape on the weather map as the cold descended into Canada, then crossed the border at International Falls. It didn't have that much farther to go before it reached Minneapolis.

"The restaurant business is not going to flourish this week," said Phil, seemingly inspired by the business analysis he had just been reading. "People don't go out in weather like this."

"That's because they don't like to *die*," Fowler said, and Jay could see that she had walked into an ongoing philosophical debate in which Phil was grudgingly coming around to the idea of suspending business as usual, while Fowler was advocating apocalyptic panic.

Fowler, of course, was not a native. He kept glancing at the window, the way the snow kept coming and how the wind rattled the loose sill. Jorge, for his part, seemed resigned to his fate, although if he were going to freeze to death, it would not be before he had made clear his disdain for the entire project of having settled this plot of land at some point in the wilderness of the past.

"My cousin talked me into moving here," Jorge explained to Jay, refusing to include the men. "Lots of work. Nice in the summer. And now look."

He motioned at the window. Fowler let out a snort of derision.

"Would you stop it?" he barked. "You sound like a little girl!"

"Actually, my little girl is taking it all pretty well," Jay observed.

"You can call me all the names you want," Jorge said calmly. "Because you are a fucking crazy man. I don't even listen. To him."

That last part was delivered, of course, for Jay's benefit. There was no settling things between Fowler and Jorge—who, in fact, deep down, did *not* like each other, and were *not* establishing a warm bond beneath their constant antagonism.

"Excuse me?" said a woman's voice. "Are you open?"

She was middle-aged, in jeans and a parka, with an embarrassed-looking teenage boy several paces behind her.

She had walked right into the middle of the kitchen without anyone noticing. Now the trio who staffed Cogito wore matching expressions of shock, as though a Tibetan Sherpa had just come into the room and announced that he was setting up base camp on the cutting board.

"Yeah," Phil said, the first to recover. "We're open."

"Pick a table," Jay said. "I'll bring out menus and water."

"Oh, good," said the woman gratefully. "I was afraid nothing would be open today. You know, the weather."

"Yeah," Jay replied. "We know."

As they left the kitchen the boy shot Jay a look of profound mortification and a desperate need to convey to her that he was on board with nothing his mother did or said. He was sort of cute, in an underage, it's-all-wrong kind of way.

The day's shipments hadn't come in—presumably the trucks were spinning tires in some narrow alley and contemplating packing it in. Mother and son were generally sympathetic to this, and made do with a sandwich for the boy and a Cobb salad for his mother. Jay pretended to tally up receipts in the corner for a while—there were, of course, no receipts to tally because there had been no other diners so far—and took a kind of distracted pleasure in watching the mother's efforts to cheer up her highly resistant son. The mother, thin on top and heavy-hipped, seemed genuinely perplexed. The boy had probably been perfectly reasonable and agreeable just a couple of years before. Well, Jay thought, that's what sex did to people. That stuff going on between his legs had rendered his role in family life superfluous and ridiculous. Testosterone would take him away. That's what it was designed to do.

It was somehow like the end of things. Jay felt a sensation that eluded attempts at definition—it was the sort of sense she'd had when she graduated from high school, or when she learned she was pregnant. She was done with something. Sure, it had to do with breaking up with Stephen, but it was deeper than that. It was as though the snow was hiding an old world that wouldn't reemerge when the thaw came.

After Mom and Jake (that was his name, Jay learned by eavesdropping) were done with their unspectacular meal, Mom paid and left a halfway decent tip, then they were gone. Jay cleared their plates and glasses, the room silent and dark. She hadn't even thought to turn on the stereo.

Back in the kitchen Phil was sitting at his desk with his head in his hands while Fowler and Jorge were engrossed in an argument about which supermarket was best. Jay quickly gleaned that Jorge, despite the limitations of his salary, firmly adhered to the bourgeois creature comforts of Kowalski's. Fowler, the chef, didn't need any of that fancy shit to cook for himself and opted for the good, honest, plebeian fare at Rainbow.

"You guys will argue about anything," Jay said.

"Fuck him," Fowler said, eliminating Jorge from the world with a wave of his spatula. "Hey. You want some eggs?"

"No, thanks," Jay said, sounding more despondent than she intended. "I'm not even hungry. Hey, what's the matter with him?"

"What's the matter with *him*," Phil said, staring down at the desk, "is that I'm getting a *migraine* and I left my *Maxalt* at home and it's already too late to take it and I'm going to be in hell for the next twelve hours."

"Mother of God," Jorge pronounced, the soul of exasperation. "Go *home*, man. Get your medicine."

"It's too late," Phil moaned. "It's too late for me."

"It's too late for all of us," Fowler muttered, attacking the grill with his spatula as though it embodied Phil's headache, Kowalski's, Jorge, and the weather outside.

Well, it was official, as far as Jay was concerned. Winter psychosis had set in. There was only so much the spirit could take, and those snowy walls were more than enough without the prospect of the awful cold to come. It was the anticipation that was always the worst, the certainty of the hardship and real physical *pain* and danger that they would all be up against come morning. The air would hurt the skin, each gentle breeze would jab with invisible needles. Skin can freeze on contact—they drummed that happy little fact into Jay's head when she was a little girl. To this day she could easily conjure images of great slabs of flesh blackening and slowly dying off, then falling from her cheeks and nose. It happened to people.

There were no more customers in the next hour. Phil loosened his tie and lay prone on his desk, moaning and pitying himself with gusto. Jorge washed what dishes were to be washed, and Fowler sank into a silent funk without any pretense of preparing specials, or prepping any more food, or behaving in any manner like a chef. Instead he smoked and drank coffee and looked out the front window.

"Let's shut this place down," he said to Jay when she came into the dining room.

"Looks like the thing to do," she replied.

"Should never have come in the first place." Fowler defiantly stubbed out his latest cigarette on the wood floor, where it left a tidy little burn mark.

"I would have liked to make more than five dollars in tips today," Jay told him.

Fowler looked up at her, seemingly stunned to hear her speak of money, and apparently chagrined at the extent of his own kvetching.

"Yeah, this sucks for you," he said. "How's that beautiful little girl, anyway?"

"Great," Jay said. "You know."

"What else is the matter?" Fowler asked.

"What do you mean?"

"You have a funny look," he explained. "Like you've decided something."

"Funny, it feels like I have but I'm not sure what it is," Jay said. "You know, everything's more complicated when you have a kid."

Fowler, a compact and perpetually self-contained man, had a daughter in Milwaukee whom he saw at most once a year. The reasons for this were vague, almost certainly very complicated, and a source of regret for Fowler.

"You'll be all right," he said. "One shift does not a month's pay make."

"See, I have to be like you," Jay deadpanned. "More philosophical."

This launched Fowler into a wheezing laugh in which his end-times gloom lifted all at once. Probably it was the prospect of another day at Cogito, rather than the weather horrors, that had put him in his terminal state.

"I think I'm going to go get philosophical with a glass of Wild Turkey at the C.C. Club," Fowler said, gesturing down the street. "Want to come along?"

The thought of socializing with Fowler had never occurred to Jay—though she knew his paternal attitude toward her precluded the possibility that he was up to something.

"Some other time," Jay said. "I think I'm going to pull Ramona out of day care early. They'll probably want to close as early as they can."

"Snowed in with a bunch of screaming brats," Fowler said. "No thanks. I'd rather grill burgers all day."

"You and me both," said Jay.

Jorge and Phil emerged from the back fully done up in their winter gear. Jorge in particular was a sight—his brown face poked out from the big white puffy hood of his coat, as though he were already buried in snow before stepping foot outside.

Phil wore no hat, and walked slowly with a queasy expression on his pale face.

"You all right to drive home?" Fowler asked.

"Yeah, thanks," Phil said. He seemed to be fighting not to vomit. "Just gotta get. To bed. Take my pills."

Fowler almost laughed, but Phil's distress was too great for that. Instead he settled for a dismayed shake of his head.

"What a bunch we make," he said.

Jay put her hand on the doorknob.

"At least we have youth and beauty here to keep us from going completely crazy," Jorge said with a warm smile.

It took Jay a moment to realize he was talking about her. And there was no weird come-on beneath the surface—*that* would have come from Phil, who was effectively neutered for the moment.

"You do brighten up the place, kid," Fowler said.

"Gee . . . that's nice of you guys," Jay said, profoundly embarrassed.

"Go get that little girl of yours," Fowler said. "We'll lock up and shut everything down."

With a lightness in her step, Jay went out into the snowstorm and crunched her way down the sidewalk to her car. It was amazing, in a small and quiet way, how much it cheered her to learn that her co-workers actually liked her. They would never know how much their affection bolstered her, because now she realized she had forgotten that she had a place in the wider world outside of Lewis, and Stephen. She had assumed that the world was empty to her, and she useless to it. Now it felt different. She could grow and leave them behind—*they* could, she and Ramona. Things didn't need to stay the way they were. It was the kind of wisdom Anna used to impart.

· · ·

Jay decided to stop off at the apartment before going to pick up Ramona—she had a copy of *Lion King II* that needed returning, and she figured once they were home they'd want to lock up and let the elements conduct whatever diabolical business was at hand. She left her boots on, trailing water across the floor to the VCR. Just before she went out, she thought to check her voice mail. The dial tone gave that little stutter that indicated she had messages.

The first was from a couple of hours ago: "Jay, it's Andrea. How are you? Nice weather we're having. I thought I'd invite myself over later and bring a pizza or something. I want to hang out with you guys! Give me a call."

Jay switched the phone to her other ear as she worked the *Lion King* back into its plastic case. It might be nice to see Andrea. It might also be nicer not to see anyone at all.

It was, she thought as she pressed the button to retrieve the second of her two messages, a hell of a time to have broken up with her boyfriend. She might have liked to split a nice Barolo with Stephen in front of the electronic hearth that night, and a warm body would be nothing to turn down.

"I'm calling for Jay Ingraham," said a woman's voice on the line. "I'm a nurse at North Memorial Hospital. This is in connection with Stephen Grant."

Jay put down the video.

"We got your name from a secretary where he works," the woman went on. "There's been an accident and we're trying to locate Stephen Grant's next of kin for medical authorization. Please call as soon as possible."

The woman gave a phone number. Jay frantically repeated it to herself over and over until she could find a paper and pen. Then she let out a cry she wouldn't have believed had come from her, had she not been entirely alone in the room.

19. IT FELT LIKE A VISIT TO A CHAPEL OF HELPLESSNESS.

Lewis found that parking his car in the driveway was not unlike leading a dog-pulled sled up a narrow mountain pass while blind drunk and incapacitated with a fever. Somehow he managed it, though for all he knew his car was now installed on his, or his neighbor's, lawn. None of the familiar visual markers were visible. All was white.

He rushed inside, slipping on the steps. The wind had whipped the snow into piles on his porch, and he had to sweep away a drift with his foot to get the door open. When he stepped inside, Carew came rushing up in a panic.

Geez, Lewis, where have you been? What have you been doing? Do you see what's happening out there? the dog said, shifting back and forth on its feet, tail twitching with anxiety.

"Hey, boy," Lewis said, bending down to take its head in his hands. "Don't you worry about a thing. Lewis is here."

The dog actually seemed *skeptical* of Lewis, but mellowed

out after Lewis refilled the big food bowl in the kitchen. Carew set upon his snack with the lust of the condemned while Lewis went to the living room.

What had he done? *Killed* Stephen? For the crime of turning Lewis's daughter against him? For challenging the bonds of loyalty from which Lewis derived all his sense of self and worth? Stephen had to die for *that*?

He turned. She had been there, he was sure of it.

Lewis paced a path from the front window to the side window, monitoring the storm, imagining Stephen breathing his last breath in those shallow frigid waters. He replayed those moments, the way he'd charged Stephen, then seeing Stephen fall and witnessing the terrible momentum of the younger man's body down the wooded slope. The worst part was not going down to help. Lewis knew. He was not in full control of himself, but he had made a conscious decision to leave Stephen down there, alone, with no one around.

With no one to bear witness to what Lewis had done. Unless Anna had been there.

"Come on," he said to the empty room. "Where *are* you?"

Worse still, perhaps, was that in searching his heart (pacing now to the sunroom, which was dark and snowed-in), Lewis could not locate any feeling of remorse. Regret? Yes, maybe, he would rather that *that* had not happened. But there was no deep remorse in his emotional terrain at the moment. It may have been a matter of shock. It may also have been that he did what needed to be done.

Like before.

He had to operate on the assumption that he would be caught. There was the matter of the restraining order—yes, that was public record and would immediately come to light after Stephen was discovered. Stan, trusted Stan, would not lie if the police asked him about their conversation of the day before. He was too honorable for that. Lewis would be jailed, tried, and sent to prison.

It was unacceptable—not just the prospect of losing his freedom but, more important, losing his ability to care for Jay and Ramona. They would be alone, Jay losing both her parents within a year. At her age, with her disposition, it would be a devastating blow.

Where *was* she?

Lewis went upstairs to the room he'd shared with Anna. The bed was made and unslept-in. The curtains were drawn wide to the silent storm outside. Lewis went to the small box of Anna's things that he kept on the dresser—some of her perfume bottles, little boxes where she kept her pins and female things—and touched each item carefully, as he did when he desperately missed her and wished she were there.

"I know, I fucked up," he said softly. "I've got to find some way to make it better. I've got to think."

His mind was not working properly. That was clear when he flashed on the gas can in the garage and considered the possibility of filling the downstairs with gas and setting the house on fire. He saw smoke pouring from the windows, the roof collapsing, himself driving away hard and fast with Carew in the back.

"No, that's not the way," he said. He put down Anna's things, carefully arranging them the way they had been.

"Think it through, Lewis," he said.

What this boiled down to was *responsibility*. Stephen had gotten in the way of Lewis discharging his responsibility to Jay and Ramona, and he'd gotten himself hurt. Dead, rather. First hurt, then dead, immediately thereafter. That was the usual order of things.

Lewis stifled a laugh. It was not the time for laughter.

Women and children first. Was that not the motto for any husband and father—for any good man? He had helped Anna, in his way, when her body broke down and betrayed her. He had done his best.

"You know I did my best," he said to the empty room.

His breath was even more ragged than usual. Lewis leaned against the wall as he endured an attack of dizziness, then a series of sharp stabbing pains in his chest. It didn't seem psychosomatic, but then who knew? He was willing to accept that these might be his final moments on planet Earth—but if they weren't, he was at least going to do something meaningful until his body broke down.

He didn't believe in an afterlife, but if there was one, surely he was linked eternally with Stephen and Anna. Actions might indeed reverberate through eternity, with meanings and linkages spiraling and intersecting beyond space, time, and meaning.

"Stop thinking like a hippie," he whispered.

Lewis went into the bathroom, took out his little basket of pills, and sat down on the edge of the bathtub. There on top was the antidepressant. He had already taken his dose that morning, his carefully monitored and calibrated chemical ration that was supposed to fend off all the guilt, anger, and fear.

"Well, gee whiz," he said.

Opening up the childproof jar, he looked inside. The pills were white, scored in the middle, and inscribed with some manner of pharmaceutical arcanum. Lewis popped one out and, lacking a glass in which to place water, chewed it up and swallowed it. It tasted strange, which was to be expected, but not entirely terrible. It was actually a fairly evocative flavor, tinged with an exotic complexity. Shrugging, he flipped out another one, chewed it, and swallowed it.

"OK, now I'm going to be *really* well adjusted," he said, getting up and putting the remaining pills in his shirt pocket. He saw Carew watching him from the hall, his head cowed, nervously pacing, watching Lewis with supreme uncertainty.

"Wait until I get everything figured out," he ordered the dog.

Downstairs he had that glass of water and chased it with a small glass of whiskey. It was the wrong order, sure, but these were desperate times. The whiskey tasted good, as whiskey often did, so he poured another one, bigger this time.

Ordering things, that was what was important now. Time was short. Someone was going to come upon Stephen, and then things were going to change drastically and, almost surely, very quickly.

The most important thing in his life, from the moment of her birth—that blessed, sacred moment, the sight of her clenching hands and the shock of dark hair on her precious head—was Jay. It was paramount that he do everything in his power to help her be happy and whole—and, in the most stark and unsentimental analysis, he had taken a step in the right direction by dispatching Stephen. It had taken him a step closer to finding Anna.

No, that was crazy, wasn't it? There had been a fight and Stephen fell. Lewis might get a sympathetic jury to acquit him.

But he couldn't count on it. A prosecutor could make Lewis out to be some sort of unhinged, vengeful father.

He laughed a little and took a long drink of his very good whiskey.

Now that Ramona was in the picture, there was a new balance to Lewis's world. He had to look out for her. And she had been so close to Anna. In a rush of clarity he realized that Ramona was a key to finding Anna.

He had some more whiskey, which did wonders toward quelling his chill and the pains in his chest. You could never tell that to a doctor, though, they'd all become teetotal, marathon-running health doctrinaires.

Back to Ramona, who was the point, after all. She needed protection and nurturing—two things that Jay was only sporadically able to provide, given the fact that she was not exactly doing a bang-up job of looking after *herself*. Now, should Lewis be locked in a cell and the key at least metaphorically thrown away, said chain of events would likely lead to Jay becoming even less capable of providing Ramona with the sort of environment she needed.

On the surface, it was a knot no man could unravel. But Lewis had faith in himself. It appeared that he was going to have to improvise.

A little more whiskey tended to free up the mind, or so he had heard.

The phone rang. Lewis ignored it.

This was looking more and more like the kind of situation in which a man had to play it by ear. Ramona came first, and he couldn't help Ramona if he was an inmate upstate for the remainder of his useful days. So he had to get to Ramona, and he had to get himself out of the reach of the authorities.

He looked out the window. Anna was in the snowy garden. Then she was not. He opened the window, letting in a rush of snow and icy wind.

"Lewis," Anna said. "Come on. I'm outside."

Lewis pressed his face to the screen. He squinted and focused, but could not see her where she had been.

She hadn't been wearing a coat. That was all wrong.

None of this was Jay's fault. Lewis, feeling better by the moment, was going to make life better for everyone.

"Come on," he said to Carew. "We're going for a drive. We're going to get Ramona. Then we're going to find Anna."

Yeah yeah, Lewis, good idea, Lewis.

Just getting to the hospital was a terrible dreamlike odyssey, with Jay's car skidding along Broadway through the north end of town like a bobsled, and about as controllable. Every other driver seemed to be going fifty percent too fast or too slow. The storm had shifted gears into the truly surreal; more than a foot was on the ground, and the radio announced that at least another foot would fall before it was all over. The schools were closing down, and there were power failures all through the city and the suburbs.

Jay called Ramona's day care on her cell phone along the way. The worker who answered—her name was Janet—sounded irritated at first when Jay said that Ramona would have to stay late, but softened considerably when Jay gave her the reason. Jay also explicitly told Janet not to tell Ramona what was going on.

Lewis, normally omnipresent, was still lying low. His cell phone rang and rang, which meant that he had it turned off. He wasn't answering at home, either. Jay couldn't remember Lewis's schedule well enough to figure out whether he was working, and she didn't have the number at Marshall Field's. Lewis's disappearance was a source of anxiety for Jay, though it was doing battle with a couple of others against which it stood little chance.

An accident. The nurse on the phone had refused to get into specifics, which apparently was a matter of policy. But it had sounded serious, and after Jay dredged up the names of Stephen's parents and where they lived—Bob and Cathy Grant, of Mendocino, California—she left right away.

Finally she saw the hospital on a small hill like an Alpine castle, lights shining from windows through the veil of snow—which meant at least *their* power was on. She negotiated through a series of turns and switchbacks seemingly designed to repel visitors; twice her wheels bumped into curbs or barriers, she couldn't be sure which. This day was turning out to be sheer hell on her suspension.

After parking on level three of the ramp—crowded, since

obviously the business of sickness and dying was not deterred by bad weather, and might have even been enhanced by it—Jay followed the signs to the emergency room. When she got there, she found herself immobilized.

There was a little African-American boy holding a bloodied cloth to his mouth. Nearby, a woman stretched out over three open seats, her eyes closed and her lips moving. Down the way, a guy intently picked shards of glass out of his arm and dropped them with dainty care on the tiled floor.

All of this was within the bounds of what Jay could handle. But it was the smell of the place, and the low acoustic ceiling, and the way the light seemed to come from nowhere at once, that brought Jay suddenly back to the countless hours—weeks, probably, totaled up—that she had spent in hospitals during Anna's sickness. Jay had never set foot in one until then. Each time she had come with her mother, or to see her, felt like a visit to some chapel of helplessness staffed by secretive clergy who barely understood the mysteries they dispensed.

She went to the desk. There was a woman there, middle-aged, wearing one of those smocks all the nurses wore, talking on the phone. She wore glasses on a chain, and held up a hand to tell Jay to wait.

Which Jay did. She put her hands on the countertop and took a few deep breaths. Stephen was in here somewhere. She had to quell the urge to go looking for him. That was not a good idea. There were surely terrible sights behind the curtains that ran down the hall.

The nurse finished her call. "Can I help you?" she asked, managing to act as though Jay wasn't a complete intruder.

"I got a call," Jay said. "I'm a friend of Stephen Grant."

Farther down the desk was a young woman in boots and a parka. She had short blond hair and was watching Jay closely.

"Stephen Grant. Yes," the nurse said, her manner rapidly

shifting to guarded warmness. "Wait here a minute. I'll be right back."

The blond woman took this opportunity to approach Jay with an outstretched hand.

"Gretchen Nelson," she said. She had that Viking pixie look so common in those parts, a flawless hardy beauty that Jay had always felt herself somehow in futile competition with.

Jay shook the woman's hand. Under these circumstances, it seemed not at all odd that a perfect stranger should come up and introduce herself. Jay shifted so that she could see little other than the bureaucratic mess behind the desk. The sight of the sick and ailing was more than she could comfortably take.

"I'm with the *Star Tribune*," Gretchen said. "We picked up Mr. Grant's . . . *situation* on the police scanner. Are you related to him?"

"No," Jay said.

"Do you know what happened?" Gretchen said, obviously uncomfortable with the prospect that she was talking to someone who knew even less than she did.

"They haven't told me," Jay said. She realized that Gretchen was probably just out of school, and roughly her own age.

"Um . . . well." Gretchen took out her cell phone and looked at its screen as though some answers were to be found there. "There was an accident. He fell into the river."

"The *river*?" Jay repeated. "You mean the Mississippi?"

"Yeah, over by the U. He was wearing some kind of running outfit." Gretchen put the phone back in her pocket and fumbled until she found a pad of paper. "I don't know why he was out running in this weather, but he fell into the water. Someone spotted him and went down and pulled him out. I don't know how long he was under, but . . . well, it sounds pretty bad. I'm sorry."

The magnitude of what Gretchen was saying settled over Jay

like a soft linen sheet, the air in the room holding it aloft and allowing it to fall in gentle folds. Under the *water*? Well, the cold had just settled in—and the *real* cold was coming that night. The river would have been frozen only on the surface. But how had he fallen all the way down?

"Are you the girlfriend?" Gretchen asked, wrinkling her nose at all the messiness her question implied.

"Used to be," Jay said.

The nurse returned with a woman wearing a white lab coat and actually sporting a stethoscope around her neck, like some fantasy of a doctor. She put her hand on the small of Jay's back.

"I'm Dr. Ellis," she said. She had bland brownish hair and a hint of a mustache on otherwise quite pretty features. Jay got an intense lesbian vibration from her, as well as a sense that she was someone who was proud of how much she could cope with.

"Jay Ingraham."

"The girlfriend," Ellis said.

"Formerly."

Ellis reacted not at all, at first, then chewed on her lip as though this might be the development that put things over the edge.

"You contacted Stephen's parents?" Jay asked.

"One of the nurses did," Ellis replied. "They're going to catch the first available flight out of San Francisco. I got the impression that might be difficult, though. They're closing runways at the airport here. On account of the weather."

Ellis seemed to be one of those semiautistic people who were remarkably effective at their jobs. Jay hoped so, anyway.

"Where is he?" Jay asked.

Ellis frowned as though this was a matter she had hoped could be avoided.

"He's been seriously injured."

"How seriously?" Jay asked. "He was underwater? Is he conscious?"

"Gretchen, I'll make time to talk to you later," Ellis said suddenly, and quite severely.

"I'm not trying to intrude, Doctor," said Gretchen, whom Jay had forgotten entirely but who was indeed still hanging around.

"This is not the time," Ellis said. "Go get a cup of coffee or something. I'll talk to you when I'm done here. Your deadline's a few hours off, right?"

"Right," Gretchen said, not at all unpleasantly.

Jay took a moment to register this level of cooperation and familiarity between reporter and physician, the way that they were symbiotically linked by other people's misfortunes. For a second she wondered if there was more between them, but decided against it. She had Gretchen pegged as engaged to a golf-loving college boyfriend.

But then, what did she know?

Gretchen left them, and Ellis folded her arms and let out a surprisingly weary sigh.

"He was underwater for quite some time," she said in a bland tone of recitation.

"How long?"

"We don't know for sure." Ellis put her hand on Jay's back again, slowly leading her into the corridor. "He was hypothermic when the EMTs brought him in. He's going to lose at least a couple of fingers and toes. As for the extent of the brain damage, we can't be sure at this time. We'll keep him warm and wait for any brain activity. There's no way of knowing when or if he's going to regain consciousness."

Jay was somehow moving into the hospital corridor—precisely how, she couldn't have said. Snow had melted from the hem of her skirt and run down her tights and seeped through a small hole somewhere in the vicinity of her calf. It was about all she felt. She wasn't even certain about the floor under her feet.

She felt the presence of her mother. But that was ridiculous.

When she got to the room she was aware of *something* against the far wall, some mass of machinery and a glimpse of flesh, but she could not bear looking at it. Her strategy of complete avoidance was abetted by the presence of a nurse (another one, unfamiliar) talking to a uniformed police officer by the window. When Jay came in, they stopped their consultation. The cop was writing something on a pad of paper, and he approached Jay with a polite nod.

"Wife?" he asked in a husky voice. "Girlfriend?"

"Girlfriend," Jay said robotically. "I mean, *ex*-girlfriend."

The policeman seemed quite confused by this distinction, and was moved to rub his brown mustache in a manner that apparently brought him a good deal of comfort.

"I'm probably the person closest to him in Minneapolis," Jay explained. "His parents are on their way."

Still she managed not to look at Stephen, but the sounds were terrifying. He was somewhere over *there,* and she managed a glance at all the machines around him. She heard an awful variety of beeps and mechanical gasps.

"Well, they're going to have a hard time getting here," the officer said. He was burly, slightly fat, and no more than an inch or so taller than Jay. "I'm pretty sure the airport's going to shut down for a while, especially with the cold coming in."

"Do you know what happened?" she asked, and now she looked. She saw Stephen, or something that she was to take for Stephen, wrapped in heavy blankets and attached by tubes and wires to machines that made him look like some sort of inert cyborg. She could see the narrow band of his flesh around his eyes, which were closed, and his skin was a dark bruised violet.

"Oh, shit," Jay said. "Can I . . . he doesn't know I'm here, does he?"

The nurse was standing behind Jay. "No, I don't think so," she said.

"You said you and him broke up?" the officer asked.

"Yes."

"Was it messy?" he asked. "Were there any indications he might have been emotionally distraught?"

"Emotionally . . . no, well, I don't really know." Jay went to the foot of Stephen's bed.

"Is he prone to extremes?" the cop asked, looking down at his pad. "I'm not trying to be rude, it's just that—"

"Do I think he jumped in the river?" Jay said. "No. I do not think he jumped in the river."

"Was he involved in any disputes?" asked the cop. "You know, over money, or property. Over you, maybe?"

Jay stared at the cop, who seemed used to being stared at and didn't mind at all. She tried to wrap her mind around what she was being asked. Could someone have possibly *pushed* Stephen into the river? That was preposterous.

Lewis. She didn't know why, but she thought of Lewis and the way he had disappeared over the last couple of days.

"No," she said slowly. "Stephen didn't have any enemies or anything like that."

"You're sure?" the cop asked. "You seemed to hesitate for a second there."

"I beg your pardon," Jay said. "I apologize for not behaving in precisely the perfect way at the moment, but I am trying to come to grips with the fact that someone I love is lying in front of me and might never wake up again. So please. Accept my apology."

The police officer's hand went back to his mustache, and he

flipped shut his notepad. He had the manner of someone who could be spoken to in pretty much any manner at all.

"Of course," he said quietly. "I'll be in touch if I need anything else. I'm sorry for what happened."

"Yes, of course, thank you," Jay said. "I'm . . . I'm sorry I talked to you like that."

"No apology necessary," the officer said, the soul of blandness, then excused himself from the room.

Jay was alone with the nurse. "How bad is it?" Jay asked.

The nurse looked at Stephen, then looked away, as though she, too, could barely take the sight.

"Very bad," she said. "He was under nearly freezing water for a while. We're lucky he's still breathing."

"Should I . . . *talk* to him or something?"

"It wouldn't hurt," the nurse said. "Do you want me to leave you alone with him?"

"Yes, please."

When the nurse had gone, Jay pulled up a chair as close to Stephen as she could, between the machines and monitors. He was breathing on a mechanical respirator, and his body was submerged beneath thick thermal blankets. All the devices made his body pulse gently. Jay reached out and touched the exposed skin by his temple. It was cold and felt lifeless.

"Well, Dr. Grant," she said.

He was there but not there.

"I've really missed you," she told him, glancing at the doorway to make sure they were alone. "I wished you were with me last night. You know you're . . . you're such a wonderful man, Stephen. I'm sorry I hurt you."

Her words felt and sounded cheap. But what else was to be said?

"You know, you'll like this," she said, thinking of the night before. "I mean, it's a little sad, but it should make you feel good. Ramona cried when she found out you weren't going to be coming around anymore. I know you thought she didn't like you. I thought so, too. Sometimes. But it isn't true. She loves you, Stephen. And I do, too. You have to hold on and find a way to come back."

Stephen showed no sign of having heard a word. At least it had made Jay feel a little better. She took off her coat and got out her cell phone, then dialed the number for Ramona's day care. Janet answered on the second ring.

"Jay, what's happened?" she asked. "How is he?"

"I'm here with him," Jay said. "It's bad. He's . . . I guess he's in a coma or something. He was underwater for a long time."

"Oh, no," Janet said. "I'll be praying for him."

"Thanks," Jay said. "I have to stay here with him. I'm going to try to get my dad to pick up Ramona. Is it OK if she stays with you until then?"

"Of *course,*" Janet said. "Don't worry about a thing. All the other kids have gone, and me and Ramona were cuddled up together watching TV when you called. I'll make dinner for her. Don't worry."

"Thanks," Jay said again. "Thanks so much. You know what my dad looks like, right?"

"Tall, dark and handsome?" Janet said with a laugh. "Yeah, I remember what he—"

Janet paused.

"Oh, hang on, there's someone at the door," Janet said. "It looks like . . . oh, *hi,* Mr. Ingraham. I'm on the phone with Jay. Do you want to talk to her?"

There was some muted background conversation.

"Um, he says he'll call you later," Janet said. "But he's going to take Ramona."

"Well, OK, fine," Jay said. "Tell him what happened and that I'll call him later."

"Will do," said Janet.

They hung up. It was strange that Lewis hadn't wanted to talk, but it was not a worry that stuck in Jay's mind. This was, after all, going to be a day in which strangeness was a very relative thing. She'd had days like this before. And now here was another.

Stephen stood at the head of the class with a piece of chalk in his hand. His students were arranged in expanding concentric circles rising in great tiers in the distance—the ceiling was too high to see, and the thousands upon thousands of pupils rose up until they became a great massed blur.

"Good morning," he said. He could not feel his hands. How, he wondered, did one illuminate a room that had no end?

The class was silent, expectant—what a responsibility. There were so many of them.

"Today I would like to talk about perception, reality and memory," Stephen began.

"You should talk," said a voice from the front row.

Stephen looked across the black void that separated him from the students.

"Not now, Mother," he said. She was sitting there knitting, not even taking notes. "I'm trying to conduct a class."

"I'm just saying, you're a fine one to teach about memory," she said in her relaxed California syntax. "You've been trying to forget who you were since high school."

"He never calls," said a man's voice.

"Dad?" Stephen said. "Look, you don't call *me*—"

"Don't try to turn things around," his father said. He had a brush and a can of wood stain in his lap. "You're my son, Stephen. It hurts to have you shut me out of your life."

"This isn't the time," Stephen said.

"All right, go ahead, teach your class," his mother said. "I'll keep quiet. Just the way you like."

"He's been terribly disrespectful to me," said Lewis. He unfolded his lanky body and turned to face the thousands.

"Manipulating. Arrogant. *Cowardly.*" Lewis spat out each word with outrageous venom.

"Now you wait—" Stephen began.

"I loved him."

Stephen turned. Seated five rows back was Jay. She held Ramona in her lap.

"You—"

"I hurt him," said his Jaybird, in a slinky dress, radiant and gorgeous. "But I loved him."

"Me, too," chirped Ramona. She smiled and waved. "Hi, Stephen. I think you're a good teacher."

"Oh, thank you, Ramona," Stephen said, feeling tears well up in his eyes. "That means so much to me."

"I was kind of mean to you sometimes," Ramona added. "But it was just because I wanted to know if you liked me."

"I like you very much," Stephen said, and Ramona smiled. "It . . . it would have been such an honor to be your daddy someday. I used to think about that."

"Hijacker!" Lewis shrieked. "Interloper!"

"You sit down!" Stephen yelled.

"Lewis, you never gave him a chance," said Anna Ingraham, who was seated behind Lewis. She looked healthy and whole, and quietly beautiful, just as she had before she turned ill.

"Why should I?" Lewis asked, still standing.

"He's a good man," Anna said. "You never allowed yourself to realize that. You had too much anger."

"Why *shouldn't* I be angry?" Lewis shouted. "You *died*! You weren't supposed to do that."

"I know," Anna admitted. "I didn't like it, either."

"I'm looking for you," Lewis whispered.

"Mom, I really wish you'd stayed," Jay called across the aisle. Anna shrugged.

"Grandma Anna, I saw you the other day!" Ramona cried out joyously.

"I know, honey," Anna said. "I saw you, too."

"You were so pretty," Ramona squeaked.

"Not as pretty as you," Anna said.

"Class, class!" Stephen said. "This is getting out of hand."

"He was always like this," his mother said. "He always had to be the center of attention."

20. TRANSMITTING WHAT SHE TOOK TO BE PERTINENT FACTS.

"Here, put your boots on, honey," Lewis said. "Carew's waiting for us in the car."

"Carew!" Ramona yelled, her tinny voice echoing in the entry chamber of the big house that served as Ramona's day care.

"Mr. Ingraham?" said Janet. She was about forty, with thick glasses and an indeterminate figure hidden beneath a big sweatshirt. "I need to speak with you for a minute. There's something you need to know."

Ramona looked up from wrestling with her boots and fixed Janet with a quizzical upturning of her nose.

"Now?" Lewis asked. He stifled a belch and hoped this woman wouldn't smell the whiskey on his breath.

"Yes, it's important." She turned to Ramona and, in a supremely condescending tone, said, "Can you stay here and get your coat and everything on, sweetheart? I just need to talk to your grandpa for a sec."

Lewis hated it when people talked to children like . . . like *children*. Even Jay did it sometimes, addressing Ramona in this syrupy singsong that infantilized everyone in its hearing radius. Well, there was no point criticizing her about it.

"Yes, well, all right," Lewis said, not entirely sure what was going on. He followed Janet through a big playroom full of toys and coloring books and a computer—but no children, apparently they had already gone—into the kitchen. There were kid-sized dishes stacked in the sink, along with those cups with the plastic lids so they wouldn't spill. Lewis spotted a carton of milk, open and sitting out on the counter.

"You should refrigerate that," Lewis said.

"What? Oh, sure, all right."

She put the milk in the refrigerator with a hint of irritation.

"I don't mean to be annoying," Lewis told her. "It's just that it'll go sour."

"Mr. Ingraham, there's been an accident with Stephen Grant, Jay's boyfriend."

Janet spoke with such an exaggerated solemnity that Lewis almost burst out laughing. *Of course! That* was what she wanted to tell him.

"Well, sister, I beat you to it. I was there," Lewis did *not* say; instead he contorted his features into some approximation of concern and worry—this Janet wasn't going to be chairing any Mensa meetings, but she would certainly notice if Lewis showed an inappropriate reaction.

"Stephen?" Lewis said. "My goodness."

"He fell," Janet said. She hugged herself. "He was underwater, and he's in a coma. Jay is with him."

"I'll have to take Ramona," Lewis said.

"Yes, until Jay has a better idea what's happening." Janet

paused to shake her head. "It's awful. I only met Stephen a few times, when he came with Jay to pick up Ramona. He seemed like a very nice guy."

"Nice guy," Lewis said. "Yes, yes."

The sun had set outside, and the snow still fell. Lewis glanced out the window at the lunar landscape of the backyard.

"Jay wants to protect Ramona from this, at least for the time being," said Janet. "So you shouldn't go to the hospital. I'm sure you want to."

"Do they know if he's going to wake up?" Lewis asked.

"I get the idea they don't know much right now."

"And he fell?"

"That's what Jay said." Janet's eyes narrowed behind her glasses.

"That's kind of odd," Lewis said.

"Maybe he had a blackout or something," Janet offered.

"Could be." Lewis made a show of thinking about it for about fifteen seconds, then turned on his heels. "Thanks," he said.

Ramona was waiting by the front door, done up in her thick pink coat, pink hat, pink gloves. Lewis took off his cashmere scarf and carefully wrapped it around her nose and mouth.

"It's windy out," he explained. "Your mother should have dressed you better."

"I had a scarf but I lost it," Ramona said, guiltily.

"Well, that's neither here nor there," said Lewis. He straightened and, not knowing what else to do, reached out and shook Janet's hand. Her hand was limp and clammy, which was pretty much what he had expected.

"Where's Mama?" Ramona asked.

"She had to do something, honey," Janet said, taking it upon herself to butt in for some unfathomable reason. "But your grandpa is going to take good care of you. Right, Grandpa?"

"Right," Lewis said.

"Bye!" Ramona shouted at the top of her lungs.

In the car Ramona wanted to sit in the back with Carew. Lewis couldn't begrudge their passionate love for each other. Ramona stroked the scruff of his neck and he responded by licking her giggling face and pressing her into the seat with the force of his affection.

"Are we going to see Mama?" Ramona asked in between courses of Carew's banquet of adoration.

They were still in the driveway. Lewis's headlights sliced the snow and mounting darkness. The strangest feeling came over him—the best way to describe it was that he had ceased to exist for a moment. There was a nimbus around things. *Ah*, he thought, remembering the pills.

"Not right away," Lewis said. "What do you think about a little Ramona-Grandpa time?"

"Sounds good," Ramona said.

"You know what I like to do when it's snowy and yucky outside?"

"What?"

"Go to a movie!" Lewis shouted. Ramona pumped her fists in the rah-rah fashion that Lewis had taught her.

"What movie?" she asked.

This hadn't occurred to him. "I don't know," he admitted. "Why don't we go downtown and see what's playing at Block E?"

When they parked beneath the big shopping block an unforeseen problem arose: Carew. The mutt had been perfectly serviceable to Lewis during the snowy drive into downtown—keeping Ramona occupied and happy, giving Lewis time to think—but now his nonhuman status made him a definite fifth wheel. There was no question of bringing him into the movie—for a moment Lewis considered putting on sunglasses and pretending to be blind, but that was the medication talking. He settled for cracking the window and giving the beast a pep talk.

"You're not going to like this, but we're going to leave you here for a while," he said.

Yeah yeah yeah—What?

"But we're coming back. Here—" He found half a granola bar in the passenger's seat and gave it to Carew. He had half an old water bottle, which he poured into a plastic cup.

"I know you can be mellow," he told Carew. "Be good."

When he closed the car door, Carew started barking. Lewis hurried Ramona over to the elevators, hoping that the dog would take a nap or something. When he got into the elevator with Ramona, he took one look back and saw that the beast was still yapping.

"Well," Lewis said. He looked down at Ramona, who was staring up at him with an expectant look. "Yes?"

"I saw Grandma Anna the other day."

Ramona delivered this news in such an offhand way that Lewis was forced to ask her to say it again. When she did, Lewis touched the wall of the elevator to keep his balance. They stepped out into the walkway by an upstairs bookstore.

"You mean for real, honey?"

Ramona nodded.

"Did she . . . did she *say* anything?"

"No. She just smiled and waved at me." Ramona walked quickly, so fast that Lewis barely had to slow for her.

"Where was this?"

"At day care."

Ramona didn't seem to be looking for any sort of comment or sign of credulity on Lewis's part. As she often did, she was simply transmitting what she took to be pertinent facts. Lewis took a deep, ragged breath and caught himself just before it turned into a sob. He wasn't sure at all about what to do after the film, but he knew that he had to keep Ramona happy—and that she would eventually lead him to Anna. The end was coming, he knew that, but before it was over Ramona would lead him to his wife.

There was only one kids' movie showing. It turned out to be some rot about a talking tree and his forest animal friends and how they had to band together to save their plot of woods from the despoliation of humans. It was a pretty blatant work of PC pro-environmentalist brainwashing, and none too subtle about it. The weather was keeping people away, though, and Lewis and Ramona pretty much had the place to themselves. Ramona noshed her way through a small bucket of popcorn and a soda pop, raptly staring at the screen without a word throughout the whole thing.

Every once in a while Lewis would steal a glance in the darkness at Ramona's profile, her upturned nose, the bangs that fell over her forehead. She looked so much like Jay.

After the movie they got back in the car—Carew wasn't asleep, but not screaming his head off, either—and drove out into the night. Lewis could tell it was getting very cold just by the look of the streets; there weren't very many people out, and the ones who were bore the expression of individuals suffering an exotic generalized torture. Lewis flipped on the radio and heard the local news. No mention of Stephen yet.

"Where are we going, Grampa?" asked Ramona from the backseat. "Are we going to see Mama?"

"Not yet." Lewis fingered the cell phone in his pocket, but he didn't turn it on.

"Why?"

"Mama has something she has to take care of," Lewis said vaguely.

"Are we going to your house?"

"You ask a lot of questions, kiddo."

He had meant that to be lighthearted, but he was quite un-hinged and it came out harsh. There was silence in the car as Ramona brooded in the back.

"Hey, I know," he said. "How about one of those Happy Meal things you like so much? Would that cheer you up? And maybe after that we can try to find Grandma Anna?"

Lewis looked in the mirror. She wasn't speaking to him for the moment, but he saw her smile as she stared out the window.

INTERLUDE. HE REALLY NEEDED SOMEONE TO TAKE CARE OF HIM.

Grampa could be mean. That was the thing about him that she always forgot, and then he would say something, do something—usually to someone else, but sometimes to her. What he said hadn't been very nice. And so she was going to punish him for a while. She didn't punish him when he was mean to Mama, or to Stephen, or to the girl at the ice cream store, since that was *their* business. But sometimes she wished she could punish Grampa Lewis for them.

She put her hand on Carew's back, which was furry and rough. She liked the way he smelled, and she liked smelling her hands after she had been petting him.

Grampa was acting weird. He was nervous, and Ramona was pretty sure that there was something he wasn't telling her about Mama. At least she was getting a Happy Meal. Sometimes they even had stuffed animals in them—little ones, but for some reason she liked the little ones best. It was like the squirrel in the tree movie she just saw. She liked small furry things that made her laugh.

One thing that Ramona didn't understand was why Grampa Lewis wasn't taking her to his house, or at least to hers. It was snowy. Grown-ups were always saying it was hard to drive in the snow. It seemed to Ramona that they shouldn't be out going to the movies and driving around. But she wasn't sure.

Grampa got her a cheeseburger Happy Meal and paid for it at that funny window. He usually said it wasn't good to eat in the car, but now it seemed to be OK. Ramona tried to eat her food while Carew tried to take it away from her. Grampa stopped the car a bunch of times to yell at Carew, which was funny.

But what wasn't funny was what happened next: instead of going toward home (Ramona knew the way), he went the other direction. Pretty soon there were fewer and fewer buildings. It started to look like the country, and Ramona felt a little scared.

"Grampa?"

"Yes, dear?"

"Where are we going?"

"I thought a drive would be nice."

He had talked about finding Grandma Anna, which was exciting—it meant he believed Ramona had seen her. But it was also strange for a grown-up to be looking for a dead person, since grown-ups believed dead people didn't come back. They rode for a while without either of them saying anything. Ramona thought about things. Grampa Lewis loved her and would never hurt her. That wasn't the problem. The problem was that Grampa Lewis was sort of . . . upset, in a way that made him act like maybe he didn't know what he was doing. It had kind of been that way since Grandma Anna died, but now it was getting worse. She tried to make things better earlier, when she told Grampa about seeing Grandma, but it just seemed to make him more confused.

The thing about Grampa was that he really needed someone to take care of him. Grandma used to, and it really helped him. She sort of took care of everyone.

Grampa *thought* he took care of a lot of things, but really *he* needed a lot of help. Ramona wasn't sure she could give it to him. It was awfully hard.

In the backseat, driving into the night, the Perfect Princess took charge.

"Grampa?" she said.

"Yes, honey?"

"Everything is going to be all right."

Grampa didn't say anything at first; he held on to the steering wheel for a while, then glanced back. His eyes were shiny.

"Can I take your word for it?" he asked.

"Yes," said the Perfect Princess. "Because I know."

"We're going to find her, aren't we?" said Grampa Lewis. "We're going to find Grandma Anna. She's somewhere out in the snow."

"Yes," the Perfect Princess said.

"She wants me to find her," Grampa Lewis said, driving.

"She wants you to find her," said the Perfect Princess, said Ramona.

21. NOTHING BUT THE CRYSTALLINE FORBIDDANCE OF THE BAY.

After a few hours of watching Stephen—immobile, not a sign of movement behind his closed eyelids—Jay decided that it might be appropriate to succumb to panic. She couldn't get in touch with Lewis to check on Ramona, which was increasingly a cause of distress. She managed to get through to Stephen's mother, who had left her cell number on Jay's voice mail. Stephen's parents were on their way to San Francisco to catch a plane, but for now the Minneapolis airport was shut down and there was little hope of getting a flight anytime before midday tomorrow.

Jay had made two trips downstairs to smoke, but the Canadian air mass was coming and, as advertised, the temperature was already around zero. She could barely taste the cigarette, nor feel its pleasant burn—she was preoccupied with pain as she inhaled an atmosphere colder than the inside of a freezer.

There were plans afoot to move Stephen to another room; the

one he occupied was a temporary staging area for the severely injured, and someone out there in the city was going to be severely injured anytime now and would need a bed.

Where was Lewis? She dialed his cell number again, listened to his voice mail pick up. She didn't leave a message. She'd lost track of how many she'd left already.

A nurse came and hovered over Stephen for a while. She checked out the machines and wrote something in Stephen's chart. Stephen continued his slow, mechanized breathing. Jay had never imagined seeing him like this—even in his deepest sleep, and he was a deep sleeper, Stephen had always seemed somehow composed, very much *himself.* Whatever she could call this human form laid out next to her, it bore little relation to Stephen.

"How are you holding up?" asked the nurse.

Jay realized she had been staring at Stephen. "Can't really say."

"The doctors here are excellent," the nurse said. "They're going to do everything possible to bring him out of this."

They exchanged names. Hers was Norma. She looked like a Norma, with dyed-blond hair pulled back in a bun, and a shapely figure neutered by her smock and heavy blue slacks.

"What do you think his chances are?" Jay asked her.

Norma thought for a moment. "He took a lot of trauma. The time underwater has possibly damaged his brain. You know, we get a couple of cases like this every year—usually because someone steps on thin ice and falls through. Each one is different. Sometimes they're fine. Sometimes they never wake up."

Jay listened to this as calmly as she could, relaxing her hand when she realized she was clutching like an animal to the edge of Stephen's blankets.

"You love him," Norma said.

"Yes," Jay replied. "Well, yes, I do. But we had just broken up."

"They're not mutually exclusive," Norma said. "Listen, hang in there. We'll know more soon."

Jay thanked Norma, who came over and squeezed Jay's shoulder. When the nurse was gone, Jay felt enveloped by the fluorescent light and the ambient grumble of all the medical devices. She supposed she could go for another cigarette. There seemed no point, though, not if that meant going outside again.

She flipped on the TV, which had a channel selection like Romania's in the seventies. All the local news anchors were going on about the snow, and the cold, with a surprised gravity that suggested they never considered such things happening. Jay turned it off.

It was tricky, figuring out the etiquette for a bedside vigil. Stephen was lost to the world, so sealed off. She wanted to go, but it seemed deeply wrong to leave Stephen alone. She hungered to hold Ramona with such palpable fervor that, she knew, meant she needed consolation from her child.

In the bathroom down the hall she had a look at herself. It was an unpleasant reconnaissance over a blotchy terrain and a lost, fearful expression she didn't recognize. When she went back to Stephen's room, the cop from earlier was there, along with a female partner.

"Hey, we were looking for you." He held out his hand. "Officer Wallace," he said.

"Officer McInnis," said the woman, also wanting a shake. She was almost as tall as her partner, and wore her hair in a ponytail.

"What do you want?" Jay asked. "Nothing here has changed."

"Is Lewis Ingraham your father?" Wallace asked.

Jay said he was. Wallace and McInnis exchanged a satisfied look.

"Why?" Jay said, trying and failing to quell a wave of unspecified alarm.

"Were you aware that Stephen filed a restraining order against your father a couple of days ago?"

"I . . . well, actually, no I wasn't."

Wallace weighed this for a little while, hiding whatever conclusions he made behind his cop impassivity. "Where is your father right now?"

"I'm not sure," Jay told him. "I've been trying to get in touch with him. He picked my daughter up from her day care. I imagine he just took her out to eat or something."

Jay felt inordinately intimidated by the police uniforms, the black leather belts housing handcuffs and God knew whatever other sadomasochistic implements. And then there was the matter of the thick metallic gun handles that protruded from twin holsters.

"This restraining order," Jay said. "What did my father supposedly *do*?"

"Nonspecified threats," said Wallace. His mustache gave a little quiver. "The details would come out in a hearing next week that Mr. Grant would attend. And Mr. Ingraham, if he wanted to rebut the allegations."

"So you don't know what happened, exactly?" Jay asked.

"Your dad threatened your ex-boyfriend," McInnis offered. "And scared him enough to get a restraining order. What was going on between them?"

"There was some friction, but nothing—"

"Define 'friction' for me," McInnis said.

"*Friction,*" Jay said. "I guess it was coming from my dad. He thought Stephen was . . . that he was getting between members of my family."

"He didn't like Stephen," Wallace suggested.

"It's not as simple as that!" Jay said, rapidly shocked by where this was going. "Look, my father can be a little . . . intense. He lost his wife—my mother—within the last year. He's very protective. But if you're suggesting he had anything to do with—"

She pointed at the evidence: Stephen, the sleeping man.

"I'm not suggesting anything," Wallace said. "But I want to talk to your father about his whereabouts earlier today."

"It's only procedure," said McInnis, flipping her ponytail.

Jay knew people well enough to understand that the police had started to formulate a hypothesis, and that they were looking for clues to build up and bolster it. And that idea was, apparently, that Lewis had done something to Stephen.

It was impossible. Lewis wasn't a violent man. He had been so strange at times recently, though. And the restraining order—he had done, or said, *something* sufficient to frighten Stephen. Who didn't easily admit to being afraid.

And Lewis had been unavailable to her all day.

And he had taken Ramona.

"Look, I'm sure this was an accident," Jay said, trying to sound like she believed it.

"It's a shame we can't ask him," McInnis said, more to her partner than to Jay.

"Yeah. A shame." He nodded at Stephen. "What are they saying about him?"

"As far as I can tell, they're just going to wait and see," Jay told him.

"Can you give me your father's address?" McInnis asked. "And yours, as well?"

Jay complied, and the officers seemed satisfied. Wallace gave Jay a card. "We're going to look for your father," he said. "If you see him first, tell him to call that number right away. If he doesn't turn up soon, we're going to start thinking about an arrest warrant."

How many hours ago had it been when it all made sense—she was going to pick a city, move, start over. Learn to do something, figure out how to make life work for herself and Ramona. And now this.

She picked up her keys from the bed stand and kissed the narrow patch of Stephen's exposed skin.

"Sorry about this," she said. "But I have to find Lewis. I have to believe he didn't do this to you. I have to."

He walked the slope of the mountain over the dull California scrub brush and the gentle slopes leading down to the familiar view that he . . .

Wait. That wasn't right. He looked around. No people, no cars, no *road* where there should have been one, winding up to the top. And no sign of anyone . . . and no—

No San Francisco. No Golden Gate Bridge. Nothing but hills and the crystalline forbiddance of the bay. He was standing on Mount Tamalpais, there was no doubt of that, but there was no human imprint on the landscape. He was looking out over the vista as it was before anyone populated it. Which meant—

What, exactly? Where *was* everyone? Stephen walked faster now, up and up, trying to remember.

He had been in a very cold place. He knew that. And now he looked up and saw Jay walking slowly down a rise toward him.

He was filled with an immense sense of relief. Surely Jay would be able to help him. But she was taking such a long time. Stephen sat down on a big rock and passed the minutes letting his eyes wander over the water to the unfolding land on the other side. Sausalito used to be there. Or *would be there* someday. It made his head hurt, and he didn't want to think about it at all.

"Have you seen Lewis?" asked Anna Ingraham, standing right next to him. She wore chinos, a linen blouse, and a sun hat.

"No, I don't think so," Stephen said. "Not for a while."

"He's looking for me." Anna peered out over the bay, the sun's radiance captured in her light brown eyes.

"Should I give him a message?" asked Stephen.

Anna paused. "He'll find me when it's time," she said. "Good-bye, Stephen."

"Good-bye, Anna."

Anna was gone. Jay seemed to be walking at a normal pace, but she was taking ages. She was wearing jeans and one of those strappy things that drove him crazy. God, she was beautiful, even at this distance. But he really wished she would hurry up and join him. He was starting to feel frightened. He had no clue how he got here, and he was sure that Jay could provide some clarification.

It was kind of like her, in an admittedly obvious symbolic manner—the way she was letting herself be seen without joining him, the way she had always held something in reserve and never given herself fully to him.

Then she was standing right next to him.

"I'm so glad to see you," he said. He made a move to embrace her, but she didn't seem willing. She stood next to him and stared out at the water, her expression blank and unavailable. In profile, she looked very much like her mother.

"How did we get here?" he asked.

She said nothing, maintaining her stony appraisal of the spectacular view.

"Jay, the cities are gone," Stephen told her. "Tell me why. Please. Tell me where we are."

"What do you think his chances are?" Jay asked in a far-away voice.

"Whose chances?" Stephen asked. "Jay. Please."

"We had just broken up."

"Who had just broken up? Us? Are you talking about us?"

She didn't reply, and she wouldn't look at him.

"I'm right here!" he yelled out. "Over here! Look at me!"

And then she started walking. Stephen jumped off the rock and followed her. He reached out to touch her but there was something stopping him; as soon as his hands got near, she was no longer there.

"What do you want?" Jay asked, her voice distant. The wind started to pick up. "Nothing here has changed."

Clouds had rolled in, and the hillside darkened.

"I've been trying to get in touch with him," Jay said. "He picked my daughter up from day care."

Her words were being carried off by the wind. Stephen had to jog to keep up with her, and he was suddenly crushingly exhausted.

"What did my father supposedly do?" she asked, turning her face away.

"Lewis?" Stephen stopped running after her. Lewis had done *something*, hadn't he? Stephen tried very hard to remember. There was cold, and snow, and there was Lewis.

"Wait!" Stephen screamed. "I remember something."

"He thought Stephen was—"

But the last part was cut off by the wind, which had picked up even more, and smelled of the sea.

"It's not as simple as that," he heard Jay say, moving away from him.

"Jay, I think your father hurt me," Stephen called out. "I'm remembering now, and I think that's how we got here. I really do. I think that's why this place exists."

"He's very protective," Jay said. "But if you're suggesting he had anything to do with—"

"No, there was the snow, and the water." Stephen shivered.

"Look, I'm sure this was just an accident," Jay said.

"No! It was no accident!"

Then she was standing right next to him again. He didn't know how she had traversed the space between them, but now he saw her hair, her face, her beautiful eyes looking not at him but through him.

"Sorry about this," she said. "But I have to find Lewis. I have to believe he didn't do this to you. I have to."

And then she was gone.

22. THE RUSH OF RUNNING TO SAVE HIS OWN SKIN.

His dreams were of the snow and the void of whiteness. Lewis wandered through fields of white, exposed in its reflective glow, denied the solace of the dark. In his sleep he *dreamed* of sleep, yearning for rest, tired beyond all measure, wanting nothing more than to stop moving.

Then he woke up, and in the process of remembering who, and where, he was, he pieced together what had happened since he and Ramona left the movies the night before and set out for the countryside in search of Anna.

It seemed like many hours they were on the road, though it wasn't much later than ten when they had stopped. He'd kept off the interstate, opting for a two-lane road heading first west, then south, a lane through the farmlands with no lights and very few other cars. Snow had fallen the entire time. Ramona had slept with Carew in the backseat, and for a while they were lucky enough to travel behind a snowplow moving slowly and noisily through the night. The black canopy above met the snow at the horizon like its sedate twin.

Carew, on the floor, got up when he saw Lewis stirring and came over to begin slavering all over his master's face. At first Lewis was too sleep-struck to do anything about it, but he soon marshaled enough will to push the dog's head away.

"Get off me," he said, his voice a thick mess of phlegm. "Carew. Damn it. I mean it. Get away."

So had begun many of his recent mornings. But now he opened his eyes all the way and saw the desk and chair, the innocuous art on the walls, the gleaming light through the crack in the curtains, and came fully to grips with the fact that he was in a motel in south-central Minnesota. He half-remembered the check-in, then sneaking in Carew and Ramona.

"Mama?" Ramona mumbled, her eyes closed as she gave a long shivering stretch.

"It's Grandpa, honey," Lewis said.

"Where are we?" Ramona asked, still mostly asleep.

"In a motel," Lewis told her. "We're having an adventure, remember? Do you want to watch TV?"

Lewis flipped on the set and found a cartoon involving pastel dragons that seemed to be pretty firmly aligned with Ramona's current aesthetics. Then he went into the bathroom, fumbled around with his face for a while, then took three times his usual dosage of his antidepressant. If he'd had whiskey, he would have taken some of that, too, but never mind.

He knew himself well enough to understand that he was not in his right mind, and probably hadn't been since Anna died. A cogent argument could be made for the period before that—the festering resentment, the salaryman's double-life of despair—but he had functioned well in those precancer days, so the death of his wife was an effective cutting-off point.

Just thinking through all of that took a hell of a lot of effort, and Lewis rewarded himself with a long pee and a prolonged session of hand washing. The cartoon was going in the next room, and the door was cracked, but there was no sign that Ramona had gotten up.

He couldn't hurt the girl, could he? No, never. But would it be hurting her to reunite her with her grandmother, if they could all be together again? Would it be a kindness to spare her all the uncertainty of life with Jay?

Carew poked his head through the door. He looked like he had to move his bowels or eat something. It all boiled down to one or the other.

"In a minute, boy," he told Carew. The dog looked so agreeable that Lewis felt his heart soften. "Hey, you've been great through this. I couldn't have asked for a better dog."

Yeah Lewis, yeah. But—

"Just give me a minute," Lewis said. "I have some matters to think through. Executive decisions, boy."

Carew skulked off. Lewis could have done with a shave, or a toothbrush for that matter, but such things could be remedied. It would have helped if he'd planned this out, instead of staggering off half-drunk and picking up his granddaughter with only the scarcest clue regarding what came next.

Yes, right. What came next. That was the key, wasn't it? Lewis took another of his pills. He was going to need all the optimism he could muster.

In the last twenty-four hours Lewis had managed to violate a restraining order, commit what could be called an attempted murder, and effectively kidnap his granddaughter. Jay must have been in a terrible state.

The guilt threatened to crush him, but he splashed cold water over his face until the wave crested. He rode it out. He wondered what Anna was going to say about all of this—probably she would be mortified. He'd blown up his life, hadn't he?

He'd had dreams in which he was being hunted for committing some crime, usually a murder, and experienced the rush of running to save his own skin. But he always then woke up in his bed, or on the sofa, tucked up like a bug in a rug. And although some part of him wished to scream out that this could not possibly be real, the solidity of the sink and the ragged sight of himself in the mirror testified otherwise.

How was he going to find her?

"Grampa?" Ramona said sleepily from the doorway. She was wearing the pants and T-shirt she'd slept in.

"Yes, my dear," Lewis said. "What is it?"

"I got to go potty."

"Oh, my, of course," Lewis said, excusing himself from the room and closing the door to give her privacy.

He sat down on the edge of the bed and stared blankly at the TV. The dragon show had given way to something about a little round-faced boy and his parents. Lewis tried briefly to grasp the plot, but was distracted by a wave of shivering and chest pains that migrated up into the regions of his jaw and teeth.

Surely none of this was doing Jay any good. But he would make things right once he found Anna. Yes, she was dead—he *knew* that. Of all people, he knew that for certain. But she was revealing herself to him gradually, he was sure of it. He would find her, sort things out once and for all, then disappear for good. One thing he knew: he could not deal with going to prison.

"The big house, boy," he said to Carew, who was waiting at his feet. "The hoosegow. Can't have it. Who'd take care of you then?"

Carew writhed with confusion but his mouth pulled back in a doggy smile. Carew: the indefatigable optimist.

"Bless you, boy," Lewis said.

Ramona emerged from the bathroom looking alert and confused. She glanced around the room, then came and sat beside

Lewis on the bed. Soon she was immersed in the TV show. Lewis tried not to shiver. He didn't want to worry her.

"Are we going home today?" she asked during a lull in the cartoon.

"Not yet," Lewis said. "I was thinking we'd go get a big breakfast and then do some driving. Maybe some toy shopping. We'll see if we run into Grandma Anna along the way."

"I want Mama," she said, her gaze still locked on the screen.

"Well, naturally," Lewis told her.

Ramona's sharp eyes fixed on Lewis. "Why can't I see Mama?"

"Oh, you will," Lewis said, alarmed by, and proud of, the girl's sharpness. "We're just going to have a little fun time. Maybe we can see another movie."

"Really?" she said. "And get some toys?"

"Anything you want."

"Anything?" She pumped her fists in triumph, and Lewis did the same. In unison they shouted, *"Anything!"*

Their good cheer ebbed temporarily fifteen minutes later when they stepped outside. Ramona let out a gasp, and Carew danced on a sheet of ice before taking a copious crap. Lewis let out an involuntary curse and rushed them both to the instinctual safety of the vehicle, where he carefully put the key in the ignition (metal was prone to snapping in these temperatures) and turned on the recalcitrant, grinding motor. It was some time before anything other than horribly frigid air came through the dashboard vents.

"Oh, *man!*" Lewis shouted.

"Man!" Ramona chirped.

It was one of those mornings when the air cut through clothes and skin, when it felt like the chill was pervading one's essence—when, in fact, the pain located an essence previously unknown. The parking lot and the two-story motel were covered in snow and ice that had frozen into semipermanent shapes, broken castles and unlikely slopes. When a car passed by, it created a bass rumble of breaking ice and the flopping sound made by tires in which pockets of air had frozen.

"It's cold, my dear," he said to Ramona.

"*Real* cold," she replied, breaking out into a laugh.

The girl had obviously inherited his mental instability. There they were, on the verge of freezing to death, and she found it humorous. She reached out and tried to write her name in the flaky ice on the window formed by their breath, and pretty soon Lewis was laughing, too. Carew paced back and forth on the backseat, in a rapture of pain and delight.

Things inside the car improved considerably once the heater started blowing warm air. The tremors in Lewis's chest subsided, and he actually felt a bit warm, which necessitated taking off his gloves and partially unbuttoning his parka.

"Hungry?" he asked Ramona.

"*Real* hungry!" she shouted.

"How about you, mutt?" he said to Carew, who responded by licking the back of Lewis's head.

"That's the spirit," Lewis said as he put the car in gear. He had to concentrate all his will not to drive them headlong into a ditch.

When they stopped the night before, Lewis had been progressively more terrified by the blowing snow and deepening cold, and had little notion of where he was when he saw the motel sign from the road. Now it turned out they were in a little town bustling enough to support a couple of markets and fast-food joints. He and Ramona had breakfast in one of the latter, which featured an indoor playground where Ramona burned off some energy.

He was familiar with this part of the state—he used to bring his family to a little place owned by Rebecca Demos, a manager at work with whom Lewis had had an affair about eight years before. He'd made a couple of solo trips down south to the same place, to avail himself of Rebecca's ample hips and deep need that sprang from her unhappy marriage. Lewis sat with a cup of coffee, listening to the news piped in through unseen speakers.

"It's fourteen degrees below zero out there," said the announcer, a female public-radio type with a northern accent. "And the National Weather Service says it's going to get colder, with *highs* through the week well below zero."

Lewis blew steam from his coffee up into his face. It was not good driving weather. The smart thing was to keep heading south. He vaguely wondered what had become of Rebecca. She'd moved to Seattle after her marriage finally exploded. As far as he knew, the husband never found out.

He waved at Ramona, who was hanging with surprising strength from a couple of rings suspended over a lake of multi-colored plastic balls. When she let go, she disappeared into their midst. Lewis smiled.

It was probably advisable to keep an ear pecled to the regional news, to see if he was featured in it. Lewis looked out over the parking lot as a pickup truck equipped with a snow-plow pushed all the snow into a small mountain over by the Dumpster. First was a story on budget cuts in state agencies—the usual woe-is-us, end-of-civilization stuff. There was a story about a murder that did not involve Lewis, instead the by-product of a Hmong turf war in St. Paul. There was the usual propaganda about the Vikings, then a prolonged explanation of what Lewis had learned when he stepped outside that morning—that it was ungodly cold out there, and that attaching hope to the immediate future was futile.

There was no mention of Lewis or Stephen. Which was excellent since it meant that Stephen was most likely alive. Of course, Stephen being alive meant Stephen could tell the police what Lewis had done. But Lewis was not so far gone that he wished death on Stephen. He no longer cared about Stephen. What mattered now was Ramona. And Anna.

It felt like a certainty now. He and Anna and Ramona were going to end up together. He allowed himself to remember the Sundays when he and his wife babysat Ramona, how sacred and rejuvenating it had been. What would it be like to make that feeling go on forever?

Ramona came out of the big enclosed play area and started tugging on Lewis's arm.

"Come on!" she said. "Come play with me."

Her hair was tousled from sleep, and she made an exaggerated face of steely determination while she pulled with all her might in an attempt to get Lewis to stand.

"Oh, I'm too old for that," Lewis said. "I'd probably break a bone."

Ramona stopped pulling and considered what he had said. "Really?" she asked with wonderment. "Gross!"

"Oh, yes, old people like me have to be very careful," Lewis told her. "We can fall to pieces. We can blow away in the wind."

"You can *not*," Ramona said, delighting in this stuff. She loved it when Lewis played the bad boy.

"I can't see! Where are my glasses!" Lewis shrieked in his foggy old-man voice.

"Stop it," Ramona said, putting a finger over his lips.

They hung out in contented silence while Ramona polished off the last of her pancake sticks, meticulously dipping each bite in syrup. There were plenty of ways to pass the time. They both needed new clothes, for instance, and then there was the driving. He felt pleasantly as though time had come to an end. Finally Ramona looked up and said his name.

"Yes, my princess?"

Ramona paused and shot Lewis a weird look.

"What's the matter?" Lewis asked.

"Nothing," she said evasively.

"Well, what did you want to say before?"

"This is fun," Ramona told him. "This is like a vacation. I'm glad Carew came with us, too."

Lewis put an arm around her. "I'm glad," he said.

"Maybe today we'll see Grandma Anna," Ramona added.

Lewis felt his breath catch in his chest. "I really hope so," he admitted.

23. YOU HAVE TO BE CAREFUL ABOUT PEOPLE LIKE THAT.

J ay woke after her second night without Ramona. She had spent the day before in a horrid circuit between the hospital, her apartment, and her parents' house. Stephen hadn't woken, or stirred, or done much of anything. He'd been moved to a room upstairs and was no longer entombed in heavy blankets. Still, machines breathed for him, and he was wrapped in sheets that spared Jay the sight of his lost fingers and toes.

She had spoken again with officers Wallace and McInnis. Police in the Twin Cities were looking for Lewis and Ramona, they assured her, and come morning they were going to set off a regional alarm that would notify law enforcement in five states—and attract the attention of the media. Jay had given the cops pictures—a head shot of Lewis in front of his house, and Ramona's photo from her last birthday party.

"We'll find them," said McInnis, with girl-to-girl reassurance.

When she had first gone to Lewis's house she found the door partway open to the cold. That scared her more than anything, because Lewis was an obsessive door-locker and window-latcher. She knew that no intentional harm would ever come to Ramona at Lewis's hands—really, wasn't the problem that he loved them *too much*?—but there was a very real possibility that he had lost his mind. The question of whether or not he had hurt Stephen hung over her like a pale shadow. Only he and Stephen knew.

The Lewis she knew would never hurt Ramona. But was that the man who had her little girl?

Not having Ramona nearby was like losing a limb. She got in her car and drove, the air crystalline and inert. She shivered hard in her seat, the temperature too low to be believed. Steam vented from apartment building rooftops. The streets were tunneled by plowed and shoveled snow, which was piled high and frozen hard. It had gotten down to twenty-one below during the night.

It was hard to say precisely where she had spent the previous night; she stayed at Stephen's side for several hours—his parents had arrived, two amiable granola types who knew almost nothing about Stephen's life in recent years. She dozed, then drove home in the dark, her poor car sounding like it was barely able to go on, and slept for a couple hours on the sofa.

Lewis had yet to turn on his cell phone.

Bastard. Hands gripping the wheel at a red light, she tried to fight off tears. All that overbearing love. She had taken it, she had drawn strength from it. She was like Lewis, as Stephen had pointed out.

But to take her daughter away from her? To disappear without a word, however benign his motivations surely were? It was fucking inexcusable. When she saw him, she was going to slap his face. She was going to . . .

Of course there was the possibility that something had happened to them. For a black flash she entertained the notion of their deaths. But no. Not Lewis. He was too strong.

She pulled up into the driveway of her parents' home. It was just after eight in the morning. She almost slipped on the ice on the steps, which gave way with great fissures and cracking sounds. Someone was scraping their sidewalk down the block, and the sound of it sent a jolt of electricity up Jay's spine.

Inside it was warm—Lewis kept the thermostat on a timer, and lately had kept the house hot at night and tropical during the day. Jay dropped the newspaper and mail on the table inside, going through the motions as though tending the house while her mother and father were on a vacation.

The house was silent. The place was tidy, much neater than when Jay was growing up. She knew Lewis took a certain grim satisfaction in his particular brand of fussy order. Upstairs she went into the closet where all her mother's things still hung. She ran her hands over the dresses, the suits, the blouses hanging in a double row all along the walk-in. Then she took a step into their midst, feeling the fabric against her neck and face, breathing deep, trying to get a faint smell of her mother's ghost.

It was almost like she was there.

In the back was an old burgundy dress that Anna used to wear, years ago, when Jay was just entering adolescence. In the years that followed Anna had put on weight and favored roomy slacks and sweaters. But in the last flower of her beauty—and it wasn't unfair to say so, for Anna had abdicated conventional sex appeal in favor of sensibly short hair and studied plainness—she had worn clothes like this dress, which showed off her arms and the slender lines above her knee. Anna had been breathtakingly beautiful once, to Jay's young eyes a standard to which her daughter could never aspire.

The dress smelled like that Japanese perfume Anna preferred—Jay couldn't remember what it was called. She took the dress off its hanger and laid it out on the perfectly made bed. Stark light streamed in through the windows. Jay stepped out of her jeans, slipped off her sweater and T-shirt. She looked at herself in the mirror dressed only in panties. To her eyes she looked small and plain, her hair hanging straight and un-washed, her nipples red and round. She put on her mother's dress.

It was almost too big for her—Anna had been a couple inches taller. But Jay filled it out, and its lines rested well on her slim figure. She found a bottle of perfume on the dresser, still there, and sprayed herself on her neck and between her breasts. Then she stood in front of the mirror, wrapped her arms around herself, and swayed in a slow comforting rhythm.

How could Anna have left? Now Jay ran her hands over the dress, half-closing her eyes until she saw her mother in the mir-ror. Being in the dress was like being inside Anna, the place Jay had started her life. She closed her eyes and listened to her heartbeat in her ears, imagining the time before she was born, when her heart beat in time with her mother's.

Some time had passed when she realized someone was knocking on the door. As though waking from sleep, she started at the sight of herself in the mirror. Anna stared back at her.

Jay rushed downstairs, thinking it might be Lewis—al-though, come to think of it, why would Lewis be knocking at the door of his own house? She saw the figure of a lone person out-side as she threw open the door. She didn't bother to hide her disappointment when she saw who it was.

"Hey, Jay," said Stan. He took in what she was wearing, visi-bly blanched, but didn't say anything. "Can I come in? I'm freezing to death out here."

The blast of cold air shocked Jay, with her exposed arms and legs in Anna's lightweight dress. She stood aside for Stan to come in, then slammed the door.

"I saw your car," Stan said. He took off his fur-lined Russian-style hat, wheezing and clenching his stout body tight to rid it of the cold. "Is Lewis around?"

"He's not here," Jay said.

"Hey, kiddo," Stan said, looking at her eyes. "You've been crying. What's wrong?"

"Oh, *shit*, Stan."

Before she knew it she was in her old neighbor's arms, sobbing like a little girl and streaking his coat with tears. She tried to talk but he told her to stop, hugging her tight. She remembered how, as a little girl, she had instinctually known that Stan was to be trusted; he was entirely without the reserve and mixed motivations that a child can sense in an adult. Although he had never seemed to like himself particularly, she had always liked him.

After a while she had gotten whatever it was out of her system. She mustered as much dignity as she could, smelling of her mother's perfume, dressed in her mother's clothes, distraught and acting like the helpless young woman she was trying extremely hard not to be.

"You freaked me out really bad when you opened the door," Stan said, releasing Jay from his arms. "You look . . . you know, you look like Anna. I thought I was seeing a ghost."

"Oh, Stan, don't," Jay said. "Not now. I'm trying to keep it together."

"What's happened?" Stan asked, his big lined face creasing with concern.

So she told him about it: about Stephen, and the cops' suspicions, the restraining order, Lewis's disappearance and the two nights without Ramona. Stan slipped out of his coat and landed heavily on one of the living room sofas, shaking his head.

"Crazy son of a bitch," he said, then quickly reversed himself. "I'm sorry, kiddo. That was a stupid thing to say."

"But it's true," Jay said. She sat down on the edge of the dining room table in the next room, ten feet from Stan.

"Well, anyway," he said. "I knew about the restraining order. I was here when he got served with it."

"What did he say happened?" Jay asked.

"I don't know," Stan said. "Lewis wasn't talking. But I found a gun there on the sideboard."

Jay turned to look. There were newspapers piled with assorted mail. "A gun?" she said. "He doesn't have a gun."

Stan gave a guilty shrug. "Men do things they don't tell their kids about," he said. "Anyway, I took it away from him. He got pissed off at me, but I was doing him a favor. I told him not to fuck up and do anything rash. Now it looks like he has."

"You think he hurt Stephen?"

Stan held up his meaty palms in a who-knows gesture.

"Lewis has always been different," he said. "I don't have to tell you that."

"What do you mean?"

"Look, I love your dad." Stan looked around, as though worried that Lewis would hear. "But he's a little nuts. I used to tell him that. I'm a licensed counselor, I used to say. I have a certificate on the wall that entitles me to make professional judgments."

Despite herself, Jay allowed Stan the pleasure of making her laugh.

"No, but seriously," he went on. "I was a marriage counselor, you know. Used to listen to people's shit all day. I shared offices with a chiropractor and some guy who handled finances or something. I quit when I had to get the bypass."

"Stan, what did you think of my parents' marriage?" she asked. She tugged at the dress, wishing it covered more of her. Stan impeccably managed not to give off any sexual vibrations, but still.

Stan let his head wobble back and forth in comical equivocation. "How much you want to hear?" he said.

There were a lot of years and volumes of unspoken knowledge in Stan's question. Stan had known Jay's parents as peers, as fellow adults, a level that a child can never attain. Jay's lens for viewing Anna and Lewis had by necessity been warped by need, and dependence, and then the setting-apart of adolescence.

But those lenses, those habits, had not served her well. Getting pregnant had been bad luck, sure, but she had let it provide her with an excuse for quitting college. Perhaps she had felt safe to drift by the power of her parents' embrace, especially by Lewis's stifling assurances that he would never let her fall. She remembered her resolve of the other night, to find a new town, to become a new Jay Ingraham, to be Ramona's mother and no longer anyone's daughter.

Lewis, in his way, had made that not just possible, but unavoidable. Because it was quite likely that Jay was never going to speak to him again once he and Ramona were found.

"Just tell me what you think," Jay told Stan.

Stan nodded. "All right. Maybe this will do you some good." He got up, an effort that required a couple of attempts before meeting with success. He lumbered across the room, then back again, talking as he paced. "You grew up in a nice, loving family, Jay. A lot of people would have killed to get such a setup. *Most* people."

"Then why am I so fucked up?" she asked.

"You're not fucked up," Stan said. "You don't know what the hell you're doing. So what? Who does? I don't."

"You're not going to charge me for this, are you?"

Stan smiled. "The first one's on the house."

"Sounds good," Jay replied.

"Well, you might not believe this, but I used to lecture your dad." Stan paused. "I know. It took some doing. But I had to say something. I used to tell him he was lucky Anna didn't leave him."

"*Leave* him? But—"

"Look," Stan interrupted. "Lewis is a great guy. Smarter than hell. But he drove Anna into the ground with all his criticizing, all his little grudges. I swear to God, the man spends all his time figuring out how people have wronged him. Here he had this gorgeous wife—talented, faithful—and what did he do? Pick on her morning noon and night. Nothing was good enough. The house was a mess. She was letting herself get fat. Why did he think she let herself go like she did? Because it didn't *matter* anymore. She gave up because he was never going to let himself be happy about anything."

Hearing the history of her family dissected in this manner produced more of an impact on Jay than she thought it would; she leaned back on the table as though pushed back by Stan's breakdown of her father's failings. She thought of Anna, how quiet she had grown over the years, retreating to the sunporch and the paintings she never showed anyone.

"But Mom could have *said* something—"

"She did," Stan countered. "I saw it. She got mad at him, she argued with him, she laughed in his face. Didn't matter. Some people are like a battering ram, kid, and your dad is one of them. I saw it all the time in my practice. One spouse chips away at the other one for twenty years, and what's supposed to happen? No one's getting beat up, no one's getting drunk all day, they have a nice house, they remember enough about the good days to live in a reasonable facsimile some of the time. You know, *life*. That's just the way it is."

"You don't know—"

"Of course I don't," Stan said. "No one does. Lewis surely has a thousand and one arguments that would counter everything I just said. People don't add up, Jay. They don't make sense. They remember what they remember and they make up reasons for what they want to do. I'm just saying that Anna got *tired*. Lewis wore her out. Maybe he was better at generating versions of reality than she was. You have to be careful about people like that. They actually *believe* what they're saying."

Jay let her shoulders slump; she looked down the front of the dress and saw the soft line of her belly rising and falling as she breathed.

"I'd better go change," she said.

"OK." Stan sat down again. He looked up at her with an expression of profound sadness. "It was shit luck the way Anna got sick," he said. "None of this would have happened if she was still around."

Before Jay could answer there was another knock at Lewis's door. Stan got up to answer it, stiffening when he saw police uniforms. Wallace and McInnis came inside dressed in light police jackets and wearing vivid expressions of pain.

"Oh, *God*," McInnis said. When she had pulled herself together, she looked at Jay. "Nice dress."

"Stan Garabaldi," Stan said. "Family friend."

"Nice to meet you," Wallace said with a suspicious narrowing of the eyes.

"Did you find Lewis?" Stan asked.

"No, but we're going to," Wallace replied. "We've listed him and the girl as officially missing, and there's a warrant out for Lewis's arrest. It went out to the media first thing this morning. It'll be all over the news, along with their pictures."

"Good," Stan said with satisfaction.

"Oh, God," Jay said.

She ached for Ramona so hard that she had to cut it off; otherwise she would start crying again, or worse. She wandered upstairs, leaving Stan to deal with the police, and made her way back to her parents' room.

The dress fell to the floor with a muffled sound. Jay put her own clothes back on and lay in her parents' bed. It creaked beneath her. She curled up on the side where her mother used to sleep, where she would come on Saturday mornings and tickle Anna's nose until her eyes opened and they embraced.

When she went back down, Stan was sitting alone in the living room.

"The cops split," he said. "You want me to get you something to eat?"

"No, thanks."

"Well, good news." Stan put his hand on her elbow. "They said that Stephen might be getting better. He's been stirring. He hasn't woken up, but they're thinking that he might."

Jay blinked and let her mouth fall open. She realized that she hadn't even considered the possibility that he might come back.

"I'd better change and get to the hospital," Jay said.

"Sounds like a good idea," Stan replied. "Look, Lewis gave me an extra key to this place one time when he went on vacation. I'll keep an eye on things here."

Jay thanked him, then jogged upstairs. If Stephen awoke, she had to be there—she had to learn whether Lewis had hurt him. But in a sense it didn't matter. Whatever had happened, she was going to find Ramona and take her away from Lewis forever. She would take Ramona and leave this place. There was no longer anything there for her.

24. LIKE BEING ANYBODY ELSE, MAYBE A LITTLE MORE *INTENSE.*

Stephen awoke from a long sleep. He had dreamed he was Lewis driving through the snow at night, with Ramona and Carew in the backseat, looking for signs that Anna Ingraham had come back to him.

But Lewis wasn't going to find her, not right away—because here she was, kneeling next to his prostrate form. She was Anna but wasn't—she was her younger self, with long hair and a slender waist, the Anna Stephen had only seen in photographs.

"You look great," he told her.

"Thanks." She smiled and held out her hand for him to stand. "There's someone I want you to meet."

Standing next to her was a slender older man in a strangely formal suit adorned with cowboy edging. His face was creased and lined, and he wore a pencil-thin mustache. He squinted, his expression Sphinx-like and unreadable.

"Bob Dylan," Stephen said as he got up. "How did you get *here*?"

"Beats me, man," Bob said, his hands in his pockets. "Where *are* we, anyway?"

They were on the main street of a little town, somewhere in Marin or the wine country. The shops were shuttered, there were no cars, and no one walked the boulevard.

"Creepy," Bob observed.

"I saw Jay, but she was saying strange things," Stephen told Anna.

Anna fixed Stephen with a surprising look of frustration. "You have to wake up," she told him. "There are certain realities you have to face up to."

"Like what?" Bob asked. He seemed cautiously interested, as though a desire to get involved in the affairs of others had burned him in the past.

"We're not really here," Anna said.

"Well, I could've told him *that*," Bob said dismissively.

"He's gotten lost," said Anna.

"Who *hasn't*?" Bob snorted.

The town was gone, and now they were on an empty grassy plain someplace. The breeze stirred the tall grass, and the sun shone in a cloudless sky. Bob Dylan wandered off, his head drooped, his lips pursed with impatience.

"That's a little better," Anna said. She was smiling again, which filled Stephen's heart with gratitude.

"I think I'm in love with you," he said.

"Of course." She grazed his cheek with her fingertips.

"Where do I need to be?"

"Think," she said. "Try to remember what happened."

Bob Dylan returned with a smile flickering across his face. "If it's all the same to you two," he drawled, "I've got my own story to be in."

"What was it like?" Stephen asked.

"What do you mean?" Bob asked, defensive, his eyes narrowing.

"He means, what was it like being you?" Anna asked.

Bob thought about this for a moment, seemed about to speak, then stopped himself. "I don't know, man," he finally said. "Like being anybody else. Maybe a little more *intense.*"

"That's about what I thought," Stephen said.

"Don't get distracted," Anna said. "Try to remember."

"Why don't you tell him what he's supposed to be remembering?" Bob said.

"Am I in the hospital?" Stephen asked.

"That's a start," Anna told him, nodding.

"Man, you don't want that," Bob said. "Steer clear of the hospital."

"Don't distract him," Anna said.

Bob folded his arms and looked at the grass.

"Something bad happened," Stephen said. "Something so bad that I've been trying to forget it."

"Story of my life," Bob chuckled.

"Don't be a wiseass," Anna told him.

"You have to find Lewis," Stephen blurted out. "He's looking for you."

"I know." Anna sighed. "He'll find me when he's ready, I suppose. It hasn't been easy, waiting for him."

"That's your husband you're talking about?" Bob asked.

"One and the same," Anna replied.

"Too bad," Bob said with a flattering smile.

"All right, I'm going to forgive you for being obnoxious," Anna said. "Wait until I tell Lewis you flirted with me. His head will explode."

"I have that effect sometimes," Bob replied.

Now they were someplace else, as flat as before, but snow-covered and icy. The wind blew chill, but Stephen didn't feel cold. The landscape was deserted, and big clumps of snow fell lazily from the sky.

Bob frowned. "Looks familiar," he said.

"You're getting closer," Anna enthused.

"Closer to what?" Stephen asked. "Waking up?"

"Sort of." Anna moved behind him and put her hands over his eyes. "Try to remember sort of sideways."

"This is getting *interesting*," Bob observed.

"There was a path, it was snowing," Stephen said. "And then Lewis was there."

"That's a start," Anna said impatiently. "Remember more."

Stephen removed Anna's hands from his eyes. Bob was kicking at a chunk of ice with his pointed cowboy boots.

"Mr. Dylan?" Stephen asked.

Bob winced. "You did *not* just call me that."

"Do you know what she's talking about?" asked Stephen.

Bob moved the snow around with his boot, seeming to take in Stephen's question in degrees.

"I got sick a few years back," he said. "Thought I might die. The pain was *terrible*."

"What happened?" Stephen asked.

"I thought I was going to meet Elvis," Bob said, his eyes turning wistful at the memory. "Not that I'm on a level with Elvis, but that's just the way it was. I knew the pain had to end one way or the other. I was going in either direction."

"What are you trying to say?" Stephen asked. "What does that mean?"

Bob shrugged. "Hey, man, this is *your* dream. Who knows where I'm going when you wake up?"

"Wake up," Anna said.

"You look so much like Jay," Stephen observed.

"She has a daughter?" Bob asked.

"Don't," Stephen said.

Bob chuckled.

"No more dreams," Anna told him.

"I can't stand too many more," Stephen said sadly. "Anna, I'm so *tired.*"

"That's the way it gets," Bob told him.

"You can make it stop," Anna said.

"It's about time to go," Bob agreed. "There's nothin' going on around here."

Stephen stepped into the wind, leaving Bob and Anna in the snow, and he walked with his eyes closed. He struggled through a dark space, stumbling and afraid, and then came to a painful awareness of his body. When he opened his eyes, he was in a room with his parents. He blinked and saw Jay moving toward him—she was wearing her coat and hat, as though she had just arrived.

"Lewis," he whispered. "It was Lewis."

Jay kissed him on his forehead, deep and tender, then took his hand.

"I'm sorry," she said.

"Don't go."

"I have to," Jay said. "He has Ramona."

"She's not safe," Stephen said.

Jay just looked at him, then she nodded.

Stephen looked at his parents, who were teary and distraught, then back to Jay. Even in his state he longed for her.

"Then go," he whispered. "Go get your little girl."

He closed his eyes, felt his parents' touch, and knew that Jay was lost to him forever.

25. HAPPY TO HAVE EVEN TRANSITORY COMPANY.

Lewis spent another night in a motel with Ramona and Carew, perhaps seventy-five miles from their lodgings of the night before. The cold snap had locked in, and sunrise saw the advent of stiff winds that whipped the snow into near-blizzard conditions. They set off in search of breakfast with the car buffeted by gusts, and with few other vehicles braving the southern Minnesota roads. The prospect of driving far enough to escape the weather seemed impossible.

"How're you guys back there?" Lewis asked of the backseat, trying to keep his voice chipper. "Hungry for breakfast?"

"Sure!" Ramona shouted, with her own version of false enthusiasm.

Lewis glanced in the mirror. Ramona and Carew were huddled in a sleepy ball. The dog had his big head pressed into Ramona's belly, and the girl was stroking his ears.

He wished he could reach out to the sky and peel it back,

because surely underneath he would find Anna. She had revealed herself to him in brief flashes, she had spoken to him. But how was he to search for her when he had no idea what she had become? She wasn't a *ghost*, he knew that. He was looking for *her*.

Where?

"Ramona, honey?" he said.

"What?" she said from behind him.

"Remember when you saw Grandma Anna?"

"Sure!"

"She didn't say anything to you?"

"No, she just smiled," Ramona said. "She was so pretty!"

"It would make her happy to hear you say that," Lewis told her. "But honey, I need you to think. If you had to guess, where would you say Grandma Anna is right now?"

There was silence from the backseat. Lewis looked back and saw his granddaughter lost in thought.

"I don't know," she finally said. "Heaven?"

She was obviously searching for the right answer, the one that would earn Lewis's approval.

"What do you really think?" he said after a pause.

No answer. Lewis steered carefully on the two-lane road, its edges obscured by drifting snow. If he lost concentration, he knew, they would end up in a ditch.

"Honey?" he asked.

"I don't know," Ramona said in an odd voice. "It's like she's here already. It's like she's everywhere but I can't quite see her."

Lewis knew exactly what she meant. It was as though if he listened hard enough, he would hear her voice. He squinted into the stark whiteness that surrounded them, sensing her close by. Anna was so close, like an oasis just over the next rise of the desert in which he now lived.

. . .

Ramona was worried about Grampa. He didn't seem like himself. And she knew they shouldn't be out, driving and driving, without at least calling Mama and letting her know where they were.

It was so important for him to find Grandma. Ramona had figured that, since she saw Grandma at day care, her reappearance in their lives would take place anytime. She hadn't thought of actually *looking* for her, but there they were. Grampa was smart, and he always knew what to do. It made her feel kind of excited to think they might find her, maybe that morning. Ramona had doubted, in a way, whether or not she would really see Grandma again. But Grampa Lewis was so sure they would.

She rubbed Carew's head while he slowly wagged his tail. Carew would be very excited to see Grandma again. He would probably slobber over her.

But then an idea occurred to Ramona, one that made her sad: Grampa *was* going to find Grandma Anna. Ramona didn't want to go with him. She had to go back to Mama. Mama was looking for *her*, for Ramona. She didn't know why she thought this, but she was sure of it. It was like the snow and the morning sun.

"Grampa?" Ramona said.

"Yes, dear?"

"Go there," she said, pointing at a gas station approaching by the side of the road.

"Why?" Grampa asked. "Do you have to go to the bathroom?"

"Maybe?" she said.

"Maybe?"

"Yes! Slow down!" she yelled.

Grampa tapped the brakes and the car skidded and slowed.

He said something to himself, kind of mad, and Ramona heard cuss words.

"Go in there," Ramona said. "You have to go in there."

Jay was on the highway heading south. She had the radio on to an all-news channel, and she gasped when she heard the first mention of Lewis and Jay Ingraham.

"WMIN has just received confirmation that Lewis Ingraham was involved in a recent assault in Minneapolis," the announcer said. "Police had no immediate word whether he's considered dangerous, but he was last seen picking up his granddaughter from a day care center and she hasn't been seen since."

Jay gripped tight the steering wheel and peered into a cloud of snow kicked up by a passing truck. The radio announcer sounded bland and unconcerned—it was the kind of story he'd read countless times, another instance of family life gone bad.

Hopefully it will turn out for the best, his tone suggested.

In the summer Lewis, Anna, and Jay used to go to a cabin owned by one of Lewis's coworkers at American Express— Lewis would take a week off and the three of them would picnic and ride their bicycles in the bucolic countryside, feeling fresh and expansive after escaping the city.

Jay remembered these roads, and she knew Lewis did as well. Lewis loved familiarity. He might have taken Ramona in this direction.

A squall of wind pushed her little car and she felt her wheels spin beneath her. She slowed down to sixty. White blanketed everything, and the fresh-plowed road was already covering up with snow.

"Hold on, baby," she said through clenched teeth. "I'm coming for you."

. . .

Strange girl. Lewis pulled up to an empty gas pump—they were down to a quarter tank—and let the engine idle before switching it off. Ramona had said nothing about needing to use the restroom. Now it was apparently urgent that they go into this little minimart.

It was squat and shaped like a shoe box, just like every other gas-station convenience store for the next thousand miles. There were only a couple of trucks parked in the lot; all around snow-covered farmland stretched out to a horizon blurred by wind-whipped powder.

"Let's go," he said to Ramona, opening the door and taking her hand. He pressed Carew back, promising the dog to bring him a treat.

The journey from the car to the door was far more difficult than Lewis had anticipated. From the safety of the driver's seat he hadn't realized how cutting and severe the winds were; he had to hold Ramona close as he leaned into the squall, his breath fleeing from him in a startled gasp. Ramona was shouting something he couldn't understand.

Once they were inside, the door shut behind them and all was peaceful. The clerk looked up from a small TV on the counter and said good morning. Lewis got the bathroom key and led Ramona to the ladies' facilities, making sure she was alone inside before leaving her to her privacy.

"Some morning," the clerk said, startling Lewis.

Lewis looked up. The clerk was stocky, about his age, and seemed happy to have even transitory company. A pair of truckers were engrossed in conversation by a counter full of coffee and doughnuts.

"Yes, it is," Lewis replied. "A hell of a time to be out driving."

"That your kid?" the clerk asked, motioning to the restroom.

"Yes. No, my granddaughter, actually," Lewis said.

The clerk was still smiling, but only with his mouth.

"We were taking a trip to see my . . . my former wife," Lewis explained.

"You from the cities?" the clerk asked.

"You guessed it." Lewis affected calm.

Lewis looked down at the newspaper on the counter, folded open to the local news. There was a picture of him next to a photo of Ramona. The headline read:

MINNEAPOLIS GRANDFATHER, CHILD MISSING: ABDUCTION FEARED

Lewis looked down. Ramona was poking him with the big plastic shingle that secured the restroom key. The clerk's eyes moved from the newspaper to Ramona, then to Lewis.

"Well, thanks," Lewis said. "You have a good day."

"Wait a minute," the clerk said, getting off his stool.

"No need," Lewis told him. "Thanks again."

He led Ramona back out into the swirling winds, his chest locked tight with panic. Halfway to the car he looked back and saw the clerk waving his newspaper, talking to the truckers and pointing at Lewis. The truckers put down their cups of coffee.

Lewis got Ramona into the car and crouched next to her. She looked over her shoulder at the men in the store.

"Are we in trouble?" she asked.

"No. At least *you're* not," Lewis said. He sighed. "Shit. Ramona, honey, I wasn't supposed to take you away from your mama."

"I know," Ramona said.

Lewis blinked in surprise. In the girl's eyes was an expression of perspicacity that was wholly new. She sat back in her seat, snow clumped to her big pink hat, and held out her arms.

"Hug," she said.

Lewis took her in a long embrace, feeling the contours of her narrow shoulders and the press of her soft cheek against his own. She was a creature of perfection.

"Come with me," he told her. "We're going to find Grandma Anna together. It's the right thing. It'll be like old times."

Lewis looked over his shoulder. The men were making for the door. Carew moaned with anxiety.

Ramona was staring into his eyes. She shook her head. He grabbed her hand.

"Is this good-bye?" he said, not knowing why.

"She's out there," Ramona said, pointing to the field beyond the convenience store, where visibility quickly faded to nothing in the tornado of snow. "Go find her."

"I love you, my dear," Lewis told her.

"I love you, Grampa," Ramona said. "Now go."

Lewis dropped the car keys next to Ramona and looked back. The three men had just come out of the store, flinching in the wind. Lewis broke into a sprint in the other direction. The men shouted at him, but he had the advantage of surprise. Quickly he was off the concrete and running hard over the furrows of a farm field.

The angry voices behind him receded quickly as Lewis vanished into the whiteout conditions of the open field. Lewis ran as hard as he could, slipping and sliding, snow stinging his face like needles, his chest burning hard with the threat of an imminent explosion. He knew the clerk would call the police, and that Ramona would be returned safely to Jay. Anyone would be crazy to venture out into these fields in pursuit of Lewis; finally, he was alone.

He began to call out Anna's name. A huge gust of wind smacked into his face by way of reply, and he staggered. He could see no more than a few feet in front of him, but he continued to run.

"Anna, please!" he yelled.

The wind replied angrily. Lewis ran more, he wasn't sure how far, maybe a half mile, then passed over a small rise and let himself sink down into the snow on the other side.

He reached into his coat pocket and upended his pill vial into his mouth. There were about a dozen left, and he crunched them with his teeth and washed them down with a handful of snow. He lay on his back, the cold seeping in through his ankles and neck like a caressing hand.

It was over, all of it. He felt the pull of exhaustion and, with it, sleep. In somnambulant torpor Lewis rolled over onto his side and hoped that no one found him before his heart stopped. He shivered and felt his pulse race. He unzipped and slipped out of his coat to better embrace what was coming.

Time passed.

Lewis rolled over onto his back with what remained of his strength. His ears had grown used to the howl of the wind, and his eyes were nearly frozen shut with icy tears. With what he imagined was one of his final thoughts, he regretted not saying good-bye to the dog. No matter. Jay would see to Carew—and herself. They would be fine.

"Yes, they will," Anna said.

Lewis slowly sat up with a groan. Anna was standing on top of the rise, looking as she had when they first met.

"Took you long enough," he said.

"Don't start," she frowned. "I could say the same about you."

"You look so pretty," Lewis told her.

She spread her arms wide and looked at herself. "I *was*, wasn't I?"

She wore only a sleeveless dress.

"Aren't you cold?" he asked her. "Look—the snow isn't sticking to you."

She shrugged. "Special dispensation."

Anna came down to where he was and sat cross-legged in the snow by his side. She brushed her hair off her forehead and gazed at Lewis with a look of infinite understanding.

"I'm so sorry," Lewis said.

"For what?" she asked.

"For all of it," he said, the words coming out in a rush. "For being such a shithead."

"Well, we could all say the same," Anna told him.

The wind battered his spent frame, and Lewis pulled his arms tight around himself.

"I think I'm freezing to death here," he said.

"Ignore it," Anna commanded.

"That's easy for you to say."

Anna laughed, and suddenly she looked as she had in her thirties: her hair lighter and shorter, her clothes plainer, a hint of weariness in her thickening features.

"I'm also sorry for . . . you know."

"What?" Anna asked innocently.

"For what I did," Lewis whispered into the wind. "That night."

"Oh, *that*," Anna said. "Well, it's important that you remember. But there's no need to apologize."

Lewis flashed back in his mind to Anna's final night. She had been moaning in pain, begging for release from the cancer that had invaded all parts of her body, the disease that was starving and choking her and turning her reality into an endless barrage of pain.

He remembered finding the needle that the doctor had given

them and loading it carefully with her next dose of morphine. Then, without thinking, he had continued to pull back the plunger until it was entirely full. He had then stuck the needle into her arm and listened to her tortured breathing turn slow and shallow. He had pulled her into his lap like a child, whispering into her ear until the breaths stopped coming.

Then he had laid her out on the bed in a position of peace.

"I'm sorry I killed you," Lewis said.

Anna shook her head and smiled, radiating peace. "Silly Lewis," she said. "I could hear you talking to me while I was slipping away. It was a wonderful way to die."

"You mean—"

"Lewis, you took care of me until the very end. And since then you've been wandering around worrying about all the bad feelings you kept inside. Don't you understand? You made mistakes, but they were mistakes of love. If your greatest sin was loving us too much, then you should be at peace."

"I was unfaithful," Lewis blurted out.

"I know," Anna replied, very serious. "I didn't like it at the time. It doesn't matter much now."

"But Stephen—"

"Stephen is fine."

"But I pushed him. He fell."

Anna tapped on her forehead. "Remember," she said.

"I *do*. That's what hurts so much."

And now the wind stopped. The land extended around them to all sides, but there wasn't much to see. It was as though the snow had risen up and engulfed the totality of the landscape; Lewis could see around them, but in the near distance a fog of blank whiteness obscured the world beyond.

"What just happened?" he asked.

"Think," Anna ordered him.

He remembered arranging Anna's body, thinking about calling Jay and realizing that he might be arrested for killing Anna, no matter how good his intentions might have been.

Then he remembered all the dinnertimes, Jay in a high chair, then a sulky teenager, the way Lewis could always make her laugh even in the depths of her adolescent alienation. He thought of the decades of familiarity they'd shared, he and Anna, the deep way they trusted each other even when they didn't like each other very much. That was why he had killed her—because she would have done the same for him.

"I remember now," Lewis said.

"You finally found me," Anna said, and now she looked as she had on her last day, emaciated and ravaged, though with an expression of radiant happiness. She reached out and took his hand.

"Come with me," she said.

Lewis remembered lying down next to his wife in their bed, feeling the softness of her cheek, pressing close to her as her consciousness dissolved and her breath began to turn ragged.

He blinked and saw that room now, felt its stillness, and touched Anna's cheek.

"Not there," she said. "Here. Come on."

"I can leave there?" Lewis asked.

"You have to," his wife told him. "It's time."

"I can let go?" he said, with relief and amazement.

Lewis got up and took her hand, and together they walked into the calm. He no longer felt cold, and his steps were no longer dogged by exhaustion. They walked together across the field until all was white. There was no longer any need to be Lewis Ingraham.

EPILOGUE. HIS LOVE FOR HER TRANSPARENT AND SHINING.

The midday sun by the riverfront coursed through a low cloud cover; the light was less stark than in weeks past, during the final flush of summer when Jay spent entire afternoons by the water with Ramona. It was October, and the world had returned to business after enjoying a sweet dalliance with indolence.

Jay sat on a concrete wall where she could smell the fresh breezes and maintain a good view of the other office workers set loose for lunch. She had bought a ham sandwich wrapped in wax paper from a street vendor, and she opened it up and took a bite. It tasted good, and she washed it down with a slug of bottled water.

Ramona was in her third week of kindergarten at the public school a few blocks from their apartment. Jay had worried about her daughter all through the spring and summer, in the months after Lewis's death, but Ramona never talked about what happened in rural Minnesota that winter, and didn't seem particularly bothered by it.

Jay had heard on the radio about Ramona being found in a little town not far from Albert Lea. Jay was only ten miles away at the time. She had arrived at the gas station shortly after the police, who had made a perfunctory search of nearby fields for Lewis but were quickly discouraged by the high winds and blowing snow. It was as though a curtain had descended around the little minimart, and everyone on the scene ended up indoors for hours, drinking coffee and piecing together what had happened.

"He went looking for Grandma," Ramona told Jay and the police.

It had taken a while, but Jay had forgiven her father. The strain of losing Anna had obviously been too much for him. His actions with Stephen were bizarre and reprehensible, but it was over now and there was no point in harboring resentments or waiting for apologies that would never come.

They found Lewis the next day, frozen stiff on his back in a furrow in a soybean field. He was almost entirely covered in snow, with just his face and extended arm visible.

He was smiling.

Jay polished off her sandwich, surprised as she often was lately by how hungry she was. She had a job answering phones and sorting mail at a downtown non-profit. Sometimes she made field visits, bringing canned food to elderly people and little bundles of clothes to newly arrived immigrant families. It was nice to feel like she was helping people who needed it.

When she had time to herself, she walked the streets of this new city. Every time she turned a corner she saw something new. She thought a lot about Minneapolis, but it was two long days away by car and she didn't want to blow money on airfare—anyway, who would she visit? People there had receded for her into fond, comforting, but ultimately irrelevant memories.

She would have money soon. Her childhood home had sold, for a relatively huge sum, and once her attorney sorted out the thickets of outstanding debt, Jay was coming into decent cash. She figured she'd buy a condo where she and Ramona could spread out and have enough space to grow together—someplace where she wouldn't have to worry about a landlord tolerating Carew, who was in heaven now that he had Ramona's daily companionship.

Ramona seemed to be doing fine in kindergarten. Her teacher said she was quiet, but that she did all her work and seemed very intelligent. The teacher and principal seemed unaware of what had happened last winter. Jay planned to keep it that way.

A young guy in office wear sat down close to Jay and made a show of checking text messages on his cell phone. Jay smiled at him as she wadded up her wax paper and sipped her water.

"Got the time?" the guy asked. He was about Jay's age, and was affecting a great deal of confidence.

"Don't you have it on your phone there?" Jay asked.

The guy blinked. He looked down at the device as though it had betrayed him.

"A quarter after twelve," Jay said, still smiling.

"Hey, I guess that was a pretty transparent excuse for talking to you," he said.

He was good-looking, with an appealing sheepishness now that his bluster had been blown to shreds.

"Pretty transparent," Jay repeated.

"Here's the thing," he said, still clutching the phone. "I've seen you out here a lot. You seem really interesting. Would you like to have dinner sometime?"

Jay folded her arms and looked into the guy's eyes.

"Maybe," she said. "Ask me another time. Right now I just want to sit and think."

"That's totally cool," he said. He held out his hand. "My name's Andy."

"I'm Jay," she said, shaking his hand. "Nice to meet you."

"See you around?" he asked.

"I'm not going anywhere," she told him.

"Good," he said, grinning with apparent relief. "Don't."

When Andy was gone, Jay realized she wished she had accepted his invitation for a date. Next time she would. Her next-door neighbors at her apartment building were a newly married couple who were always offering to babysit Ramona. They told Jay she needed to get out and meet people. They were probably right.

Stephen was settling into the fall term with a new batch of students to obsess over and fixate upon. He really loved them, a fact he assiduously tried to hide from them lest they realize their power. He was a figure of legend on campus now, having survived a near-fatal attack by the father of his younger lover. He was missing a finger, walked with a cane, and suffered bouts of headaches and memory loss that would probably never entirely clear up. Still, he was about to publish his book and had moved in with a female faculty member whom he rarely talked about during his and Jay's monthly phone talks. Their conversations were already becoming more repetitive and distant, and soon he would be able to live without the sound of her voice. It was perfectly natural. Jay didn't mind.

She got up and started walking in the general direction of her work. She knew it was just the power of novelty, but everything around her seemed so fresh and vital—the air, the countless lives all around her, the sparrows flitting in the square dining on crumbs. She felt an absence of worry and emotional oppression that had to be very close to happiness. In a few hours she would see Ramona, and they would have dinner at the little pizza place downstairs from their apartment. Already everyone who worked there knew them, and the staff would make little swans out of paper napkins for Ramona and bring her free cups of lemonade. Ramona would tell Jay about her day at school, and Jay would hang on her every word.

About a block from the building where she worked, Jay stopped short. She saw a man holding a rail by the waterfront with his back turned to her. He was tall, standing very erect, dressed in a herringbone sport jacket and wool slacks. He was smoking a cigarette, his full head of hair blowing gently in the breeze off the river.

Of course it wasn't Lewis. He was much thinner, his hair was much darker. The lines in his face marked him as at least a decade older.

The man stubbed out his cigarette and took the railing in both hands. He seemed lost in thought as he squared his shoulders and tapped one foot against the pavement.

Jay supposed that's how it was going to be—seeing shadows of her father, and her mother, everywhere she went for the rest of her life. It wasn't necessarily a bad thing.

She knew that it would only be in her memories that she would see Lewis again, and see the way his face would brighten in the instant that he recognized her, his own memories ignited and his love for her transparent and shining. It was the same look that Ramona would one day remember about her.

ABOUT THE AUTHOR

Quinton Skinner is also the author of *Amnesia Nights,* as well as other nonfiction books. He lives with his family in Minneapolis.

ABOUT THE TYPE

This book was set in Bodoni Book, a typeface named after Giambattista Bodoni, an Italian printer and type designer of the late eighteenth and early nineteenth centuries. It is not actually one of Bodoni's fonts but a modern version based on his style and manner and is distinguised by a marked contrast between the thick and thin elements of the letters.

m88